DOCUMENT OF EXPECTATIONS

DOCUMENT OF EXPECTATIONS

Devon Abbott Mihesuah

Michigan State University Press
East Lansing

Copyright © 2011 by Devon Abbott Mihesuah

∞ The paper used in this publication meets the minimum requirements of ANSI/NISO Z39.48-1992 (R 1997) (Permanence of Paper).

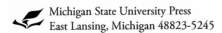
Michigan State University Press
East Lansing, Michigan 48823-5245

Printed and bound in the United States of America.

17 16 15 14 13 12 11   1 2 3 4 5 6 7 8 9 10

LIBRARY OF CONGRESS CATALOGING-IN-PUBLICATION DATA

Mihesuah, Devon A. (Devon Abbott), 1957-
    Document of expectations / Devon Abbott Mihesuah.
        p. cm. — (American Indian studies series)
    ISBN 978-1-61186-011-5 (pbk. : alk. paper) 1. Anthropologists—Crimes against—
Fiction. 2. College teachers—Fiction. 3. Indians of North America—Antiquities—Fiction.
4. Women detectives—Fiction. 5. Murder—Investigation—Fiction. I. Title.

    PS3563.I371535D63 2011
    813'.54—dc22   2011008831

Cover design by Erin Kirk New

Book design by Scribe Inc. (www.scribenet.com)

Cover art by Mike Riggs

g green press INITIATIVE Michigan State University Press is a member of the Green Press Initiative and is committed to developing and encouraging ecologically responsible publishing practices. For more information about the Green Press Initiative and the use of recycled paper in book publishing, please visit www.greenpressinitiative.org.

Visit Michigan State University Press at:
www.msupress.msu.edu

DOCUMENT OF EXPECTATIONS

FRIDAY AFTERNOON

The Oscar Ranger Seminar Room on the second floor of the old stone building known as Anthropology grew hot after a day under the late spring sun. Unlike other buildings on campus, which housed multiple departments, Anthropology held only one. The comparatively affluent anthropologists enjoyed the comfort of their own freestanding building, with its name newly carved in marble above the majestic front doors. A decade before, the Department of Anthropology had been just another minor entity in the College of Social Sciences at Central Highlands University, but a wealthy benefactor, a collector of antiquities, had given funds for an endowed chair and for unspecified "site improvements." The donor's only stipulation was that the funds be directed to anthropology. Because of the president's desire to please the benefactor (who also gave money to reroof the School of Hotel and Restaurant Management), the inhabitants of the College of Education were booted from the elegant stone building and transferred to a lesser structure, which had once held the now-defunct School of Drama. The anthropologists had moved in to take Education's place and were now solidly ensconced in the fine edifice.

It was early May, unusually warm during finals week, and the air conditioning would not be turned on until the first summer session began in three weeks. The students felt uncomfortable in the stuffy seminar room on the second floor of Anthropology, so the first professor to use the room that morning opened the old casement windows. At the end of the day, the professor giving the last exam of the semester, on "Southwestern Rock Art and

1

Sacred Vortexes," would normally have paid no attention to the windows. But this day was different. After the last haggard student dropped her blue composition booklet on the table next to the lecture podium and left the room, the professor picked up his thermos full of Hawaiian Punch, walked to the window and poured the red liquid on the carpet. That is how it had been planned since well before the sun had risen that morning.

SUNDAY, 11:30 P.M.

Thick Virginia creepers proliferated around the base of the old stone Anthropology building. Tiny feet of the lush, green tendrils had latched on to the century-old cement and rock outcroppings, and over a long period of time the ivy had ascended the outer walls.

In the night's darkness a figure in black pants, a black, long-sleeved knit top, black shoes, and a black mask crept along the edge of the flowerbeds, then stopped to look up. Lights in two of the offices on the third floor were still on. Stepping across a flowerbed, the intruder put black-gloved hands onto the wide sill of the eastern window of the first floor and, with a small hop, pulled up onto the sill.

The intruder ascended from the first-story window ledge the intruder reached toward three large rocks as handholds, intending to scale to the top of the old greenhouse at the second floor, a steamy conservatory that the university medicinal botanists had insisted stay attached to Anthropology. Considering the amount of grant monies the biologists brought in every year, the president of CHU didn't argue with them. So the greenhouse had remained. From there it would be an easy step for the figure in black across the roof to the wide window ledge of the second-story Ranger Seminar Room windows.

However, the intruder found the ascent to the second floor more arduous than expected. A light rain had fallen earlier in the evening, and the trespasser struggled to hold on to the slippery, leaf-covered rocks. A gloved hand tried to grip one of the stones as a handhold, but slipped off the wet leaves. The intruder fell backwards, arms flailing, snapped through a rose bush, and landed with a splat a few feet below in the muddy flowerbed.

Cursing, the prowler stood up and reached back to pull thorns that had penetrated denim and stuck into soft flesh.

The prowler took a few deep breaths and started upwards again. This time, instead of trying to grab the top of the rocks, hands reached up under the leaves to take hold of the granite chunks protruding from the wall, and now the ascent went better. Small lizards in hiding for the night scurried away to sounds of wheezing. Holding onto the old vines and setting feet on solid stones, the climber reached the second story. Breathing heavily, the trespasser rested, then crossed over the greenhouse to the seminar room windows.

At the center window, the invader turned sideways to step through. Halfway into the room, the intruder stepped onto the floor with a right foot, which sank into the shaggy carpet.

"Shit," the prowler muttered tersely. The carpet had been steam-cleaned after the exam on Friday afternoon. A pair of socks covered the prowler's Nikes. No tread marks showed in the fluffed carpet, and measured steps made no sound in the dark seminar room as the figure walked to the outer door, passing the enormous oak conference table in the center of the room. On the walls, glare from the lampposts along the nearby sidewalk reflected off the glass-covered aerial photographs of the university. It felt strange to be inside the building during off-hours, and the prowler thought that it would be very easy for anyone to trash select offices. At the moment, however, there was more serious business to see to.

The trespasser carefully turned the interior knob of the heavy door to the seminar room, emerging into the hallway. The solitary form stepped slowly to the stairwell and silently climbed the stairs to the third floor. Again the intruder rested a few moments, breathing heavily, before tiptoeing down the hall and turning the corner to peer at the office door of Professor Roxanne Badger. This was one of the two offices with its lights visibly on from outside the building.

Light filtered out past the edges of the flyer the professor had taped over the small window in her office door. The dark figure moved quickly to the door, pulled a glinting object from a sheath attached to a belt, put a gloved hand on the knob, and tried to turn it gently. The intruder tried again, applying more pressure, but to no avail. It was locked.

The prowler would have to knock. The shadowed form gripped the shining object and tapped its handle lightly on the dark old wooden door. A few moments passed, silent but for a few labored breaths. No one answered. The trespasser leaned close to the window and peered through a thin slit at its edge that the poster did not cover. The woman was not in her office. She had forgotten to turn her lights off.

"Shit," he muttered again. He had missed one target.

The figure retraced the route down the hall, with uncertainty in every step. Stopping at the stairway, hesitating, looking down the stairs, the invader decided what to do next. Instead of descending, the infiltrator crept slowly to another corner and peeked around it. Light shone brightly through a door that was left ajar in the third office from the end of the hall. The prowler heard paper rustling inside.

A smile formed under the hot, scratchy mask as the intruder gripped a stainless steel hunting knife with laminated wood handle and a five-inch blade with a gut hook.

It was just a few steps down the hall to the lighted office. *It's just not safe to work at night in this building* the mind thought as the face grinned.

MONDAY, 4:00 A.M.

Monique Blue Hawk opened her eyes and saw the outline of her Afrin squirt bottle and a tumped-over plastic water cup on the nightstand. A hazy dream drifted through her mind, although she couldn't say what the dream was. She dozed and dreamed more of the same, and during her thrashings flung her arm across the table and knocked the cup off the nightstand. That woke her up for good.

The ceiling fan whirled above her, creating a pleasant breeze. Steve, her husband, snored softly beside her, holding a teddy bear with his left arm and cradling their impressively ugly cat, Foogly, with his right. Monique wasn't sure how many men slept with a cat, much less a stuffed animal, but she did know that if she took either animal away from him, he'd toss and whimper. The bear friend was one of Steve's childhood things, one she had never understood. As a kid Monique had played with Tonka trucks and frogs.

It was no use trying to sleep. Monique kissed her finger and touched

Steve's face. He slapped his face as if he thought a mosquito was sucking on his cheek. He sat up, looked around, and said, "I wanna pizza with extra mushrooms for dinner." Then he lay back down and hugged Bear. Foogly meowed indignantly and licked her calico butt.

Monique yawned and rubbed her temple. She had run too far yesterday, then lifted weights for half an hour without drinking enough water. All night she had paid for her workout with a dehydration headache that hadn't improved with the passage of time. She swallowed an ibuprofen with help from the extra water bottle stashed on the floor next to the bed, stood up, and, in the darkness, almost tripped over a pile of books, one of many stacked throughout the house. In the darkness she blindly pulled a CD from the wooden entertainment center and hoped that she'd picked Robert Plant instead of Steve's Willie Nelson.

Monique made her way to the kitchen, where she flipped on the coffee pot that she had prepared the night before. After a few seconds of waiting for sounds of percolation that never came, she realized that she hadn't put in water. "Damn it," she muttered, filling the pot. She pinned up her long hair with two butterfly clips, turned on the stereo, slipped on headphones, and read *Consumer Reports* while slowly pedaling her recumbent bicycle.

No sunlight peeked through the curtains yet. Steve and their son Robbie normally woke at 7:00, early enough for Steve to get ready for work at his auto parts store and for Robbie to finish whatever eighth grade homework he hadn't completed the night before.

She set the resistance on high and peddled hard for half an hour before venturing out to get the paper. The sun was rising and the day felt like it would bring T-shirt weather. A box turtle puttered across the lawn. She picked him up and he promptly peed on her. She opened the gate that led to the back of their home, an old rambling ranch-style house that sat comfortably behind what soon would be a riot of wildflowers, elephant ears, Crepe myrtles, and dozens of other plants that spanned the color spectrum. It had taken five years to design and grow the landscaping. If the newspaper girl threw the paper anyplace but on the walkway, Monique had to search for it in the jungle.

She took the turtle to the garden, where she had planted vegetables and herbs every place the sun shined. Sunflowers and tall cannas with orangey blossoms lined up against the fence.

"Hey Monique!" Her nosy neighbor called to her from his porch, where he drank early morning coffee and watched her. "Do you plan to enter your salsa and squash in the county fair again this year?"

"You bet," she yelled back. "And be very afraid."

Monique went inside to shower in the guest bathroom, then sat in the den lounge chair with its footrest elevated. She wore a pink camisole and girl's underwear that was supposed to look like boy's boxers. A bag of frozen peas lay across her right thigh and another on her left knee, from which most of the cartilage had been missing since a nasty fall off a horse ten years before. The permanent limp the doctor had promised her had improved into an occasional hobble that kicked in after a long run or hike.

On the end table next to Monique sat several bottles of her favorite liquids: grape Propel, Evian, V8 Splash, Gatorade, an almost full bottle of white merlot. There was another smaller container of her trusty Advil and a half empty can of Budweiser. She looked around the den and assessed what she needed to do that weekend: seal the skylight on the west side before the next rain, strip and polish the wooden floor in front of the front door, and repot the unhappy decorative orange tree.

Because it was almost time for Monique's menstrual period and therefore headaches, a third bag of peas lay on top of her head. As she flipped on the television to see a rerun of the *Crocodile Hunter,* her fourteen-year-old son Robbie wandered in, his shaggy hair tangled from flopping in his sleep.

"Good bike ride?" He yawned.

"Yes, baby. Thanks."

"Didn't you run last night?"

"Yes again. Thanks for noticing. Get ready for school."

"Doesn't your knee hurt?"

"Sort of."

"Then how come you make it worse?"

"Good question."

"Can I get a kayak?"

"You have a canoe."

"Yeah, but a kayak's different."

"We'll see."

"Ah, dang."

"I said maybe."

"*Sa-hochvffo*," he said.

"*Nanta vpa chi-bvnna-o?* Oatmeal or Cream of Wheat?"

"Total corn flakes *sa banna hinla*." He wandered off to wash his face.

The hot water heater thumped, meaning Steve was in the shower. Monique looked at the clock.

"Yikes," she said out loud. It was 7:20 already.

"Robbie," she yelled, "you're going to have to cut up your own strawberries. I'm late for work."

She dropped the television flipper on the end table, almost toppling the drinks. The bag on her head fell off onto the floor, where the peas rolled out of the split pouch like marbles. "Damn it," she muttered, hurriedly scooping them up and dropping them into the garbage.

"I heard that, Mom!" Robbie yelled from the bathroom. "You owe me a dollar!"

"Shit," she said in a whisper.

"Did you say 'shit'? Another dollar!"

Out of the corner of her eye she saw a four-foot dark ribbon moving fast along the floor, heading for the kitchen. "Damn."

"Another one!"

"Robbie, enough. Diesel's out. You left the top of his cage off. Kindly grab him before he gets behind the fridge again."

MONDAY, 8:05 A.M.

The three Central Highlands University police officers had completed the last patrols of their all-night shift when they received the call from the dispatcher about a dead person in a trashed office in Anthropology. The sleepy men jerked to attention and turned on their sirens and flashers while they sped through the winding campus streets, their elaborately painted silver and blue Ford Tauruses looking more like escorts for the Dallas Cowboys than university patrol cars.

The officers parked crookedly in the small lot in front of Anthropology, jumped out of their cars, and sprinted to one of the two front entrances. All three had master keys and they bumped into each other trying to unlock the door. Once inside, they looked cautiously up and down the corridor, then walked quickly to the departmental office to find Mary, the secretary.

"Up there," the thin, crying woman pointed. She looked ready for an afternoon of clam digging in her cream-colored Capri pants, brown mules, and a black T-shirt. "Third floor. The door's open." She sobbed wetly.

Jeff Ogden took charge. "Okay, men," said the lanky senior officer. His prominent Adam's apple moved up and down as he spoke. He wore thick glasses and carried an old .38 Smith and Wesson in his holster, a tear gas canister strapped to his belt, and a snub-nosed .22 Charter Arms velcroed above his left ankle. He backed up those weapons with a blackjack and heavy-handled flashlight. "You never know how belligerent a college student might get around finals week," he once told his inquisitive wife.

"I'll get tape to cordon off the stairs," he continued in a calm voice. "Richard," he said to sweaty rookie officer Richard Snelson, a big bodybuilder, "you call for backup now. We need guards at the front entrances and one in back to keep out faculty and students with keys." Snelson thought he might be sick. He'd never investigated a violent death before.

"Frank," Ogden said to Frank Villario, the jumpy Puerto Rican native who looked ready to make a quick draw if necessary, "sweep the building. I'll be back to help you in a minute." Frank stood with his shoulders hunched forward and fingers twitching in anticipation of finding a lurker in the hallways.

Ogden sprinted up the stairs to the third floor hallway. He pulled his Smith and Wesson from the holster as he reached the top. He cautiously but quickly made his way to the office third from the end. The door was open. He looked in and saw the dead man, his throat deeply slashed. There was no need to check for a pulse. Ogden turned and walked quickly back down the hallway, his weapon poised as he breathlessly looked in potential hiding places, in case the perpetrator was still in the building, waiting to strike again. Satisfied that he was alone in the hallway, Ogden hurried back down the stairs to the second floor, where he conducted a search of that floor, figuring that no one could get off that level without being heard. He then returned to the stairway, taking steps two at a time back to the first floor, heading for his patrol car and the yellow barrier tape.

As he walked back through the front door, he heard Frank Villario yell, "Here's one!" Frank crouched, his P-89 blue Ruger 9mm pointed at a small figure standing in the middle of the first floor hallway. "Halt!" Frank ordered, shrill enough to be heard throughout the building.

"It's okay, Frank. Put that away." Ogden walked towards the wide-eyed blond, who held steaming coffee from the South Student Union in one hand and a gooey chocolate éclair in the other.

"What's going on?" the woman whimpered, her voice quivering. Frank's yell had caused her to spill most of her coffee onto the shiny floor.

"Who are you, ma'am?" Ogden asked.

"I'm, I'm just a graduate student," she stammered. "I'm here to print out my thesis."

"Come this way, ma'am," Ogden said, sidestepping the puddle of coffee. "For the moment let's put you someplace where it's safe." He looked sideways at Frank and motioned for him to holster the weapon. Frank complied but kept his hand near the gun as he turned to escort the frightened women to the mailroom. After considering Frank's posture a moment, Ogden called dispatch to report what he had found. He hoped the Moose City PD would hurry the heck up and get there. And he had someone specific in mind.

Monique limped to the kitchen and turned on the teakettle for her husband, then went down the hall to the bedroom to dress. She had finished brushing her hair and was twisting it into the usual bun when Steve came into the bedroom holding in one hand his Fort Worth Zoo mug full of steeping tea and in the other a banana.

"You look tired," Steve said while he studied the circles under her eyes. He finished the banana and dropped the peel into the wicker basket.

"I'm okay." She picked up her pills off the dresser, an acidophilus, two Metamucils, an all-purpose vitamin, and her birth control pill and washed them down with Diet V-8 Splash.

"How come you hit me last night?" Steve put down the tea and struggled with an impressive spider web of hair that had matted behind his ear.

"I didn't hit you, Stevie. Your hair is all tangly again. You need to use my conditioner and braid your hair before bed."

"Yes you did hit me. I sat up and saw you looking at me." Steve was a

9

big, burly guy with large arms he had developed from a lifetime of physical activity, not the least of which was lifting weights. After he broke his femur playing college football he learned the crafts of tree trimming and roofing prior to opening his own auto parts store. People told him he looked like a Native Hulk Hogan, except smaller, darker, and not as annoying. He peeled his banana as delicately as a gorilla.

"Steve, you hit yourself. Gotta eat that honeydew today before it goes bad, honey. And the grapes."

"Yeah, I cut up the melon. Uh, forgot to tell you. The truck's smoking."

"What do you mean? From the engine or the tailpipe?"

"Back end."

"I'll look at it tonight. Take the Bronco to work in case there's a problem with the truck." Before entering the police academy she'd wanted to be a truck mechanic, so she took two years of auto mechanics at a community college. That was before she decided to be a marine biologist. She earned her bachelor's degree in biology, but her oceanography goal got nipped her senior year when she decided that her calling should be zoology or forestry so she could save the environment. After a year of intense graduate course work the shooting happened, and she changed her mind once again.

"Mom!" Robbie yelled from down the hall.

"I'm in here," she yelled back. "*Hash chilika-na!* Come down here if you need to talk to me!"

He strode down the hall, talking as he approached the bedroom. Diesel the snake coiled around his wrist. The big water snake's tongue darted in and out. "I need some money for cookies. The cheerleaders are selling cakes and stuff today."

"Ask your dad."

"But you always tell me that you manage the money."

"True."

"Can I have an iguana?"

"No."

"How come?"

"Because they grow to be six feet long, that's why. I found a turtle. I put him in the garden."

"Cool. Thanks. Dad, can I have a power saw? I want to make a tree fort."

The phone rang before Steve could answer. He stopped combing his hair and stared at the phone as he always did when it rang early in the morning or late at night.

He knew it was best to let Monique answer. "I'll get it," she called. She picked up the bedroom line, said hello, and listened. She put on her jacket as she balanced the phone between her ear and shoulder. If Robbie had not been in the room she would have pressed the speaker button.

Monique listened for a minute. "I'm on my way." She hung up.

"Where you going, Mom?"

"Campus. They had an, uh, event during the night."

"Mom," whined Robbie. "Money?"

She fished out from her pants pocket three dollars and thirty cents. "Put that snake away and wash your hands." Robbie dropped the money in his backpack, then put on his headphones with one hand and turned on some music that Monique couldn't identify.

After she saw that Robbie had reached the end of the hallway, she turned to Steve. "Someone found a body at CHU," she told him.

"Was it murder? You don't need to go in, then. I think that . . ."

"Hush." She gave him a quick kiss and snapped shut her holster. Then she quickly walked down the hall, not only to see what the day might bring, but also to avoid an argument with Steve.

MONDAY, 8:15 A.M.

It took forty-eight-year-old Monique Blue Hawk, Chief Investigator of Moose City Homicide, six minutes to drive to her partner's house. Detective Charles T. Clarke, fifteen years her junior, jogged from the front porch with a white powdered-sugar donut in his mouth and a jacket over his arm. Clarke got in the car and Monique watched sugar flutter down onto his shirt and her seat.

"Got a homicide," she said. "Get that donut under control."

"University, huh?" Clarke mumbled through a mouth full of dough.

"We'll be dealing with inflated egos and large salaries, so try not to get pissed off," Monique said as she gunned the white Impala. It would be just a five-minute drive to CHU.

The Arkansas-born Clarke nodded. "My college professors were like that." "Professors" came out "perfessers," with the accent that Monique called "Oklahomaese." The thin man sat sideways in the front bucket seat, leaning back against the door without his seat belt fastened.

"You sound like one of those guys on a Sunday morning fishing show." She was especially amused by Clarke's use of "boy howdies" and peculiar Oklahoma witticisms.

"Why sure, I can speak like I went to charm school. But that's too hard," Clarke rationalized. "You know what I'm sayin' anyways, right?"

They reached the main drag of restaurants and shops. "Let them blabber on about themselves," said Monique. "Be patient. They'll probably tell us all kinds of information, and we won't even have to ask."

Monique tolerated long silences. Most people got nervous and talked more than was good for them. She also had the advantage of looking a bit exotic, which made people attentive. With dark skin, dark eyes, and long straight hair, she was clearly out of the mainstream, and people had a hard time placing her ethnicity. A few people asked if she was Italian or perhaps part Middle Eastern. In her home state of Oklahoma, the land of mixed-blood Indians spanning the spectrum of colors, people pretty much knew she was a mixed blood, although sometimes they'd ask hopefully if she was Cherokee because they also had a Cherokee princess grandma. Then she'd sigh and say, "*Chahta sia anoti ahattak-vt Pawnee*—I'm Choctaw and my husband is Pawnee. *Chukka chuffa-yt Okla humma micha Texas*—My family lives in Oklahoma and Texas. *Chi yalhki yammi am-ahowa*—And I think you're full of shit."

Monique was a direct descendent of a *Nanulhtoka*, a Choctaw light-horseman, one of the men who enforced tribal law. She took much pride in stories about her great-great-grandfather Wood Nall, a man who rode through the Choctaw lands in Mississippi doling out the law to transgressors, and who survived the nightmare of removal to Indian Territory. He rode through the Nation as a Lighthorseman until 1861, when the war started and his family needed him to stay on the farm. Monique was most proud of Wood's stance against the Progressive Choctaws who favored statehood and the break-up of tribal lands into allotments. According to her great-auntie Rosalinda, Wood was a traditionalist Choctaw who, along with twenty other Nationalist tribal members, murdered several pro-Oklahoma state Progressives after the contested tribal election of 1892. He was in his nineties when he made his stand.

"He knew what to do, Monique," her great-auntie told her when she was fifteen. "Don't you ever doubt yourself."

"I won't," Monique promised. So she carried herself tall and straight and never backed down to anyone. She spoke *Chahta anumpa*, knew her tribal history and stories, and spent as much time as she could around the community in Oklahoma. Monique felt comfortable with her identity and harbored little patience for those with no connection to the cultures they claimed.

On the other hand, the younger, chatty Chuck Clarke felt less sure of himself. He had little education in homicide investigations, but he had read murder mysteries and hoped that one day he'd encounter a case with circumstances similar to those that Kinsey Milhone and Dave Robicheaux dissected and solved. Clarke had not yet seen what humans were capable of. Monique, however, had encountered murderers, rapists, and thieves and had managed to help put away most of the ones she pursued. She made Clarke nervous.

Clarke worried with his tie knot and adjusted his belt badge. He felt more comfortable in shorts and no shoes. "I got a hard time with eggheads," he said. He ran long fingers through short surfer-blond hair, wiped his face to brush away crumbs, then unwrapped a piece of Double Bubble and popped it into his mouth.

Monique chuckled in her deep voice. "They're like everyone else, partner. They just act like they're more important."

Clarke mussed his hair again. Monique smiled when she looked Clarke in the eyes. They were pale green, like ocean shore water, an eye color unlike any she had seen. His lashes were long and black, almost as if he wore mascara. He was cute, all right, but his skin was too pale for her taste.

Monique said, "You look swell. Would you like to stop at Bonnie's Beauty Boutique on the way?"

"Just jumpy."

"Let me tell you something, Clarke. For the most part, Ph.D. stands for 'Post hole Digger.'" Monique pushed up the right turn signal with her index finger, even though few cars were on the street. The sirens blared. "A lot of these people think they're better than you because they have a degree, but framed diplomas on the wall don't mean crappoola right this minute."

Clarke smacked his gum and watched a jogger sprint across the street to beat the police car.

"Jerk," said Monique. "I could bust him for that. He heard us coming a mile away. Anyway, if I see you looking intimidated, I'll step on your foot. They're used to students kissing their rears, so don't you do it."

Actually, she had had a few run-ins with professors in school who thought they knew everything about Indians. She had only met a few academics that she respected and that included self-identified Native professors who were so far removed from the realities of tribal life that they might as well be Norwegian.

"Don't step on my foot today. Man, I really hurt it this time."

"I hadn't planned on it," she replied. "Now what happened?"

"I ran with my laces too tight, and I think I may have a stress fracture."

"So, Clarke, tell me—why didn't you stop and loosen the laces?"

"I got that half-marathon coming up and I was timing myself. Takes too long to stop and re-tie laces when you're in a hurry."

"Clarke, that is the dumbest excuse I've heard in a long time. Now you hurt yourself."

"Yeah, okay. So, what's the deal in this case here?" Clarke asked.

"Murder in the Anthropology building."

"Anthropology," Clarke repeated. "You mean like Indiana Jones?"

"Yeah, I'd say that. Some anthropologists loot burial sites. But they tend to be a bit more careful in how they describe what they're doing—how they acquire remains and sacred burial items. They say 'excavation' instead of 'looting.' Some anthropologists study Indian skeletons, and are interested in some pretty weird stuff about them. Hardly any normal people understand what they write about."

"You don't like them. But how come you know about what they do?"

Monique sniffed. "I've dealt with way too many pot hunters and bone collectors. They're scavengers."

"And anthropologists are like that?"

"Well, there's differences, I guess. But anthropologists have the same thoughts about Indians as the pot hunters in one way. They think Natives are valuable only for studying."

Monique paused to think about what she just said. She better remain fair and not generalize, otherwise she'd come across as ignorant. "Some are sensitive to what Indians think about using their ancestors for study. Hopefully that's who we'll encounter here."

Clarke stared at her, as if he knew she really didn't believe what she was saying. "Who's dead in the Anthropology building?"

"Don't know." Monique took a last swallow of her V-8 Splash and threw the plastic container in the back with the rest of the garbage piled in the trash box she kept in the floorboard. On Wednesday she'd sort out the recyclables from the trash and vacuum the car.

They arrived at Burnett Street, the main entryway to south campus. Monique turned off the sirens and kept the lights on. She admired the university grounds and felt invigorated at the sight of green grass and flowers of rainbow colors. Droplets from the water sprinkler sparkled on the petals, and the damp air smelled like a nursery.

Monique slowed the car in front of Anthropology and stopped where a campus officer motioned her to park behind a CHU police car sitting cockeyed to the curb. She turned off the lights and tucked into her jacket the Sponge Bob note pad she had borrowed from Robbie. Her regular pad had run out of paper. Before getting out of the car she looked into the rear-view mirror and, even though she didn't wear much makeup, checked her mascara and then readjusted her sunglasses.

Two other police cars, an ambulance, and a fire truck were parked in the street. Monique didn't see their drivers, which meant they had to be in the building. She patted the holster that held her Glock .40 semi-automatic, felt for the outline of the old .38 Charter Arms revolver back-up strapped to her leg, straightened her jacket, and exited the car in one smooth motion.

Clarke got out too and they stood in the sunshine. As usual, Monique wore a white French-cuffed shirt with dark trousers and jacket. She had taken Clarke's advice and ordered some dressy-looking New Balance Trekkers that felt as comfortable as her running shoes. A tall CHU officer strode down the sidewalk to them.

"Detective Blue Hawk," he greeted Monique. "Glad to see it's you. We've met. I'm Jeff Ogden." He stuck out his hand to each officer.

"Sure. How you doing?" They had met two years before when Ogden still worked in the Moose City Police Department. He had never met an Indian cop and figured she had to be one because of her name. Ogden had looked her up and down, assessed her height and straight posture. She stood confidently. Like a fighter. He liked Detective Monique Blue Hawk even before she had showed him what she was made of by solving a strange case. A man appeared to have hanged himself from the rafters in his boat shed, but it turned out his wife had laced his tea with arsenic, then strung him up after he was unconscious. Monique found slight bruising under the man's armpits and across his rib cage. Although a kitchen chair lay on its side under the suspended body, Monique was suspicious and inspected an ATV that was parked nearby. She found a few strands of rope that had torn off in the washer at the base of the hitch ball. Using the ATV and a rope was the only way the small woman could have dragged her husband's large body from where she had poisoned him.

"Looks like a male professor was killed sometime during the night in his office up on the third floor," Ogden was saying.

"During the night?" asked Monique. "What was he doing in his office so late?"

"Some professors work here at night. I remember seeing his light on a lot. Same with another office on that floor, down the other wing."

"Who has keys to the building?" She talked fast in order to garner as much information as she could before looking at the murder scene.

"Faculty and staff for sure, and most of the graduate students. The keys say 'do not duplicate,' but that doesn't mean they don't get stolen or loaned out. We get lots of calls about missing keys. Sometimes the locks are changed after a wad of keys get lost or lifted, but usually not."

"Insecure system," Monique said as they briskly approached the entry. Colorful flowers surrounded the base of the old stone structure while ancient oaks provided shade and homes for lizards and mourning doves. Colorful and loud birds flitted across the front of the building then darted into the thick green ivy growing around and over the two glass doors. The three stepped in the small puddles left from the sprinklers set every six feet down the edges of the sidewalk.

"Could be better, yeah. It's hard to keep track of keys since there're so many of them. Costs CHU a lot to change locks because departments also have to pay to make new keys."

"So anyone with a key could have gotten in."

"Well, yes, ma'am."

"What I mean is, over time you have a lot of non-university people with keys."

"Yes. Faculty, graduate students, staff, custodians, service people all have keys."

"And you said not everyone gives their keys back when they graduate or leave CHU?"

"That could be. Although I think that giving keys back is a requirement for graduating and getting retirement money."

"But no one watches to see who comes into the buildings, right?"

Ogden shook his head. "There's no way to do that. We continually circle the campus, which takes about twenty minutes if we don't see anything suspicious." They paused at the front door before entering, and Ogden handed Monique a master key he had borrowed from Snelson.

"How many campus police officers?"

"Maybe five or six. If the weather's good we might bike through campus and that takes longer. There're eight or so security guards who go from building to building. But I think they only manage to visit each building once a night 'cause they go in pairs and it takes a while to go through everything."

"There are what, a hundred buildings on this campus?"

"At least. Some are connected by second-story passages or basement tunnels."

"No security cameras?"

"Only in a few buildings where departments have issues with people using other peoples copy machine codes or are stealing food from the department lounge refrigerators. The School of Communication had their potted plants stolen last Christmas break so they put in a few cameras."

Clarke snickered.

"Actually, it's a serious problem," Ogden said solemnly. "Plants are expensive. Plus people put their lunches in the department refrigerators, then a few hours later find them gone. Last summer the biology faculty found a bunch of empty beer cans in the paper recycle bin, so the department chair installed a video monitor. He caught some grad students drinking in the middle of the night."

Clarke laughed again. "College days. I remember when . . ."

Monique cleared her throat and Clarke stopped talking. She looked at Ogden and nodded toward the front door. "We need to hurry."

Ogden swallowed and took a deep breath. "I'll show you where he is." He glanced to the glass doors and gestured with his bony elbow.

Inside the building light shot through the open door and bounced off the polished wood parquet floor. It was very quiet. Stained wood wainscoting and the cherry wood office gleamed. Framed paintings of local landscapes and university dignitaries hung on the walls between offices. Tall plants in terra cotta pots sat to the side of each doorway. The spacious entry featured a large cement fish fountain that poured water from its mouth into a foot-deep marble pool. A tangle of large-leafed green plants grew in a planter box. Cool humidity rose from the moist garden and wafted down the hall.

"Looks like an attorney's waiting room," observed Clarke.

"Yep," agreed Ogden. "They don't like to save money around here. You should see the College of Business. The plants in this building are worth about ten grand."

They walked past a wall case of kachinas, pottery, and baskets (*not approved for display by the tribes that created them*, thought Monique), then another glass case that held faculty portraits. They turned at the wide stair-case, ducking under the yellow tape that stretched the width of the stairwell. They climbed the polished wood steps and Monique noted the careful décor on the landing.

The trio took a left at the top of the stairs, then walked to the end of the corridor. Although it was less elaborate than the ground level, framed pictures and lush plants decorated the hallway, and the comparatively plain floor was still more sophisticated than the floor in any school either Monique or Clarke had attended.

"Down there," said Ogden, pointing to the obvious place of activity. Monique saw from a distance that the medical examiner, Archie Klaus, was just exiting the dead man's office and pulling the door just about closed.

There were so few murders in the city that the ME arrived quickly at the scene and rarely sent an assistant.

"Hey, how'd he get here so fast?" Ogden asked out loud. "I never even saw him."

"Nature of the business," answered Monique as the three walked towards the end of the hall.

"Whoa," Monique said. "Look down." Monique put her arms out to stop Clarke and Ogden.

They saw faint but distinct footprints in the shadows leading away from the office for about twenty feet. Someone had stepped in blood, and the prints revealed that the feet had shuffled a bit. Then the prints petered out. There were no apparent prints leading to the door.

The medical examiner, a little man with a blond ponytail and round spectacles, folded his hands together. He wore a maroon button-down Oxford shirt with the sleeves rolled up. Monique wondered if the color was chosen for the obvious reason. His black and blue windbreaker lay on top of the black bag at his feet.

"How'd you get in here?" Ogden asked.

"South door was open."

"Dang." Ogden turned and hurried down the hall so he could chastise Snelson.

"This man has been dead about nine to ten hours," Klaus said matter-of-factly in his deep voice. "Almost complete rigor. Looks like multiple stab wounds with a big blade. One hand is lacerated, indicating that he tried to defend himself. The cut to the neck is deep and is a fatal wound. But so are the stab wounds to the heart and liver. I don't know for certain the sequence of events in this attack yet."

"Nice to see you, too, Klaus," said Monique.

Klaus smiled grimly and handed them a small box of white plastic gloves. Monique always carried some in her pocket but took what Klaus offered. The two police officers pulled on gloves, and Monique pushed the door open all the way with her index knuckle. She looked into the room before entering, and even though she saw a body out of the corner of her eye, she first noted the strewn papers, the blood-splattered walls, and then turned her full attention to the dead man on the floor. His long black hair was tied back and appeared thick, like a horse's tail. The kind of hair that looks pretty blowing in the wind.

The man lay with one arm across his chest and the other stretched out behind his head, atop his hair. He wore two silver earrings in each lobe, a large silver and turquoise bracelet on his left wrist, and a thick silver wedding band on his third finger. The heavy oak filing cabinet lay across the man's hips. The blood ring emanating from the neck wound extended to the bookcases. Dead brown eyes stared up at the water sprinkler on the ceiling. Monique assessed that he was a tall, dark, and good-looking guy in life. Now he was just pale and dead. He also looked a lot like her brother Brin after he had been murdered and left in an Oklahoma City alley. Monique held her breath and felt a wave of dizziness sweep through her. She stepped out of the room and looked at the name plate on the door on her way out. It read, "Associate Professor Anthony Smoke Rise." She leaned on the outside wall.

"Big humdinger of a mess in here," Clarke said, looking around the doorway at her. "You okay?"

"I'm good," she said quickly. "I'm getting water." She took deep breaths as she made long strides towards the water fountain across the hallway.

"See, his neck's cut," she heard Klaus tell Clarke. "That's arterial spray on the walls and window glass. The windows are open, so some droplets may be on the outside wall or some may have made it to the ground."

Monique gulped cold water and watched the water swirl down the drain. The vicious murder of Smoke Rise had made her dizzy. Indians and anthropologists. *God, what a combination.*

She made her way back to the dead man's office. This time she looked around to notice details. A three-foot high castle constructed of empty Advil bottles sat on a small, undisturbed table in the corner. "Headaches." she said.

"Yup," agreed Clarke. "A *lot* of headaches."

"Stressful job, I guess," said Klaus.

"His name is Tony Smoke Rise," said a new voice behind them. The detectives turned. Ogden had returned, accompanied by a man who wore knee-length flowery shorts and a polo shirt. He extended his hand and spoke again. "Mark Fhardt, department chair." He looked down at the dead man, fascinated. "My Lord. He really is dead."

Monique didn't take his hand. She looked at the floor to see what

Fhardt's flip flops had stepped in. At least he'd walked around the prints. "What did you say your name was?"

"Fhardt," he said, then spelled it, slightly defiant. His curly brown hair and chubby cheeks made him look he had never quite grown out of childhood.

"Okay," said Monique.

Mark Fhardt continued. "Smoke Rise was associate professor of anthropology. Been here for eleven years."

"He married?" Monique queried.

Fhardt stared at Smoke Rise's body, then looked up. "Yes, he is. Was, I mean."

"Has his wife been informed?" Clarke asked Ogden.

"Actually," Fhardt interjected, "her next-door neighbor heard about it over the radio. I guess she listens to the police dispatches. Then she called here to ask. She told me that Tony's wife has the flu and she took some medication and didn't realize he hadn't come home last night."

"And how did you know it was Tony?" Clarke asked.

"Uh, well, I came in early and Mary, the secretary, told me."

Monique wondered how a wife would not know her husband didn't come home, even if she was sick. Monique possessed an internal radar system that alerted her anytime Steve was in the vicinity.

"Thanks for the information, Mr. Fhardt, but I need you to wait back there please," Monique motioned to the middle of the hallway, where several campus police now milled around. "Officers," she called out to them. They turned and Monique pointed to Fhardt.

"Sure, I'll go," Fhardt said. "Of course." Then he realized how it might look, him being in the building. "Hey, wait. I just came in to get some things for a trip."

Monique asked, "Where are you going?"

"Bahamas." Fhardt did indeed look ready for an island vacation.

"Not today you're not. I'll speak with you in a few minutes. Officer Ogden, escort the gentleman to his office and make sure he stays there."

Ogden motioned to the expressionless Frank Villario, who moved close enough to Fhardt that the chairman backed up a few steps. Fhardt then walked hurriedly down the hall with the intense policeman tailing him like a shadow.

"Hmmm. That boy's slicker'n okra, I'd say," Clarke said as he stepped back into Tony Smoke Rise's office.

"Yes," agreed Monique. She turned back to the mayhem in the office. Even though it was spacious, there wasn't much room to move. Books had been tossed off the shelves and file drawers pulled out. A well-tended hanging ivy basket appeared untouched, the long tendrils of green leaves gently moving with the breeze blowing through the open window.

"He was dead by the time that cabinet fell," said Klaus.

"You work fast," said Clarke.

"Seems obvious. He was stabbed multiple times and the wounds are grievous. Didn't take long for this poor fellow to die."

Monique looked again at Tony Smoke Rise's face. She sighed. *Who did this? A white man or another Indian?* After what she'd seen in her life and career, neither would surprise her.

Prior to moving to Moose City, Monique had worked in Oklahoma City and spent a few short years in Phoenix, where she met law enforcement officers who worked in the White Mountains of Arizona. She was still, years later, coming to grips with the reality that that job had shown her, that many insecure Indians who believe they are indeed inferior to white folk make life hell for each other. She had grown tired of seeing dead Indians. She had been emotionally drained, down to the dregs, trying to discover who left them so many Indians dead in dark alleys. She had grown weary of the whiskey smell and odor of dead men whose lives could have been meaningful to themselves, their families, and their tribes if only they had believed they were worthy.

The worst part of her job was finding abused Native children and women beaten and raped by men with no respect for females or for themselves. Despite the heartache she kept encountering, Monique knew there was hope. She knew plenty of Native women and men who were healthy, smart, and kind and who worked for the betterment of their cultures. They had solid family lives and a strong sense of identity. They did their best regardless of poverty and racism. *Why can't all of us do that?* She had asked herself that question a thousand times. *What's wrong with us that makes us do ourselves so much harm?*

She had tried to stay with the job. Monique was willing to overlook a few damaged personalities to punish those who were at fault. But in the end, she couldn't take the pain of it, lying awake all night, or the dreams that haunted when she did manage to sleep. She needed a new start, and she and Steve thought that by moving to Moose City she'd get away from suffering Indians for a while. *And here I am again, looking at another dead one.*

"We're here," came a husky female voice from the top of the stairs. Megan Alter, the forensic investigator, had come to dust for prints and to vacuum for samples. Jeremy Foreman, the photographer, trailed behind her like a faithful dog. His blond floppy hair and wide face made him look around seventeen. To counteract that impression, Jeremy dressed meticulously in pastel shirts with a colorful tie, pressed black pants, and jacket.

"Hey dudes," Jeremy grinned good-naturedly. "And Lady Detective," he smiled at Monique.

She nodded, smiled back, and wished he'd stop calling her that.

"Hey, Meg. Jeremy." said Clarke. "How 'bout dusting this doorknob and knobs of the other doors up here?"

"Wow, Clarke. What a novel idea." Meg was what Clarke called a "chubbette," a cute fleshy woman with dimples and short curly hair that she pulled off her face with a pink plastic headband. She wore dresses with puffy sleeves, and her nails were necessarily short. Hot pink polish showed through her plastic gloves. She dressed as if she attended a religious seminary, but she was actually a smart-mouthed atheist. She looked ten years older than her real age, and Monique figured it was because she ate copious amounts of junk food and had a fondness for Southern Comfort and Pepsi.

"And I want prints of every member of this department," added Monique. "Including cleaning people and graduate students."

"Plus the guys who buff the wood floors," said Ogden. "They're in addition to the cleaning staff. Also the plant waterers."

"The what?"

"CHS has workers who come to each building and just take care of the plants. They have keys to all the faculty offices."

"You mean, faculty don't water their own plants?"

"Well, not the ones in the halls. They water the plants in their offices. Oh, and the painters and other maintenance people have keys, too."

"Good grief," Clarke exclaimed.

23

"Tell me again who found Smoke Rise," Monique asked.

"Department secretary," said Ogden, he had his thumbs tucked in his belt again. "She's down in her office. Mary's fairly calm, but we called the health center doctor to come over to see if she needs some Valium or something."

"Don't give it to her yet," said Monique. "I want to talk to her."

MONDAY, 9:10 A.M.

After an hour of taking photographs and bagging evidence, the police allowed the body of Tony Smoke Rise to be removed. The ambulance attendant tucked the dead man's long ponytail into the bag before zipping it and lifting it onto the gurney. Klaus also left for the morgue.

"Shame," said Clarke. "Handsome guy." He then saw a framed picture of Tony and three other people on a high bookshelf. "Look, Indians."

Monique looked up at the photo. "What a hell of a detective you are."

"Not really. Seems obvious as the balls on a boxer dog."

Monique felt her eyes water even though she didn't feel like crying.

"What's wrong? You cryin'?"

She pushed her glasses to the top of her head and wiped her eyes. "Nothing's wrong."

"Yes, there is too something."

She sighed. "An Indian. Goddamit."

"You can't take it personally, Monique."

"Sure I can."

"How can you take it personally if you don't know him?"

"I don't have to know him."

"You always feel like this when it's an Indian?"

"Yes. I do."

"That's quite a burden you're hauling around."

"It's always something, Clarke. It never ends for us. Racism, poverty, discrimination, self-abuse, stereotypes. Murder's just part of it."

"All right. So Indians get killed just like everyone else. Every day. It's not your fault."

"I'm not saying it's my fault, Clarke. We've been dying for over 500 years and it sure as hell is someone's fault. More than a few people. It's the colonizers' fault for doing it to us and it's our fault for letting it happen."

"Okay." He knew better than to argue with Monique. She'd die trying to eradicate the country of racism. On top of that, her brother had been killed by some drunken white guys and that was her main reason for turning to law enforcement. Revenge combined with intense anger towards the dominant society could be dangerous motivators. He worried about her.

"Check out this one," he said as he picked up another framed photo.

Monique looked at the five people, clearly two parents and three children. One was Tony, smiling with straight white teeth. His long-haired father smiled with the same teeth and towered over everyone in the picture. Tony looked about six feet. Dad stood three inches taller and Mom a few inches shorter.

"Mama looks like she could whip some butt," said Clarke. The woman's dark brows framed intense, slanted eyes. She wore her black hair streaked with gray and pulled back at the sides, fastened with tortoiseshell clips. She appeared dangerous in a mature, cat-woman sort of way.

Two young men who looked alike stood next to Tony. Both appeared to be smiling reluctantly, and Monique figured they didn't like having their pictures taken. One had sunglasses on his head that held back his hair. The other brother wore his hair in a single hair-and-leather braid that fell over his shoulder to his hip. He had inherited his mother's threatening stare.

"Imposing family," said Clarke.

Monique looked at the photo once more. She recognized the look in the woman's eyes. "Here." She handed the frame back to Clarke. "I have a feeling something significant will hit the fan when they find out what happened to their son."

MONDAY, 9:15 A.M.

After Monique and Clarke completed their initial investigation, they removed their gloves and jackets. As they left Tony's office, Meg returned from printing the doors.

"I got prints from every knob."

"Good work. Thanks," said Monique.

"Except for two."

"What does that mean?"

"This one," she said, nodding toward the dead man's door, "and the knob to the office at the end of the hall have no prints."

"No prints?"

"Nope. Someone grabbed these knobs and turned, but they had gloves on. By doing so they cleaned the handle of prints. Not only that. In the big meeting room on the second floor there are footprints on the carpet, but it looks like the perp put socks over the shoes. I can probably determine the foot size but not the treads. It's a very plush carpet for a university classroom."

"No kiddin,'" said Clarke. "Where I went to school my classrooms always had tile or a brand X carpet that never got cleaned. And we sure didn't have all this art on the walls. In the cafeteria we . . ." Monique held up her hand as a signal to hush. She nodded for Meg to continue.

"Anyway, I didn't go in, but it appears the feet belonged to someone who came through the window. Then he went down the hall." She pointed towards the end of the hallway and the stairwell.

Sunlight through some of the classroom windows reflected off the old oak floors. The faint odor of floor wax floated through the air.

"But there's only one set of footprints in the meeting room. That means," Meg continued, "our perp went upstairs to do the deed, came back down, and left the building through a door instead of going back into the seminar room to climb down the wall."

"Ogden!" Yelled Monique. The gangly cop jogged over to her. "I need you to post someone by the meeting room one floor down. No one goes in."

"Okay. Anyplace else?"

"This floor for sure. Keep the first-floor doors closed. No students allowed in unless they have information for me." Ogden repeated the orders to Richard Snelson, who had regained his composure and stopped sweating, though his armpits revealed plate-sized stains. Monique wondered if hers looked the same. She felt hot, and a throb had started in her left temple.

"Meet us down there in a minute," Ogden said to Snelson's back.

"Why come through the window in the first place and not through the front doors?" Clarke asked aloud. "That late, nobody would see him come in."

"Always the chance that someone else might come in too," Meg reasoned. "Climbing up this way is unexpected and less chance someone would see. It's looks hard to climb up here and even worse going down, so maybe our perp changed his mind and thought about an easier way to get out." She cocked her solid hip and rubbed her chin with the back of a gloved finger.

"Climbing up the side of the building would leave more clues than coming through the front door," Jeremy said. "Down there's grass, dirt, crushed plants, all kinds of things that pick up parts of our perp." With his surfer drawl and choppy hair, Monique had at first thought Jeremy a doofus, but he did offer intelligent commentary.

"Maybe the *tankla binili* wanted us to think that an outsider did it; someone without keys to the building," Monique said.

"The what?" Clarke asked.

"Intruder."

"Oh, okay. Well, you're probably right about why he went to so much trouble. So, what's in the room the perp used as an exit?"

"Dunno," said Monique. "Let's go down and see."

The five walked down the hallway and descended the stairs, agitated and determined. On the first floor they stopped in front of two large white doors, one adorned with an engraved metal plate that read "Foghorn Memorial Dining Hall." It wasn't locked. Monique pulled open the door and cool air rushed outwards. Clarke looked around quickly in case someone undesirable was still lurking in the dark room.

"Lights here," Clarke said as he felt along the wall. He flipped the three switches. Light shot down from half a dozen chandeliers made of tear-shaped crystals, illuminating the dozen banquet tables and glass-covered cabinets along the walls that displayed gaudy china and silverware. Little side tables decorated with lamps and coasters sat on the oriental rugs atop the gold carpet.

The enormous room was partially underground. The bottom of the large windows sat level with the ground outside. "Cool. You could play basketball in here," Jeremy observed.

"Dining hall for faculty on south campus," said Ogden. "Ugly, isn't it?

Lots of money went into this. The kitchen's in back. Most mornings there's coffee on that long table back there and then lunch is served from eleven to one. There're double the coffee urns because last week was finals week. There's only lunch on Wednesdays in the summer."

"Just faculty members eat here?" said Monique. "Isn't the student union next door?"

"Students and a lot of faculty eat in the union. But the older faculty, the emeritus guys from other departments who get along with the anthropologists, eat here. Only four bucks a plate and I hear it's pretty good. Sort of a tradition to eat in the Foghorn Dining Hall. For the stuffy folks, that is."

"Jeremy," said Meg, "let's do a quick walk-through. Officer Ogden, kindly tape this room off."

Meg and Jeremy confirmed that the intruder went through the dining hall and out the door in the back of the kitchen. Trash bins and a service truck almost obscured the door from the outside. "We'll come back to this room," Meg said. "I'd rather see about the upstairs first."

"Ogden," said Monique, "please call your men to cordon off this door."

"Who's in the other office?" Monique asked as they walked back upstairs to Tony Smoke Rise's office. "The one with no knob prints?"

"The plate on that office door reads 'Professor Roxanne Badger,'" Meg said.

Monique and Clarke looked at each other. "Another Indian?" said Clarke. "You think she may have done this?"

Monique chewed on her inner cheek. "Why do you think that?" she asked. Actually, the thought had occurred to her, too. She had seen many cases of Indians' ugly behavior against other Indians. Although she felt guilty thinking that a Native woman could murder a Native man whose office was just down the hall, she knew for a fact that Indians could behave as badly as anyone else. That thought made her queasy.

"Dunno," Clarke was saying. "Indians. Maybe they didn't get along. You said that happens sometimes."

"Yes, I did say that."

"So maybe this Badger lady had something to do with Smoke Rise's demise."

"Maybe." She abruptly turned and left Tony's office with Clarke close behind her. Meg, the clue-finder, dove into the challenge of locating hair, torn nails, skin flakes, eyelashes, and other miniscule body parts that might have been left behind by the killer.

They started for the seminar room, but stopped in front of a door with the plate that read "Graduate Study Hall." Monique used the master key to enter the large room that looked twice the size of the seminar hall. Three rows of study carrels divided the room, the cubicles partitioned off by floor-to-ceiling walls, each space large enough for the student to have a desk, chair, personal refrigerator and an extra table for plants, computer, and printer. Two copy machines and a fax machine lined one wall.

"Check this out," said Monique as she walked to the sliding door in the center of the west wall that led to a locked outside, enclosed patio adorned with tables, umbrellas, and chairs. "Everything a college boy and girl needs."

In one corner of the room sat a large refrigerator, a sink, full-sized oven, counter with microwave, coffee pots, and mugs. Plates, cups, and canned goods filled cabinets next to two-dozen lockers with padlocks. Behind a thick door were two other doors marked MEN and WOMEN that led the way to bathrooms equipped with small lockers, toilet, sink and narrow showers.

"Wow," Clarke said. "All this for students? They could stay here all day."

"And night," agreed Monique. "They can go for a run or play basketball then come back here and shower then eat breakfast and lunch, study and go to class. I'd wager this is intended to keep students in here and out of the faculty areas. Separate the riff-raff." She tried to no avail to open a padlock on one of the lockers. "We need to go through these lockers. Tell Ogden to put a sign on this door to stay out. If students need books or discs or something then they need to write a request and we'll screen what they take." Before they left the graduate room Monique took one last look around and shook her head.

The detectives inspected the seminar room next. Meg was right. The carpet had been fluffed by cleaning, and they saw footprints leading from the window.

"I take it the carpet cleaner didn't come and go through the window," said Clarke.

"You take it right, Clarke. Go get Meg. I want her to deal with this room now."

After a thorough check of the seminar room, Meg concluded that the person who entered the window wore gloves and a size 11 men's or 12 women's shoes. "Whoever it was wore socks over the shoes," she said.

"What for?" asked Clarke.

"Well, he may have thought the socks might hide the soles. You know, didn't want to leave detailed tracks."

"How do you know the perp was wearing socks?" asked Monique.

"There were fibers stuck to the blood upstairs and more by the greenhouse where the perp climbed up. Some good prints down there including a nice outline of a butt."

"A what?"

"Whoever the perp was, he fell off the window ledge and landed butt first in the flower bed. It was a substantial, wide ass."

Monique looked out the window. She saw the greenhouse to the side and the rose bed and green grass directly under her.

"Look down again," Jeremy said.

Monique leaned out the window. "In the dirt," Meg said behind her. "You can see prints from here."

"Monique squinted and saw the outline of feet. She motioned for Clarke to have a look. "I see four prints, easy," she said.

"Yep," Meg said. "The imprint of either running or basketball shoes comes through in here, too. There're probably more sock fibers around on this carpet." Monique and Clarke turned to leave. "And detectives," she said like a mother about to gently scold her kids, "try not to walk around out there too much. There are also traces of carpet shampoo on the floor in the hallway and I want to find out where the feet went."

Monique thought for a second. "Can you do it now?"

Meg sighed. "Cops on a case," she said. "They want all the answers right now. Do you think I'm Superwoman?"

"Yes. I do. We'll wait here."

A few minutes later Meg returned. She had determined that the intruder had headed toward the stairs, but that's as far as the carpet evidence went. "Makes sense that he was headed toward Roxanne Badger's office," Meg commented. "Tried to get in there first, but the door was locked."

"Let's check it out," Monique said, heading back up to the third floor.

At Badger's office Meg stepped up to the glass window in the office door, then backed off. "Wait a minute." She took her brush out of her bag and dipped it in a can of powder, then lightly flicked off the excess. She brushed the window two inches above her nose.

"Oh yes. Indeedy do." she said to herself.

"What?" asked Clarke.

"Someone tried to look in and left a smudge."

"A student?" offered Monique.

"No. It's not face oil. The window is dusty, and the print isn't from skin. It's from a nose, like if you pressed it up against the glass, but I think the skin was covered."

"Mask?" Clarke offered.

"I'd bet."

Monique cocked her head. She had the master key in her hand. "Let's open it."

Books and files filled the large office. On one table sat a computer with dozens of sticky notes stuck around the monitor. On top of the monitor sat a small stuffed buffalo with a tiny drink umbrella taped to his side and a troll doll, the latter's hair sticking straight up as if electrified. Manila files appeared to prop up the computer from both sides. Arrowhead water bottles, ceramic coffee mugs, and several stacks of books took up space on the second large desk. Three dried ears of colored corn lay next to one speaker and several bunches of dried sage were tucked next to the other.

Monique opened a few filing cabinet drawers to find them filled to capacity with labeled file folders. The first file in the "ANT 101" drawer said "101 Syllabi," the next was "Terminology," and the one behind that was "What is Anthropology?" followed by "Stereotypes." The second drawer, entitled "ANT 202," also began with syllabi then went on to "Methodologies," "Field Work Protocol," "Clifford," then "Guidelines for Oral Research." She shut the drawer. "This is where she keeps lectures for each of her classes."

A small brown refrigerator hummed under the computer table. Clarke opened the door. "Diet drinks, a few bottles of Gatorade, yogurts, a spicy V-8, and a bottle of, what is this?" He tried to pronounce the name, "Aci-doph-i-lus tablets. What's that for?"

31

"Digestion."

He opened a desk drawer. "Hard candy, beef jerky, hot cocoa mix, a hairbrush. Ziploc baggy of soy sauce, mustard, and pepper. Parmesan cheese packs from a pizza place. The next drawer is full of pens, pads, and stuff like that." He opened the bottom drawer. "Look at this. She's got what, a dozen bottles of Tylenol in here. And some prescription painkillers. What's with Indians and headaches?"

Monique said nothing.

Meg stood looking at the monitor. A screen saver flicked from one cartoon picture to the next. "Computer's on."

"Probably stays on," Monique commented. "We oughta check out who she was corresponding with. Jeremy can do it."

"Good."

"By tonight?"

"You don't ask for much, Monique."

The walls featured an old framed map of the American West, a colorful Stanford pow wow poster, and a poster of Einstein in a sweatshirt. To the side of one filing cabinet were stacks of back issues of *News From Indian Country* and *Indian Country Today* as well as a smaller pile of the more expensive *Indian Report*. The address labels on the two newspapers had Smoke Rise's name, while the latter said "Prof. Roxanne Badger." "They shared newspapers," said Monique. "Like friends."

Monique looked out the window that faced west. Virginia creepers framed the window from the outside. A few tendrils hung down, the green leaves looking like eavesdroppers. One floor below, newly planted posies, impatiens, and other bright flowers Monique couldn't identify looked healthy under the sprinklers. "Nice view. The tough afternoon sun gets blocked by those oaks. You can smell the flowers from here."

She turned back to the office. The full recycle bins probably meant Badger was environmentally conscientious. The battery-operated clock on the wall with farm animals at each number that hung over her desk meant she wasn't humorless. An open book, files, and copies of essays lay next to the keyboard with certain passages highlighted meant that a real worker used this office.

"Busy lady. Need to ask Dr. Fhardt about her."

"What?" asked Meg behind her. "Who the heck's Dr. Fart?"

"The department chair," said Clarke.

"Figures."

Monique directed her attention to the small desk light next to the computer. It had a snake neck and shade with glass dragonflies on it, a poor man's version of a tiffany lamp. Another small lamp with a brown base and a blue shade shaped like a flower sat atop a filing cabinet. The lamp on the desk focused down on the essay next to the keyboard.

"Light's on," Monique said.

"Why have on a desk light when there're all those lights on the ceiling?" asked Clarke, looking up at the three large light panels.

"It's too much overhead light with those big fluorescent bulbs," answered Meg. "They can give you a headache. It's more peaceful to have the shades up and the small lamp on."

"Was this Badger lady in here, then went to pay Smoke Rise a visit?" Clarke asked.

"Nope. I think our prowler came here before killing Smoke Rise and found the door locked. Badger was the intended target, or at least one of the two targets. The perp thought she'd be in here. I bet if we stand outside tonight and look up here, we'll see that this light is visible from the sidewalk." Meg walked over to the lamp on the filing cabinet and rotated the on-off switch on the cord with her thumb. "No light. Burned out. Maybe this was on, too."

"That's what I'm thinking," Monique agreed. "But we'll get a better idea after doing some interviews. We'll leave you to work, Meg. Do this room, right?"

"Yes, dear, I know."

Now the detectives could begin the next phase of their investigation. Monique found it unpleasant having to look at the dead man who died unnecessarily, but it might be even worse interviewing the anthropology faculty.

MONDAY, 9:30 A.M.

Roxanne Louise Badger, cultural anthropologist and member of the Oglala Sioux Tribe of the Pine Ridge Indian Reservation of South Dakota, normally woke early on weekdays to read the newspaper, grade student papers, then write for an hour. Roxanne's husband Warren, a mixed-blood member of the Osage Nation of Oklahoma, slept while she wrote, then she woke him before leaving to play handball with her best friend Renell at the health club. Before leaving, Roxanne fed their young daughter Giselle and the numerous animals on their ten-acre property, then dropped Giselle off at preschool.

"Sure, honey," Roxanne had told Warren, an artist and sculptor, when they negotiated duties after Giselle was born. "I'll wear myself out for the good of the family in the mornings, but you'll pull your weight in the evenings." Warren became the grocery shopper, and he approached cooking as he did art. He mastered casseroles and pies and side dishes for teriyaki chicken. To Roxanne's delight, her husband became the dinner-maker, and to her surprise he thought it a fair deal.

Roxanne and her best friend Renell had met ten years ago, the day after Roxanne had been given some tough news: despite receiving two book contracts, she was destined to teach three courses that spring semester, while her colleagues who did not write taught only one or two classes so they could "concentrate on their committee assignments." Roxanne had fumed all night and was ready to work out hard the next morning. She had discovered lifting weights the year before and became instantly hooked. She arrived at the club around 6:30 A.M. and stood by the leg extension machine, waiting for a large lady with varicose veins to finish.

"Can I spot you?" a tall, skinny woman with freckles and a red pageboy haircut standing on the other side of the machine asked the big woman.

"Spot?"

"You know. Help you lift it."

"Well," the big woman looked around, confused. The weight key was under the lightest setting and twenty pounds wasn't that hard to lift. "No, I'm almost done. But thanks."

"You are very welcome." The freckled woman looked at Roxanne and winked.

When the large lady finally got up, the redhead Renell said to Roxanne, "You first."

"Thanks. But I don't need a spot."

The skinny lady laughed loudly enough for the entire gym to hear. "No shit. Really?"

After Roxanne finished one set, the other woman hopped on, added another fifty pounds and easily did a set.

"Hey, wanna squat?" she asked.

"Not really," answered Roxanne. "Tough on my knees."

"Never mind then. Let's play handball. There's a court open."

As they walked to the front desk to get gloves, goggles, and balls, Roxanne's new friend introduced herself. "Renell Sweeney." She held out her hand. Roxanne took it.

"What's your name?"

"Roxanne Badger."

"No." Renell feigned shock. "*In*teresting name." Roxanne's new friend talked loud as a matter of course. She didn't seem to care who thought what about her. "Hey, there's my husband. Honey!" she yelled. "Come over here."

A very tall, light-haired man wearing a van dyke and basketball togs yelled back, "Coming, dear."

"This is my new friend, Roxanne."

"Nice to meet you. Roscoe Sweeney," he said loudly as he almost broke Roxanne's hand.

"I was just asking Roxanne where she works," said Renell.

"University," Roxanne told them.

"Hmmm," Renell muttered while putting on her goggles and tossing the ball up and catching it behind her back. She didn't seem to approve of Roxanne's place of employment.

"Maybe my wife can knock some sense into you," Roscoe blurted out. He pinched his wife on her bottom and said, "See you two later." Roscoe jogged off, dribbling the ball as he dodged the weight machines.

"He's a judge in town," said Renell. "Used to be the Sheriff. I'm a lawyer. Wouldn't have guessed that, right?"

"Not hardly."

So began the friendship between the American Indian anthropologist Roxanne and the Irish attorney Renell.

"What's up for this week?" Renell Sweeny asked Roxanne Badger as she dropped the small black ball and smacked it with the palm of her right hand. It hit the wall at midpoint and bounced back to Roxanne, right where she wanted it.

Roxanne had worked on her conference paper longer than she'd planned that morning, but this was finals week, and she wasn't compelled to arrive at her office early. Not only did Renell have a complex attempted murder case to deal with, her husband, the Honorable Roscoe Sweeney, rolled his ATV the night before on his quest to shoot a coyote who'd been killing his chickens, and he whined all night about his bruised hip. Both women felt like doing only an abbreviated workout.

Roxanne hit the ball low to the far left side of the wall. It bounced off and landed short so Renell couldn't get to it before it made a second bounce. "Finals week. I give a final at noon and then there's the bimonthly bullshit department meeting later this afternoon."

"You mean *all* afternoon."

Renell patiently listened with concern, disbelief, and amusement to curious stories about Roxanne's department meetings. Even in perfect weather, when the anthropologists could be outside strolling, their meetings lasted for hours because the majority liked nothing better than talking. They rehashed old business, covered the new, and found irrelevant topics to discuss. Then they devoured the 16-foot submarine sandwich and full-flat Sam's Club cake Mary ordered for lunch. And they met twice a month instead of just once.

Roxanne wiped her face with her shirt, then gently cleaned her goggles. "A meeting during finals week. Believe that? The agenda is full and I swear it's the same stuff we talked about two weeks ago."

"You're just not a committee person."

"That's not the issue. I don't have time for this."

"Maybe you should be sick and not go," suggested Renell.

"Already did that twice last year. They remember absences. Especially mine." Roxanne undid her ponytail and smoothed her long hair, then quickly braided it. "Besides, they know I give a final today and I'll be in the building."

"They're crazy, Rox. Some people have power and they use it for good. Other people get a little power and they use it for their benefit." She whacked the ball and Roxanne hit it twice as hard, a sure sign that she was pissed off.

"Missing a meeting during finals is understandable. Plus you have a conference and you have to get your paper done."

"You should be my secretary."

Renell put hands on her hips as she watched Roxanne retrieve the ball. "I see lots of off-balance people, Rox. They just want you to go to the meeting so you can't finish your other work."

"Well, maybe. But if I don't show up it'll be this year's excuse to cremate me on the merit evaluations."

"So? They always come up with something." Renell scratched her nose. "If it's not absences, then they'll find something else. Like you being uncollegial because of your clothes."

"They've done that. Except it wasn't about my clothes; it was because I wear too much silver jewelry."

"Geez, see what I mean? Or they'll make up something."

Roxanne served the ball even harder. "They always do. Every fall my Document of Expectations lists publications I intend to write, classes I'll teach, and conferences I'll attend. Not only do I complete all of that, I do even more—far more than I'm required to do and more than any one else manages. Yet the annual merit committee still ignores my accomplishments in favor of searching out anything negative they can use against me."

"Sounds like they're the ones with insecurity issues."

"Yes, and they make those issues my problem."

After their handball games Roxanne completed the weight circuit twice. She hit upper body and lower body on alternate days.

"Ever consider changing jobs?" Renell's husband Roscoe had asked her one night years before at dinner.

"And do what? This is what I'm trained for. And in theory, it's a great job. Reading, writing, teaching eager students. Undergraduates, that is. The faculty have poisoned my reputation among the graduate students."

Renell gave a disgusted grunt. She piled more spaghetti onto her plate and dusted the pasta with Parmesan cheese and crushed red pepper. "Seems to me you spend more time feeling stressed out than enjoying yourself."

Roxanne sighed. "You're right. I know. I'm trying to get used to it, but I still dread the merit evaluations, promotion applications, reviewers' reports. It's mainly political, and I guess if I was a bullshitter, I'd feel right at home."

"You couldn't bullshit if your life depended on it," Renell said before she drained her beer.

"Rox, there's gotta be another way of looking at things," Roscoe said. "You can't continue to hate your job like this. It'll make you sick."

"It already makes me sick."

"You should go to another school."

"They pay me too much here. No other place offers associates what I make."

As the years passed, Roxanne had thought about Roscoe's question. She thought about moving from Moose City, but no place in the country compared to it. This was her home. The sun shined all fall and spring, and even though Moose City stood at 7,500 feet, snow melted quickly. Summer days were warm, with cool nights. She was one-half hour from the Snow Flake ski resort, and about two seconds from hiking and running trails since her house backed up against a national forest. The trails took her up into alpine areas of the Carstoney Mountains, where she could watch for elk, or down off the rim and into a valley of streams and the best fly fishing in the west.

Moose City received its name from settlers two hundred years ago. As a group of hungry migrants sat around their campfire contemplating how they'd stay alive that winter, a herd of large animals ran through camp, scattering wood and sparks in all directions. One ember landed in the gray, flammable beard of Johnson Jackson, who lived the rest of his life with hair on only one side of his face. Some of the settlers believed what they had seen were bull elk. Others argued they were moose. No one had seen moose in the area before or since, but they still decided on the name Moose City. True or not, it was a colorful story for the tourist bureau.

Despite Roxanne's pleasant activities away from her job, department meetings and end-of-semester evaluations caused her moderate headaches, whereas the annual faculty merit reviews caused incapacitating migraines. She visited her doctor to find out if she had a tumor. The doctor prescribed a painkiller with codeine, then on the next visit upped the ante to Vicodin, a narcotic that could cause damage if taken incorrectly. But it knocked out the pain in a hurry.

"Looks like stress to me, Roxanne," her doctor said. She prescribed massages and advised Roxanne to find another job. Roxanne took the former prescription but not the latter. As long as she could watch squirrels and birds at their feeder while she typed and could spot elk and deer on her hikes, she could handle her department. Or so she told herself.

"You do too much," Renell told her. "You should lay off writing for a while and rent dirty movies. Enjoy life."

"Can't," Roxanne replied. "I don't know how to sit around and do nothing. I *need* to work hard. Tony and I are alike. We *have* to work."

"And notice that your department hates you both," Renell told her.

MONDAY, 10:15 A.M.

"Chair Fhardt," said Monique as the two detectives entered Mark Fhardt's office. They got comfortable in the soft leather chairs reserved for guests. "I'm wondering," Monique began as she took out her pen and the Sponge Bob pad. "How long have you been chair?"

"About six years." Fhardt considered leaning back in his lounge chair and propping up his feet like he did when students and faculty came to talk to him, but thought that the detectives would view him as arrogant. So he sat straight and leaned forward.

"Do all faculty members have leather furniture in their offices?" Monique asked.

"No. Just me. I'm the chair, you know."

"Did you pay for it?" asked Clarke.

"For what?"

Since Fhardt offered the possibility of answers to two questions Monique said, "Both."

Perspiration erupted from Fhardt's forehead. "The chair has a yearly stipend to buy research materials." He looked from one detective to the other. "You know, photographic reproduction, books, uh . . . travel to collections."

"And how much do chairs get?"

"Well, it varies from department to department, but here the administrative stipend over my regular professor's salary is $75,000."

Monique almost choked on her spit, but continued. "And what would you get if you weren't chair?"

"With the merit increase this next year, I think around $194,000."

The two detectives sat still. They didn't clear Fhardt's salary between the two of them.

Mark Fhardt smiled nervously. "It's a big job, being chair. I have to oversee a lot of business and a lot of people. Plus there's my research." He twiddled his thumbs while trying to justify his annual take. "There's lots of research expenses. Uh, like publishers require that authors send two copies of a submitted manuscript. You know, to send out for review. And there's postage."

"And that costs a lot?" she asked calmly.

"Well, no. Not really." He realized the idiocy of what he'd said: copies were about five cents per page and the department paid for postage. "Uh, but I can purchase extra bookcases or a new computer. And I have travel funds to go to libraries."

"And to the Bahamas?"

"No, that's my money."

Monique continued to stare at him. When she questioned a person she listened with full attention even while jotting notes. She heard everything. Then she gestured around at his vast personal library. "So what books up there are yours?" she asked. "Chairs are chosen because of their expertise in the field, right? How many have you written?"

Mark had only written one slim monograph; actually he had co-authored it and on the shelf it looked like a child's Little Golden Book. "Uh, I wrote a book called *Pot Shards in Ruin #24 at Hawikah*."

She didn't change expression. "Sounds enlightening."

Fhardt's cheeks flushed. He knew he was basically a non-scholar and groped around for something easy to write about, but he managed to keep that from students. Fhardt's brown-nosing and political connections, including agreements with the most powerful members of the faculty had gotten him to where he currently sat. In just two words the detective had sarcastically summed his career.

"You know about archaeology?" he hoped she did not.

"Some. How did you get your job?" Monique asked again.

"You can't buy jobs here." Fhardt laughed nervously. "I was appointed."

"A political appointment."

"No, it's uh, it's uh . . ." Often, interrogations take place in a stark room at the police station that is designed to make the person being questioned feel vulnerable and more likely to talk. Bare walls, nothing on the table, and doors that lock from the outside are supposed to give control to those asking the questions.

But like other parts of Anthropology, the chair's space was sumptuous with heavy, carved furniture, lush green plants, and hardbound books with imposing titles. Instead of metal, Chair Fhardt had two four-door oak filing cabinets and an expensive conference table for eight sitting regally in the corner under a chandelier made of a thousand tiny crystals. The room had been organized to create the impression of power. Monique knew the image emanated from the furnishings, not from Fhardt. He should have felt at ease in the presence of his expensive furniture and alphabetically arranged books, but instead he sweated.

"Your faculty members were not given a formal search to select a chair. That's what you're saying, yes?"

"Uh, well, yes. I guess so."

Monique continued smoothly. "Tell me about Tony Smoke Rise."

"Well, he was an Indian." Fhardt paused, realizing that was a stupid way to describe a person, especially since this detective looked like she might also be one. Fhardt knew he better be careful. One wrong statement and she'd take him for a racist. "He was a cultural anthropologist who did demographics. Population statistics."

"You mean like census stuff?" Clarke asked.

"No. Well, sort of. He researched populations that were here prior to contact."

"How do you do that?" Monique already knew the basic nuances of how because she had read Russell Thornton's *American Indian Holocaust and Survival* for a book review in school.

"I think he does research with missionary lists and other textualized materials, but he also has to look at digs and midden piles."

Clarke sat forward. "What's a midden pile?"

"Old trash piles, or pits with potsherds, sandal pieces, animal bones, scraps of hides. That kind of thing."

Monique watched Fhardt as if he was the most fascinating person in the world. She would later recall every word he said along with of the body language that went along with them. "Smoke Rise seemed to be out and about with his work."

"He does a combination of archaeology and history. You know, how many people an environment could support, was there enough water, good soil, and decent weather, I don't know. It's complicated. Yes. He traveled a lot."

"Tell me about Roxanne Badger."

"She's an Indian too." Fhardt looked up and quickly added, "and a prolific writer like Tony. She's a cultural anthropologist specializing in identity issues of Indians. Mixed heritage Indians, mainly. Her last book was about how they function in their tribe compared to dealing with the outside world. Or something like that."

"Now that does sound interesting," Clarke said. "Interesting" came out "innersting." Clarke's parents were Irish and English, the former staunchly Catholic and the latter Protestant. He dealt with heritage every day of his life.

Clarke's words made Fhardt's head hot. Anytime someone praised Badger or Smoke Rise his ears poised to burst into flames.

"What tribe?" Monique asked.

"Uh, Sioux."

"Specifically, which Sioux? Lakota? Dakota? Minneconjou? Mdewakanton?"

"Well uh, I don't know except it was Sioux."

Monique stared at Fhardt a few seconds to let him know she was displeased with that answer. Monique then asked. "What else does she do?"

"She's on her third or fourth book. She also has several dozen essays published."

"I can see that Badger and Smoke Rise work hard. I checked out their offices." The only paper she saw in Fhardt's office was a newspaper sitting on the massive desktop.

Fhardt tried to figure out Detective Blue Hawk. Clearly, she was the officer in charge, so he didn't pay too much attention to Clarke. Fhardt tried to meet her gaze but he kept looking down at his desktop. She looked like she knew what he was thinking. So he sat still and tried not to fidget. What was it that gave a liar away? Darting eyes? Licking his lips?

"Do Smoke Rise and Badger make a habit of working late?" She asked.

"Well, I don't really know. But with all the writing they produced there was no way that it could be done during the days, when they stay occupied with classes and meetings." Fhardt felt a bit queasy admitting that Smoke Rise and Badger worked hard.

"Got resumes for your faculty?"

"Yes, I have merit files from last year." Fhardt started to stand.

"Not now," Monique stopped him. "Actually, we'll need access to all the files."

"All of them?" Fhardt asked, surprised.

"Yes. For the entire department going back say, eleven years."

Fhardt paused for a second. "I'll get them ready for you."

"No need. You have to leave the building after we're through here. We'll find them."

Fhardt panicked at the thought of strangers having access to his office. "I can stay and show you where the faculty files are."

"Are the files in this room?"

"Yes."

"We'll find them," she repeated.

Fhardt shifted in his chair. He was used to asking the questions. He looked at Clarke and saw him smiling.

"Where were you last night between ten and midnight?"

The chair's eyes widened. He had only heard that asked in the movies. "I was home in bed. My wife and I watched Letterman and Conan, then uh, an old *Streets of San Francisco.* And my daughter called from Lexington during that time. There should be a record."

"Phone records don't tell us who did the talkin,'" said Clarke. "What size shoes do you wear?"

"About a ten. Sometimes a ten-and-a-half."

"Who would have been the last person to enter the big meeting room on the second floor over the weekend?"

Fhardt's heart raced. "Uh, the custodian, Mrs. Donald, cleans the rooms at night. Probably her."

Monique scribbled on her Sponge Bob pad. "Where are the graduate student files?" she asked.

"In Professor Belinda Rinds' office. She's the department's graduate director. She's pretty private. I mean, you can call her and ask if you can . . ."

"No need."

Chairman Fhardt breathed heavily through his open mouth. Nothing would be the same again. Ever.

"So when's your trip?"

"I leave tonight."

"Sorry. Can't leave town."

"Am I a suspect?"

Monique put her pad in her jacket. "Not formally. Not at this moment. But we've just started to investigate. And it would look rather suspicious to a lot of people, you running off to the Bahamas right now, wouldn't it?"

"Wait a second. If I'm not a suspect, then why did you question me?"

"You didn't have to answer. Now if you'll excuse us," she motioned with a sweep of her arm towards the door.

The red-faced chairman Fhardt was booted from his office and the detectives locked his door behind them. Policeman Villario stood outside the door next to a pear-shaped man with an enormous head. His long and narrow ears gave him a slightly alien look. He had on Bermuda shorts similar to Fhardt's and a T-shirt that said "Hard Rock Café Los Angeles." Fhardt started to speak to him, but the man ignored him as he took a step towards the detectives.

"This individual says he wants to talk to you," said Villario, his heavy moustache did not move when he spoke. He stood facing the shorter man, hands on his belt waiting to see what he might have to do.

"Yes, I'm Associate Chair Dr. Ross Clipper," the large man thrust out his right hand to Monique and squeezed it tight. Monique winced. "I had to come in and tell you."

"Tell us what?" Clarke asked without introducing himself.

"Well, Tony had lots of enemies." Clipper didn't look into the eyes of either detective. He kept shifting his gaze to objects around the room. "I mean, he was hard to get along with and a very difficult personality. Never socialized with us, never ate lunch with anyone in the department except that Roxanne Badger. No one likes her either."

"Now why might that be?"

"Those two Indians stick together. They got hired because of their race with no merit evaluation involved. The chair who hired them that year was a Black woman who hired all kinds of minorities like Roxanne."

"You mean qualified applicants?"

Clipper's face turned pink. "No. I mean people who get whatever they want around here because they're in a protected category. Not many of them left now except the three Indians."

Monique motioned to the door. Her voice stayed even. "Let's go to your office, Mr. Clipper."

"Hey, why?"

"You don't want anyone to overhear you, do you?"

"I don't care."

Monique's mouth smiled but her eyes didn't. "I do. Let's go."

Monique and Clarke followed Clipper to his office door, which was ten feet down the hall from Fhardt's office. Clipper opened the door without unlocking it. He had already been inside it that morning.

Clipper walked to the other side of his desk and sat down. He picked up a can of Coke that sat on his cherry desk. There were no coasters and between the litter of candy wrappers, used Kleenex, and packs of gum, the tabletop was stained by the wet bottoms of dozens of soda cans. Like Fhardt's office, Clipper's was well furnished with new leather chairs and wooden bookcases. The odor of sweaty feet permeated the stuffy room. Monique mentally compared Badger and Smoke Rise's office setup to Fhardt's and Clipper's and was willing to bet that the associate chair published about as often as Fhardt did.

Clipper didn't ask if the detectives wanted to sit. So Monique and Clarke sat anyway in the two chairs that faced Clipper's desk. His computer played a little song.

"Is that a card game on your computer?" Clarke asked.

"Yeah."

"You can do that?"

"Well, yeah. Lots of games on there."

Monique crossed one long leg over the other and opened her Sponge Bob pad. "You said that there are three Indians in this department?"

"Yeah. Smoke Rise, Badger, and Wenetae. Pauley Wenetae. He's okay, though."

"And what happened to the other minority faculty?"

"Quit years ago. Just like that." Clipper snapped his fingers. "Couldn't take the pressure of having to be team players. All of them were loners. Except Wenetae. He knows how to play ball around here. Those others were intimidated by the rest of us."

"Intimidated? How?"

"Some people around here are the core of the department. We do the important scholarship and we teach the most important courses."

"And that's intimidating?"

"Well, yeah. You know."

"Oh yeah. I know. What did you think of their research?"

"Minor. All about identities and not rigorous."

"And what do you do?"

"I run the anthropology lab."

"What does that mean?"

Clipper took a bag of peanuts from his top drawer and poured a large amount into his upturned mouth. "I organize the lab. I oversee the grad students."

Monique sighed. "I mean, what do you study?"

"I'm a physical anthropologist. I study human bones."

Clarke sat up. "Whose bones?"

"North American skeletal remains."

Clarke sat back with a sigh. This was Monique's territory.

"Old Indian bones," Monique corrected.

"You can say that. Yes."

"What for?" Monique asked coolly. Clarke looked at her steadily. He knew that in a situation like this, the calmer she appeared the more agitated she felt.

"What for? Ha! You can find out all kinds of things looking at them. How they died, what they ate, if they had injuries, how tall they were, how long they lived."

She didn't ask another question for about thirty seconds, which was long enough to make Clipper squirm. Clarke had learned a lot of things from Monique Blue Hawk and one of the most important was to be comfortable with silence—or to at least act like it doesn't bother you. Clarke knew that Monique could stare at Clipper for an hour and appear tranquil.

"And what do the Indians in this department think about you studying Indian bones?"

Clipper's forehead shined with sweat. "What did I tell you already? Badger and Smoke Rise are know-nothings. They don't do fieldwork with artifacts. They're just want to block us scientists from doing our work."

Monique didn't flinch. "So Tony Smoke Rise didn't like what you're doing?"

"No, he sure as hell didn't like it, and neither does Badger. I don't give a rat's ass what they think. It's for the good of society."

"How's it good for society?"

Clipper glared at her as he did at an undergraduate who asked an off-limits question. "You giving me a hard time because he's an Indian?" He paused and his eyes narrowed as he looked hard at Monique. "*You* an Indian?"

"Clipper," Monique said in a voice that dropped an octave, "I do the questioning."

Clarke had only seen Monique lose her temper once. A man they had questioned about the disappearance of his wife called Monique a squaw. She smiled, told the perp they were finished, and when he stood she walked over to him and jabbed him in the solar plexus with two fingers—not enough to make him fall down, but enough to cause the man to lose his breath and to fall against the table. She straightened him up with her left hand under his armpit and her right fingers around his nuts. "Sorry, my hand slipped," she whispered. If Clarke hadn't had gotten between Monique and the perp, the guy would have lost parts of his anatomy.

Clipper sat up straight and leaned forward. "Do you know who I am?"

"Ross Clipper."

"No, I mean, do you know that I'm a respected scholar at this university? And I'm a prominent member of this community."

"I've never heard of you," Monique said.

Clipper licked his lips. "I shouldn't have to answer these questions."

"You do. A man is dead. A man you say was intimidated by your power. A man you say challenged your work. An Indian. An individual who was your colleague and who you claim did not know crap."

"Now you're saying that he got killed because I didn't like him challenging me?"

"I'm not saying anything you didn't already say. I'm just revisiting the information I have so far."

"I'm not telling you anything else, then. I think you're prejudiced, and I'm calling my lawyer."

Clipper stood and came around to the door. He opened it and waited for the detectives to leave. Clarke and Monique stood.

Monique didn't blink. "Where were you last night between ten and midnight?"

"Hey. I came over to give you information, not be interrogated."

Monique took two steps to Clipper and put her nose a few inches from his face. "It's either here in your office where no one can see you," she said quietly, "or we can haul you to the station. And then the rubbernecks down on the sidewalk can watch." Monique stared at Clipper as she lied to him. Unless Clipper became a suspect, he didn't have to say a word, much less go to the station. Monique, however, figured that Clipper didn't know the law. She also figured that he wouldn't be so tough when a woman challenged him.

Clipper licked his lips with his big pink tongue. "I was home. Asleep. I played golf yesterday and got sunburned." He pulled down his shirt collar and pulled up his sleeves and showed them white skin that contrasted with the red, burned skin. "See? It made me sick so I took some Tylenol and went to bed early."

"You married?"

"My wife was there, yeah."

"What size feet?"

"Feet? About a nine."

"I don't mean her. I mean you."

"I am talking about me."

"Oh." Monique looked down. "Well, that will be all for now, Mr. Clipper."

"Dr. Clipper," he corrected.

Monique leaned in towards the man with ruddy cheeks and a jiggly belly. She didn't blink. "Clipper. I'll call you when I want to talk to you again." Clarke wondered what would happen if Clipper didn't back off. She would never, ever back away from him. As far as Clarke could tell, no one intimidated Monique.

Clipper blinked a few times in confusion and stepped back. Then he burped and wiped his mouth with the back of his hand.

"You have to leave the building," she added.

"Hey, I'll be happy to."

Clipper turned on his right foot. The two detectives watched the professor waddle back down the hall and out of sight around the corner of the stairwell. "Well, well. Someone's all swelled up like a poisoned pup," Clarke observed.

"A what?"

"A snakebit pup. You know."

"Right."

"I bet his daddy never smacked the fire outta him, but wishes he had."

"Maybe his daddy did smack him, and too much."

The two walked the hallway to where Villario stood outside of Fhardt's office. "Little feet don't mean much, you know," Clarke said. "It's easier to wear a bigger size than to wear shoes too small."

"Now you're thinking, partner." Monique slapped Clarke on the arm. "Let's go to Wenetae's office before anything else. Frank, do you know where Pauley Wenetae's office is?"

Clarke noticed that Monique wasn't sweating. If he had challenged a man like that, he'd for sure be sweating. She looked sweaty after seeing the dead Smoke Rise, but a run-in with a large living white man didn't faze her. *Inneresting.*

"No, ma'am. But it's probably on the third floor where they put the Indians and new people," he said with a smirk

"Is that to keep them farther from the elite anthropologists on the first floor?"

"That would be my guess. Want me to go with you?" Frank looked eager as he put his hand on his sidearm.

"No thanks. You're needed here."

"I wonder how many students get their butts kicked by Clipper," Clarke asked as they climbed the steps.

"Not just students, I'd wager. Some of these professors have a God complex. Like a lot of doctors. They get away with their arrogance because people let them."

"I bet Clipper was a handful as a kid and his momma fed him with a slingshot."

"Where do you come up with this stuff, Clarke?"

"Not hard to picture his poor momma doin' that, right?"

Monique smiled.

They walked the third floor, looking at each name plate on the doors and didn't find Wenetae's office. Then they covered the second floor, and it wasn't there, either. "Gotta be here someplace," Monique said as they went back to the ground floor.

The detectives finally found Wenetae's room two doors from the department office behind a tall, heavy cherry wood door. Monique turned the key and pushed the big door open to find a spacious room large enough for an aerobics class.

"Dang," said Clarke. "Twice the size of Tony and Roxanne's offices."

"And half the books," added Monique.

A cherry table held only a computer and printer, and the desk featured a coffee mug and one framed photo. No papers, no journals. Books filled a few shelves but nothing overflowed, giving the impression that whoever worked here didn't do a whole lot that involved documentation. Potted plants sat under the large windows that offered a view of the east lawn and flowerbeds. A faded print of Mount Everest hung over the computer table and the velvet silhouette of the Indian on a tired horse called *End of the Trail* was nailed by a window next to a "dream catcher" made of yarn and dyed turkey feathers. Except for the two lounge chairs with a small table in between, there was nothing homey about the office; it seemed merely a place for the occupant to park for the short time he had to be at work.

Clarke picked up a photo of two men on the shelf. "I take it the one on the left's Pauley."

Monique glanced at the talk dark man dressed in a thin polo shirt and jeans with an emerging pot belly and thin ponytail draped over his shoulder. "The other guy's the university president, Brion." She looked inside the coffee mug. "Coffee's all dried up. So much for Wenetae."

"I sure would like to look at Clipper's and Fhardt's home garbage," Monique said. "And I want to search their homes."

"It'll be tough getting a warrant right now, and it's a sure thing that Fhardt and Clipper won't let us in even if we ask nicely."

"Then let's get moving on the evidence."

"Will do. And we need to talk to Roxanne Badger."

"Yes, we certainly do," answered Monique. "But first let's talk to the secretary."

MONDAY, 10:30 A.M.

Tony Smoke Rise's parents received the news of their son's death a few hours after Moose City police received the call from CHU police. The Moose City police had in turn contacted the Hopi Tribe and Flagstaff police, 800 miles to the south. Flagstaff PD dispatched an officer to the Smoke Rise residence to give them the devastating news.

Justin Creamer hated the part of his job that required him to inform families about the deaths of their loved ones. He tried to wash off the residue of their sorrow, but their anguish and despair coated him. Creamer's face adopted a melancholy expression like that of mortuary workers, ambulance drivers, and attendants at animal shelters who perform euthanizations.

Creamer drove from the station in downtown Flagstaff up Highway 180, the well-traveled route that led to the south rim of the Grand Canyon. He passed Coconino Center for the Arts and the Museum of Northern Arizona, and from there it was only a few hundred feet to the entrance of the neighborhood of Cheshire. Creamer parked his car in front of the small, neat-as-a-pin home. Fortunately for the Tony's parents, they had bought a home that was not south of a once-vacant field. Residents on the south were not so lucky, and now two-story homes blocked their view of the San Francisco Peaks.

Flowers decorated the beds and fruit trees surrounded the Smoke Rise home. The wood-sided house had recently been reshingled, and the two silver maples in front looked newly planted. "Shoot," Creamer said out loud. A decent family was about to find out their son is dead.

He got out of his patrol car and walked up the sidewalk that was lined on either side with pea gravel. An evaporative cooler covered by a blue tarp sat on the Smoke Rises' roof. Not many people had air conditioning in Flagstaff. The summer temperature rarely exceeded 90 degrees in Flag, but it was hotter than it used to be. The monsoons came later, and the threat of wildfire was exacerbated by the pine bark beetle that killed pine trees.

On the porch, moss roses grew in whiskey barrels, and an engraved "No Smoking No Evangelists" sign had been glued under the doorbell. Creamer pressed the lighted button and heard pleasant chimes on the inside. The door opened and out wafted the aroma of pot roast, perhaps in a crock pot with onions and carrots, he thought. A dishwasher was sloshing and he smelled detergent along with the cooking roast.

His next image was of a huge, silver-haired man of about sixty-five with thick hair neatly combed to his shoulders, dressed in blue jean cut-offs and a short-sleeved blue T-shirt that showed his defined arms. He looked like the winner of a tough man contest, or maybe an Italian movie star, Creamer thought, but his dark skin and hawk nose were definitely Indian. The tallest Hopi Creamer had ever seen was about five-ten, and he wondered if this man was a mixed-blood. "Smoke Rise" didn't sound like a Hopi name.

"Who is it, Glenn?" a female called from a back room.

Glenn locked eyes with Creamer. "Police," the woman's husband answered in a booming, masculine voice.

"Mr. Smoke Rise?" He introduced himself and showed the man his identification. Justin dreaded this.

Glenn nodded.

"Sir, I'm afraid I have bad news." Glenn Smoke Rise cocked his head as if hard of hearing and listened to what the uniformed officer told him. "Sir, it's my sad duty to inform you that your son Tony Smoke Rise has died. Apparently, his wife is too aggrieved to call you and requested the police do so. He was found dead by a co-worker in his office at Central Highlands University this morning. Investigators are on the case right now."

Glenn stood motionless. His wife Arlene had also heard. She fell against her husband and strong arms caught her.

"What do you mean?" She asked breathlessly. "Are you certain?" Her dark eyes stared into Creamer's hazel ones.

"Yes, ma'am."

She had retrieved her breath and spoke in a normal, but dangerous tone. "What happened?"

"Well, from what little I was told, he was discovered dead in his office. The department secretary found him this morning when she came in."

Husband and wife looked at each other.

"Had he been killed?"

"Uh, yes ma'am. I don't have details on that."

Mrs. Smoke Rise looked back at the officer. She assessed him as a man who didn't have any more information than he had already shared.

"What about his wife? Is she all right?" she asked.

"Yes. Although she has the flu, I'm told."

"Roxanne, what about her?"

"I'm sorry. I don't know who Roxanne is. I can call and find out."

"Do that. Roxanne Badger. His colleague. Call me and let me know how she is, please."

"Can I send a priest or other clergy out?" asked Creamer politely. "We can recommend counselors and other services if you desire."

Arlene knew what to do and she didn't need anyone's advice.

"No. I appreciate the job you have, officer. You can tell the police in Moose City that we're on our way."

"One more thing. I'm to tell you they must perform an autopsy. They weren't sure about your religion."

Arlene stared into Creamer's eyes for two heartbeats and said, "I insist on it."

MONDAY, 10:40 A.M.

Mary, the secretary, sat sipping orange juice, the boxed kind with a straw, the same brand Monique put in Steve's and Robbie's lunch boxes. Mary had stopped crying, but her hands shook.

"Mrs. Cooper, I'm Detective Blue Hawk and this is Detective Clarke. We'd like to ask you some questions, but you don't have to answer without an attorney present."

"No, no. Ask. I'm okay." Mary was taller than both detectives. She looked to be around twenty-five, although they later learned that she was forty-one. Monique was once again struck at how quickly she had reached forty-eight. *Do I look as old and tired as I feel?*

"Please, sit down," Monique said to her. The detectives pulled up chairs and sat in front of Mary. "Tell us what happened this morning."

Mary sat and crossed her long, thin legs at the ankles. She looked as lean and twiggy as a high jumper. "Well, normally I don't arrive at work until eight. During finals week I get here early to deal with students pretending to be sick so they can miss tests they haven't studied for. Plus there's the end-of-semester financial paperwork, and I have to call the budget office to make sure everything's done right."

"I got a note from Tone several days ago asking if I'd correct an erroneous call listed on his phone bill. But I hadn't answered him yet." She took a deep breath. "Bullshit work simply overwhelms me around here and I hadn't found time to see to his request. I did make a note to take care of the phone before anything else, though. After I got the coffee pots going in the lounge I called Tone's office. He came in early a lot. Tone drank a mix of decaf and regular. He'd stand at the coffee pots and put in half a cup of one, then fill it the rest of the way with the other, then he'd add a little creamer and a shake of sugar then a packet of Sweet'N Low. It'd take him five minutes to get all that together." She smiled at the thought. "Faculty and students are supposed to give me four dollars a month to pay for coffee but a lot of them never pay. Tony always gave me more than that. I think he was afraid that someone would think he was stealing. Anyway, he and his friend Rox Badger have a conference at the end of the week and were working on papers."

"Rox and Tone?"

"Oh, I mean Drs. Badger and Smoke Rise."

"You knew them well. First-name basis. Nicknames, even?"

"They told me to call them that. We got along well."

"All right. Go on."

Mary folded her arms in front of her. "Well, I knew Tone was here because I saw his truck in the lot. I dialed his extension and got a busy signal. That's unusual. If a professor's not available to answer or if they're on the line the caller gets voice mail. A busy signal means the line's been pulled out of the wall, and it's a pain to deal with because I have to get telecom over here and they take forever. So I got the master key. It's hidden behind that metal panel over there."

Clarke walked over and looked at the small metal door but did not touch. Mary sat forward and put her hands on her knees, then straightened her back. "I locked this door behind me. It wasn't eight o'clock yet. I went up to the third floor. The lights weren't on. Tone's door was slightly open. I pushed it." Mary quickly added, "I didn't put my hands on the knob."

"Good thinking," Monique said.

"As the door opened, I was looking down, so the first thing I saw was the overturned recycle basket. I think I said 'Oh crap' and wondered if someone had robbed the office. I pushed the door more and looked up. I saw red-streaked walls, red spots on the windows, a smashed monitor screen, and papers and files strewn everywhere. Then I saw him under the cabinet. I only stood there for a few seconds. Then I turned and ran down the hall."

"Did you notice anyone else in the building?" Monique asked.

"No. I felt like I was the only one here even though I knew Tone was upstairs. No noise. I figure no one had been in the mailroom since I closed up Friday at 4:30. The mail came late and I hadn't sorted it out yet. The pile hadn't been messed with, and the late afternoon faxes from the machine were still in the tray."

"What was Tony like?" asked Monique. She had a variety of impressions, but figured Mary would have a fairly accurate one.

"Honest. Hard working. You know he was best friends with Roxanne Badger? Well, they stayed pretty quiet. Well put together, if you know what I mean. He and Rox always have a project going. You know, a book, essay, grant application. Students like them a lot. The undergraduates, I mean. They haven't taught grad courses in a long time. It was my birthday last week. Rox and Tone remembered and sent me cards. Tone remembered Secretary's Day, too."

She pointed to the bulletin board above her computer. A few cards were thumb-tacked to the cork. "Fhardt sent flowers. Of course, he's my boss and needs my support." She brushed back a few tears. Her nails were filed short and went unpolished. "Well, that's all I know. I came down here and called the campus police and they got here in minutes. I've been in here ever since."

"Did Tony have a temper?"

"Why do you ask that? Does that matter?"

"Maybe. How he dealt with others can be a factor in how they dealt with him."

"Oh. Okay then, yes, he had a temper. And a pretty good one. He spoke up a lot and had arguments with some of the faculty."

"Like who?"

"Fhardt. Clipper. Langstrome. Those three, mainly. I heard them shouting about Clipper's use of skeletons or something. I know he didn't like some of the other professors either, but he avoided them. I know he stayed away from Belinda Rinds because he thought she was devious. 'Quietly devious,' is what he once told me."

Mary paused to sip her drink, then looked over her shoulder to see who else might be listening. Monique noticed.

"It's okay. You can speak freely. Tell us about the faculty in this department. Did Tony have enemies? Sounds like he did."

"Are you kidding?" she sniffed. "That's an understatement. I recognize resentment when I see it. A lot of people here are jealous of Rox and Tone."

"You mean like Ross Clipper."

"Especially Clipper. He and those others are jealous of Paul Deerbourne and Samantha Brazzi, too, but they're off limits for harassment."

"Who're they? Why's that?" asked Monique.

"Well, they're white and tenured and well connected in the city. Paul would personally beat the peawadding out of anyone who tried to undermine him, and Sam's husband would do the same for her. Plus they get big bucks from other sources, like the Brazzi's Italian restaurant, and can afford to hire a good lawyer if they need one. Assistant and associate professors usually can't. You might spend tens of thousands suing the university for harassment or discrimination and still not win."

"Universities have deep pockets."

"This one has the deepest. Anyway, Rox and Tone often work alone up here. None of the other professors work late in their offices. Most come in only three days a week, or two if they could swing a Tuesday-Thursday schedule." She snickered.

"What's funny?" asked Monique.

"Nothing." Mary stood and walked to the switch plate by the door and turned on the ceiling fan. "I was thinking of what it's like around here when it comes time for Fhardt to schedule courses. Everyone wants Tuesday-Thursday courses and not everyone can have them. I see the course request forms before he does and included in the requests are the justifications for why faculty members need to be here for only two days a week. Clipper's really good at rationalizing why he needs just two days."

"Only two days a week?" Clarke looked incredulous.

"Oh, yes. Fraudulent reasons, too. The idea that every person in the department does intensive research and is writing every day of the week is absurd. Only four or five people do that. Besides Rox and Tone, there's Paul and Samantha and the new professor, Janine Boster. She's on fellowship leave in Mexico right now. A few others are good at writing fellowship applications but they never do anything with the money except take a vacation. The other published professors left a long time ago."

"You think some of these people are jealous enough to kill Tony?"

Mary shrugged. "Who knows what goes through some people's minds?" She dabbed her nose with the tissue." I hear a lot of things working here. Some of those professors, like Belinda Rinds, tell students all sorts of bull about Rox and Tone. That they don't know the current theories, they're essentialists, they can't help students find jobs. Blah blah." She took another draw of her juice.

"Essentialists?" queried Clarke.

"That only Indians know about Indians and therefore only Indians should write about Indians. Neither one believes that. They've said so."

"But students believe it?"

"Of course. By telling the graduate students that's what Rox and Tone preach, then students believe they can't succeed if they work with them. It's a perfect ploy to keep graduate students away from professors who threaten to make the other professors look less than stellar. Students don't know anything about departmental politics. The professors they love the most are the ones who wipe their noses. And I can see who's the next target: Janine Boster. She's young, attractive and is going to be well-published. She got a grant from the state historical society and has applications in to big agencies. I heard Belinda whining to one of her students the other day about Janine. Something about Janine getting a new telephone with call waiting."

"Hard to believe professors do that to each other," mused Clarke.

"Hell yes, they do. As soon as Janine starts out-publishing Belinda and these other professors they'll come after her. They already screwed her on the merit evaluation this year. She won a prize from Ethnohistory and hardly anyone told her congratulations."

"Tell us about the other Indian faculty, Pauley Wenetae," said Monique.

"He was hired at the same time as Rox and Tone, but he's nothing like them. He speaks around campus at roundtables, seminars, and he always does the Indian Prayer at big functions. Pauley gets along well with the schemers in the department because he allows them to use him. Pauley's never here. He takes a research trip at least once a month."

"How does he manage that?" asked Clarke.

"Courtesy of a large grant Clipper won for developing a Native Studies program or something. Pauley's supposedly out doing more fund-raising."

"Were Tony and Roxanne part of the grant?"

"I doubt it. There's quite a bit of objection in this department to Clipper's stance on repatriation. He drops prominent names in the department to get grants to do research about Indians, or to develop programs to help them, then he doesn't follow through. He uses the money to travel. Clipper's very good at writing grants. He uses the reality that there're Indians in the department, and he knows how to give the impression that they all work together and that funding will help them all."

Clarke wrote fast. Monique asked, "How can Clipper get away with writing grants using Indians if he doesn't help them?"

"Happens everywhere. Biologists do it, too, Roxanne told me. They say they're doing AIDS research among tribes. They are, but their grants also promise they'll employ Native graduate students and they don't. The internships go to white students. All of this is why Rox and Tone decided to create the institute."

"Institute?"

"Yeah, the Indigenous Studies Institute. For a couple of years they've been getting the curriculum together and raising money for a new building."

"Wait a second," Monique said. "You're telling me that Roxanne and Tony have a new program starting and have money for a new building? That takes a lot of funding."

"They've raised over one million dollars with more coming." She looked from one detective to the other. "You didn't know this, I guess."

"Fhardt didn't say a word about it," said Clarke.

"Sounds like it's colder than a mother-in-law's love around here," said Clarke.

Monique winced. Both women looked at him and said nothing.

For a few seconds the three pondered the conversation so far, then Mary asked, "Want a juice?"

"Actually, yes," Monique answered. If she didn't drink more liquid she'd have a migraine by lunch. Mary got a couple of juices from the small refrigerator under her desk.

"Did Pauley get along with Roxanne and Tony?" Monique asked as she tried to put the straw in the juice box without squirting juice on her leg.

"They're disgusted by him and stay away."

"Did Roxanne and Tony gossip?"

"They may have to each other. But I never heard them gossip to anyone else. No."

Mary wadded up her juice box then threw it towards the wastebasket across the room. It bounced off the wall and fell in. Clarke's eyebrows shot up.

Mary crossed her arms again. "I may have said too much." Mary took another Kleenex and wiped her nose. "I've been here a long time." She took a another deep breath and let it out slowly. "This place impresses you with its Ivy League looks, but it's all a façade."

"What do you mean?" asked Clarke.

"It's all about politics, schmoozing, knowing the right people.

The phone rang and Mary jumped. "Let the answering machine pick up," Monique instructed. Mary reached over and turned the volume down.

"The only reason the strong faculty members stay here is because of the environment around Moose City. Skiing, hiking, elk in your backyard. And that includes Tone and Roxanne."

"I don't get it," said Monique. "Why does the administration let this happen?"

"Easy. The upper administration lets the chairs deal with their departments, and the deans deal with their colleges and they're supposed to work together to solve problems. If the chairs and deans don't want to do anything about the problems they just ignore them. Even if chairs want to do something about incompetent teachers it's impossible to get rid of them. Some of the worst ones ingratiate themselves with the president or high-powered members of the city. The president protects quite a few of these faculty and the chairs and deans know it.

"Look," she said, opening her hands, palms up. "A lot of assistant professors got promoted to associates with tenure as a matter of politics, not of merit. With the exception of political science and biology, no department on campus has a list of stipulations the applicant has to meet prior to submitting a promotion and tenure application. Departmental committees judge the applications, but decisions are purely subjective. The committees in this department change every two years and if someone wants a promotion, all they have to do is wait for friends to sit on the committee."

"That's not fair. Is it?" asked Clarke.

"No, it's not. But that's the way it works."

"This is a very strange business," Monique said.

"There's no business like academia," Mary agreed. "The irony is that the most offensive faculty can't get jobs anyplace else. Here, they call themselves 'teacher-scholars.' At other universities, they'd be known as 'dead wood.'"

"Do you think someone on the faculty murdered Tony Smoke Rise?" Monique asked.

Mary sniffed and wiped her blue eyes with the back of her hand. She straightened her spine again and pushed back her amber bangs. "Most of these people couldn't actually hurt another person. But any number of them would have loved to see Tone and Rox gone. This place is very strange."

"Hmmm," Clarke said as he rubbed his chin.

"They're crows," Mary said.

"What do you mean?" asked Monique.

"You know, crows hang around campus, looking to steal food. They take eggs from those sparrow nests in the trees. See? Right outside there." They looked through her window to the line of apple trees. "I watch them do it every year. Flocks have sentinels that watch and analyze everything, plus scouts who come ahead to check out a scene and then they go tell the rest of the group what's going on."

Monique looked at Clarke. "Sentinels and scouts. Interesting comparison. Crows certainly are opportunistic."

Mary cleared her throat before speaking. "Yes. And so are some people in this department."

MONDAY, 11:00 A.M.

Roxanne ate a banana and drank a chocolate Slim Fast on the drive to work. She thought about how she could've parked right outside the anthropology building if she'd paid $395 for a yearly parking sticker. Most of the time she didn't have much to carry to and from her office, so walking was no big deal. Rainy days were more problematic, as were the days she had to carry her replenishments of Diet Dr. Peppers. Today she decided to take her chances on a place off-campus and found one in front of the Hole-in-the-Middle Bagel Shop a half-mile away on Pine Del Street.

She still felt hungry by the time she parked and had just enough time before class to pop into the bagel place to buy a cinnamon raisin bagel smeared with cream cheese and an orange juice that she consumed as she walked. She passed Charlotte's Web used bookstore, which featured textbooks, pornographic greeting cards, and a room for accordion and bagpipe lessons. Then she walked past Blockbuster Video and a Thai restaurant.

Roxanne passed the Pine Del Café, which invariably had customers sitting out front at the sidewalk tables whom local residents called "hippies." Their ear, nose, and lip rings shone in the morning sun, and their dreadlocks hung heavily to their shoulders. Smells of fried potatoes, coffee, and breakfast meats wafted through the air. As Roxanne passed the café windows she looked at her reflection and made a mental note to brush her hair again when she got to work.

Roxanne wore her waist-length hair tied back in a ponytail, then propped it up with a butterfly clip so that it looked like a Tennessee Walker's cut tail. The poor horses react to their tails being cut on the underside by holding them up so they look like a waterfall. It's pretty but no doubt hurts like hell. As her mother had told her when Roxanne was seven, "No one has hair this

61

thick, honey. You didn't get it from me for sure." Now Roxanne would give just about anything for her mother to be sober enough to speak.

Roxanne strolled along drinking her juice. Birds sang and played in the puddles left by sprinklers. She took note of the thick Virginia creepers covering the brick buildings' walls. Each spring she looked forward to the unfurling of the green leaves because that meant summer break loomed close. In fall when the leaves turned bright red, winter recess was just a few weeks away. The most depressing time was winter, when the vines were bare and the dead leaves hung like empty locust shells.

The perfectly healthy geraniums in the bed by the bookstore had been replaced over the weekend with purple pansies. Work crews prepared to resurface the library parking lot for the fourth time in as many years. "This university spends more money on tinkering than any place on earth," Mary had told her years ago. "In eight years we've had three different sets of shingles over us."

Roxanne used the pedestrian side of the cobblestone bike and footways that cut through each building's bright flowerbeds and soft thick grass where students studied and chatted while they tanned. She passed dorms that would fit comfortably within the pages of *Architectural Digest* and waved to a colleague standing in front of the mathematics and communications buildings, which had been featured in *The Chronicle of Higher Education*'s story about campus beautification projects.

She breathed deeply and felt satisfied that she'd exerted herself that morning. Her workouts were similar to her research and writing schedule: she wasted no time creating excuses or making promises of what she would write about. Complaints about writer's block or lack of time were out of the question. One could always find time to exercise and write.

Roxanne followed philosophies passed on to her by her major professor, Lenay McGraw: "If you don't submit a manuscript, it won't be published." "If you don't submit a grant application, it won't be funded." She knew many scholars who feared rejection, so they never took the time to write. Roxanne also feared rejection, but she wrote anyway, and every time she submitted something to a journal or book publisher, she knew there would be readers who wouldn't like her work. Readers' reports gave her a sick feeling, for invariably one reader would be anti-Indian or self-important, with nothing good to say about anyone's research. Roxanne knew from long experience that she'd forever have to defend her work on decolonization from asinine commentary. She still dreaded the process.

Roxanne had not always been so industrious. She didn't make particularly good grades in high school. Her alcoholic parents didn't pay much attention to what she and her brothers were doing at school. Roxanne fumbled through her youth, drinking, partying, driving around the rez way too fast in beat-up cars and trucks.

But at some point Roxanne grew bored with this life. She had studied the history of colonization that had led to the aimless days she was living, and she could have bemoaned and resigned herself to the reality of the colonized Indian. But instead she took her tribe's offer to pay for tuition and books, and she enrolled in a community college. It was something her parents would have appreciated had they been sober enough to notice.

Maynard Community College was located outside the reservation, about an hour from Roxanne's house, but only half a mile from her grandmother's. Roxanne's decision to "get educated" pleased the old woman, and she allowed Roxanne to stay with her while she took classes.

Roxanne found that school wasn't that difficult once she figured out the art of studying. She felt somewhat intimidated during registration, but felt better after seeing Indians going from one department table to another, choosing their classes. Roxanne followed an advisor's recommendation and enrolled in basic math, biology, American history, and literature.

She had been leery of literature, thinking that she'd not like the stories written by long-dead white men. But the harpies, Circe, and other strange creatures in *Ulysses* reminded her of some tribes' mythological players, and she decided she liked it. After that she read *Moby Dick*, then *Hamlet*. Roxanne found Shakespeare to be an extraordinary observer of human behavior and motivations. Including her own.

Roxanne took her books and notes home and read in the quiet of her grandmother's house, which sat in the midst of a cottonwood grove. When she tired of reading she'd help the old lady in the yard or drive her into town to shop. Then Grandma Fast Deer made dinner while Roxanne read some more.

Roxanne emerged into an outgoing student, not shy about asking her instructors probing questions. The second day of anthropology class was a revelation to her. Dr. Reath informed the class about the merits of physical anthropology

"Dr. Reath," Roxanne, with her hip-length hair and Red Earth T-shirt, stretched her arm up high.

"Yes, Miss uh," Reath looked at the seating chart. "Miss Fast Deer."

Even though Bill Reath was paid less than six thousand dollars to teach three community college courses, he had promised himself to make them the best classes he could. He saw no disgrace in being a good teacher who made little money. Reath believed that teaching ranked as the world's most honorable profession.

"I'm wondering," began Roxanne. "Are all the interpretations about Indians made by Indians? Or by white people?"

Reath smiled. "You've raised one of the most volatile topics in Native Studies. The answer is that it is mainly non-Indians who write about Indians. Some try to be sensitive. Some work with tribes to get information about their culture. In their accounts these scholars omit what tribes say is sensitive, or they cease to study that topic altogether out of respect, and move on to something else. Others who aren't so sensitive barge in and take what they want. Like skeletons and cultural objects. They appropriate tribal cultural knowledge and hoard it like a game of finders' keepers."

Roxanne sat, transfixed. She had never thought about how history and culture was written or who wrote it. And her mind reeled at the thought of Indians being a main focal point of anthropological study. That included her and her tribe.

"I'll be happy to discuss it with you further," Reath told her.

Roxanne took Reath up on his offer. She rushed him after class and peppered him with questions. "Can professors do any research legally?" "Do tribes have rights?" "What happens if they publish information about religious ceremonies?"

Roxanne became curious about how many other Indians were working in the field of anthropology. The answer Reath gave her was "not many." So then came Roxanne's most impressive question of all: "How can I become an anthropologist and write about Indians?"

Reath seemed thrilled to have an eager student and an Indian one at that. Roxanne was smart, enthused, and possessed a goal in life. They talked most days after the Tuesday-Thursday classes, and Reath gave her additional readings. Fortunately for Roxanne, Reath discussed issues with her that also interested him.

Six months before, Reath had written an opinion paper called "Indians and Anthropologists: Collaboration and Appropriation" and submitted it to the journal published by the Society for American Anthropology. He held little hope that it would be accepted by the editors, who were generally opposed to papers that criticized anthropologists' appropriations of Native culture. To his amazement, the editors accepted his essay. The paper got him noticed: he received a job offer as assistant professor of anthropology at the University of Texas at Grand Prairie.

In the meantime, Reath talked with Roxanne extensively and he told Roxanne to submit an application to UTGP and major in anthropology. With her outstanding grades, Roxanne received an acceptance letter.

Roxanne traveled back north to her rez three times a year because that was all she could afford. She didn't Sun Dance, but to make certain that her mind stayed spiritually and emotionally on track, twice a year she went through a cleansing ceremony conducted by Arnold Old Bull, the medicine man she'd known all her life.

When Roxanne wasn't visiting her northern home, she stayed in the library or hunkered down in the garage apartment she rented from an elderly couple who saw to it that she always had a meal. The kindly old couple knocked on her door, bringing cakes, cookies, pot roast, or whatever they were baking. In return they asked that she watch their two Peakapoos, named after *Star Trek* captains Picard and Janeway, whenever they went out of town.

Grand Prairie's fall and spring were pleasant, so she kept the windows open to catch the moist breeze coming off the green lawn. In the hot summer, shade from the Black Jack oaks and the window air-conditioner kept her comfortable and blocked out all outside noises. Her time as an undergraduate was the most pleasant time of her academic career. No fights, little stress, and good health.

She earned her B.S. degree and was accepted into the master's program. Graduate school turned out to be very different from undergraduate study.

There was more work, of course, but the students were also more competitive and judgmental. They gossiped about what their professors were up to and speculated about and criticized other students.

Roxanne grew as bored with them as she had with her teenage party life, and she began studying in places where she wouldn't encounter other students. She became a loner, which made her an attractive subject for rumor.

She also questioned her professors' use of terms such as "objects" and "tools of study" to refer to Indians. Roxanne did not want to be the political correctness police, but certain comments in lectures cried out for a response.

Professor May began: "The primitive, uncivilized cultures of the pre-contact Eastern Woodlands groups . . ."

"Excuse me," Roxanne blurted out as she raised her hand. "Please define 'primitive' and 'civilization' and explain who created the definitions."

"You can look that up in the dictionary, young lady."

"Well you're describing my ancestors and I take issue with your descriptions of them." She folded her arms and awaited a reply.

The class was silent and giddy with anticipation of an argument between the Colonialist Oppressor and Activist Indigene.

"When I use those terms, Miss Fast Deer, I mean no offense, of course. These are the terms used by the old school anthropologists and I'm simply reiterating their terms since I use their material for my lectures."

Bullshit, thought Roxanne. Roxanne let May slide with his explanation. It only took one question like that to a few professors to get them talking among themselves. At least they'd think about monitoring their language. Of course, her concern about prejudice in the classroom also made Roxanne a juicy target for professors' wrath.

Roxanne was the only Indian in the graduate program and one of the four minorities, the other three being Chinese, Korean, and Brazilian. As it happens in many graduate programs, no matter the field of study, speculation grew as to how they paid their tuition.

"All minorities get free rides," said Will Brown, a lily white New Englander, before a seminar began one afternoon on Samuel Norton's ideas about polygenesis.

"Yeah and they don't even have to apply," added Rachel Kemp from California.

The anorexic Katherine Jones from Orlando joined in. "I know for a fact Indians are recruited into graduate programs because they help fill the minority quota. Their grade points are super low, but professors have to pass them to stay out of trouble with the administration."

Because of such conversations, other uninformed graduate students came to believe that Roxanne and the other students of color were being passed through classes no matter what kind of work they did. Resentment grew and prejudices formed where previously there were none.

Roxanne was not prepared for the enthusiastic embrace of "post-colonial theory" among scholars who subscribed to the idea that Natives were no longer colonized.

"So you're telling me that there is no racism, no treaty abrogation, no mascots, no poverty, no alcoholism?" she asked Professor Jones-Smith the first day of the graduate seminar Anthropology Theory and Method.

"Well, uh, I'm not trying to tell you there are no problems, Ms. Lame Deer."

"My name is Fast Deer. You're thinking of the Lame Deer, Seeker of Visions," Roxanne responded. "Perhaps you read the book."

"Yes. Well."

"It's a different person. A different name. I take pride in my name."

Jones-Smith, a twenty-year veteran of the anthropology department who had written works on "spirit possession" among the Indians of Yucatan, thought she might faint. She sat at the head of the seminar table unable to think of what to say. She could only stare back at the living indigenous entity that had challenged her authoritative voice.

"There is no such thing as post-colonial," Roxanne continued. "We're still colonized peoples being subsumed by the colonial power structure."

Jones-Smith couldn't gather herself that afternoon, so she dismissed the class, went to the health center for a massage, then returned home for a drink. The next week she distributed a new syllabus that did not make mention of "post-colonial."

Still, Roxanne fought relentlessly each class period, correcting Jones-Smith when she spoke of tribal beliefs as nothing more than "candles in the dark." Exhausted, Roxanne lurched through the semester and earned an A mainly because Jones-Smith was too afraid to give her anything else. She left the course with a new appreciation for racism in the academy.

Roxanne knew she was changing emotionally. She had grown defensive and slightly paranoid. How this new anger might serve her into the future she didn't know. Her short fuse scared her. Still, she graduated with all As and a masters thesis on why some Oglalas acculturated to white culture while others had little interest in it.

For her Ph.D. work she transferred to the demanding Wisconsin program. There she studied hard, never missed class or guest speakers. She decided on a dissertation topic early, "Effects of Colonization: Cultural and Emotional Change among the Oglalas," a logical extension of her thesis. By the time she completed her written and oral comprehensive exams, Roxanne's graduate assistant money had run out. She needed money to complete her dissertation, so she applied for and won a Ford Foundation Dissertation Fellowship.

This set off another chain of rumors among the graduate students about minorities "getting everything and whites getting nothing." "Rox," said Dr. Lenay McGraw, "this is the kind of bullshit you'll always have to deal with. If you confront every single jealous asshole that tries to rationalize your successes, you'll kill yourself trying to convince them you're right and they're not. It's impossible to make them admit they're wrong. I know of what I speak."

McGraw was a white woman, in her late thirties and the mother of three. She was naturally thin, pretty, and smart, which made her the object of insecure women's jealousies.

"You've earned everything you've done, Rox. If you don't ignore their attempts to destroy you—and Rox, I do mean destroy—then you're going to end up like a child trying to please abusive parents. You give and give—write and publish like a maniac—and nothing will please them. The more you do, the more they'll hate you."

She leaned across her desk and planted her fist hard enough to make her Boston ivy plant jump. "They will never, ever tell you that you've done well. So don't you ever do your work with the idea of gaining their approval. You do what you want. For you."

Lenay's sudden anger stunned Roxanne. She knew her major professor wasn't friends with many of the anthropology faculty, but she chalked that up to her being busy. Now she knew she distanced herself because of something else entirely.

Lenay sat back, her chair squeaking. She took a few Tums out of the plastic bottle on her desk and chewed them quickly. She returned to her normal, calm self. "If you really want to piss them off, apply for the same grants they do. At least they can't say the only grants you can get are designated for minorities. If you care what they think, that is."

Roxanne didn't care what they thought, although she wanted to prove a point because principles mattered to her. So she applied for several grants at the same time other graduate students did. Unlike her colleagues, she met with success. McGraw was right. Hate for Roxanne circulated through the graduate student population like Mad Cow Disease.

"Just like my learned, sophisticated colleagues are doing now," Roxanne said out loud to no one as she approached the CHU anthropology building on the warm, still morning ten years after graduating with her Ph.D. Her saving grace was the addition of Tony Smoke Rise to the faculty. They had quickly become allies, and together they wrote circles around the rest of the department. And on this fine morning she knew she'd see him before he left for his trip. She had a few CDs to loan him for his long plane ride.

Roxanne normally liked to arrive early so she could check her mail and e-mail, then use the copier and pour a cup of coffee without having to run into anyone except Mary. On the rare days like this that she arrived late, she felt like she was missing out on something. Today she felt out of sorts.

Roxanne popped the last of her bagel into her mouth as she rounded the corner of the humanities building and stopped. Yellow police tape surrounded Anthropology. Students, faculty, and administrators were straining to see what happened. Roxanne saw Louis Ryan, a vague acquaintance from psychology, standing on the periphery. Roxanne didn't socialize with many faculty members. Just with a few other souls who had found their comfortable niche or with kindred spirits who suffered through their academic existence like she did. Louis was a non-published full professor who nevertheless thought he was as important as Freud. Roxanne walked over and stood by him.

"Hey, Louis. What's going on?"

Louis lowered his chin and looked over his bifocals at her like he was inspecting a booger on his finger. "You don't know?"

"Know what?"

Louis raised his chin and spoke slowly. "Tony Smoke Rise was murdered last night."

Roxanne stopped breathing and stared at him. She didn't blink, didn't move.

"Roxanne?" Louis reached out to take her arm.

"Rox!" She heard another familiar voice yelling at her from a distance.

"Warren?" she asked quietly. She briefly thought about how nice her husband looked in his tight blue jeans and white T-shirt marked with streaks of clay. His dark hair flowed behind him as he ran down the sidewalk through the growing crowd.

"Honey," he pushed his sunglasses back on his head. A few globs of modeling clay stuck in his hair. He was hard at work on a sculpture. "I heard on the radio that a professor had been murdered. They said it was an anthropology professor. Is it true?"

"It was Tone," she said as if in a trance.

Warren realized his wife was shocked. He took the bag off her shoulder and knocked the empty Styrofoam cup to the ground. "Come on, Rox." He took her arm and pulled her close to him. She felt limp, as if she might pass out.

"Oh, hey there," came the voice of Ross Clipper. He normally arrived to campus only after he'd played a round of golf; then he taught his Tuesday-Thursday class and left to meet his buddies for beers.

"Wow. What a thing, huh? Bet you're upset." Clipper grinned as if he had just been awarded a Guggenheim.

Roxanne turned her head and shook off Warren's arms, her mouth hanging open. Then she spoke. "You son of a bitch."

Clipper stopped smiling and took his hands out of his pockets.

Roxanne pushed her husband's hands away and slowly walked towards Clipper. Warren grabbed for her left arm, and Clipper's eyes widened before he turned and walked away as fast as he could without running. Roxanne fell to her knees and caught herself before hitting her head on the sidewalk.

Some of the people who milled around the building watched Roxanne as she cried. Some seemed scared. And some who wore sad faces were actually happy.

The old guard resented Deb Young from the very day she entered her position as chair of the Department of Anthropology. Young insisted that faculty give a complete accounting of their research travel. She made certain that everyone taught a Monday-Wednesday-Friday course at 8:10 A.M. once every three years, and that candidates for promotion to full professor be judged only by other full professors.

Most offensive to the status quo was her diversification of the department. In her first year she hired Roxanne and Tony. The second year she hired two African American women. Then the third year she scored what would have been a coup at any other university: she convinced a preeminent cultural anthropologist from Harvard, who happened to be Black, to teach as a visiting professor for one year.

Several months after arriving at CHU, Roxanne overheard Jerry Langstrome in the mailroom. "Badger probably screwed someone good to get this offer," said Jerry. He was surprised when he saw Roxanne peek around the corner, but regained his smirk.

"Don't get defensive, Roxy," Jerry said, looking her up and down. "Take advantage of it." Then he walked out. Roxanne yelled after him to come back and give an explanation, but he kept on going.

"Hey now," said a voice behind her. Roxanne turned to see Ben Rogers, a tanned, thick-haired Peruvianist. His pumped-up biceps looked bronzed against his baby-chick yellow golf shirt. "Don't get too upset by those guys. They have problems of their own. Don't take it personally." Rogers smiled big and fiddled with his wedding band. He smelled of warm cologne. "If you need anything, let me know." He touched Roxanne gently on the arm before turning to retrieve the mail from his box.

At Roxanne's first departmental retreat, the faculty divided into clusters of five to talk about upcoming issues. Instead of focusing on their assigned topic, what color carpet to install in the faculty lounge, Rhonda Cartwright blurted out to Roxanne in her high-pitched voice, "You have more travel funds than we do."

An excitable personality, Rhonda dressed the part of an applied forestry professor. She wore long skirts and baggy sweaters, thick slouchy socks, and Teva sandals. She was perpetually sunburned, with chapped lips and premature wrinkles framed by thin brownish hair. Her specialty was earth mother goddesses in indigenous cultures.

"For God's sake, Rhonda," Roxanne replied. "I'm giving papers at three conferences, all in one week. For your information, the Ford Foundation Conference of Fellows is in between two of them and is footing most of the bill for my transportation."

"Well, see! The department still has to pay for some, and it cuts into trips some of us really need to take."

"What did I just say, Rhonda? I'm saving the department money. I'm also making it look good. For a change."

Rhonda stood up so fast she turned her chair over. She stormed out the door, the soles of her Tevas whacking the floor.

"Anyone else want to accuse me of something? Now's the time to do it," Roxanne said.

"Enough," a voice said from the breakfast buffet table. The group turned to Paul Deerbourne, a Regents' Professor two years away from retirement. He'd published at least thirty articles on Khufu's Great Pyramid, had written a text on Egypt's Old Kingdom (the royalties paid for the addition on his house), and received enough fellowship money to travel to Africa at least twice a year.

"Come off it, Paul," said fifty-two-year-old Leo Harding. He wore a religious-looking beard but no moustache and tried to hide his slick head by combing long hairs over his balding pate. In contrast to Deerbourne, who spent his energy writing, Harding preferred to devote his time to campus committees. "Roxanne has no business talking to Professor Cartwright like that."

"Yes, yes," said Ben Rogers, the Peruvianist who had visited Peru once in his career. "Remember though, that it's easy to produce conference papers when you have time off." The tall, fit man with perfect posture and a strong jaw was referring to Roxanne's Ford Foundation fellowship.

Frank Smithers, the San Ildefonso potsherd specialist, said, "I could publish a lot too if I got favored treatment." Smithers was flabby and obese, and styled his thick curly red-blond hair in an Afro. He dressed in a tight T-shirt with stains at the armpits, khaki shorts, and sandals that showed dirty toenails. He had traveled the Southwest twice in his career and based his essays on secondary materials. As part of the merit file each member of the faculty assembled every year, he turned in Christmas cards he'd received from prominent Moose City citizens.

"You have to apply for grants to get grants," said Roxanne. "You've been here for over twenty years Frank, and you have never won a grant or published in a refereed journal."

Smithers ate cheese and crackers and belched. "That Ford thing is only for minorities. I couldn't ever get one of those, and neither could anyone else but you, your friends," he motioned to the two Black women and the Aussie, "and Smokestack, there."

Daniel Harwood, the visiting professor from Harvard, stood and cleared his throat loudly. The dark-skinned, white haired, bearded man who looked like Santa's shorter Black brother leaned forward, glared at Smithers, and quietly said, "Show respect to my colleagues or by God, I'll flatten you." He glared at Frank who held his crackers aloft.

Lester MacKenzie, the Australian aborigine sat quietly, his eyes widening as the conversation heated. He tucked his curly hair behind his ears and kept eyeing the door as if measuring how many paces it would take him to bolt out of there.

"Stop showing your ass, Frank," said Samantha Brazzi, a fifty-five-year-old Catholic who specialized in the Mormons' influence on the peoples of Polynesia. She had received full professorship five years before, but only because she threatened to sue the university for discrimination because her department had voted 'no.'

"Not everyone has to beg for money," Leo Harding interjected. "You women seem to have a need for it."

Harwood slammed his mug of hot tea on the polished table. "I am astounded at your rudeness. But I'm not surprised. I also know that someday your comments will come in useful. Idiocy has a way of turning on itself."

"Look, Paul," said Frank. "If you got colored skin, you have it made regardless of whatever else you got going."

"Watch your mouth." Harwood removed his beige jacket as he stood. Brown suspenders held up his white pants. Harwood clenched his fists and Smithers moved to the other side of the table.

"It takes brains to actually write grants," said Bobbie Rennard, one of the African American women Deb Young recruited that fall. The tall, lanky 26-year-old with dozens of thin braids to her waist played basketball through her university years, had six protective brothers, a physician father and attorney mother, and she took no insults from anyone. She also was just off an American Association of University Women post-doc, and in that short time she had completed the revision of her dissertation, "The Unkindest Cut: Female Circumcision as Expression of Patriarchal Influence in Ethiopia." She was being courted by a number of presses.

"She's right," said Roxanne. "I also got a National Endowment for the Humanities Fellowship and one from the AAUW. Those aren't just for minorities. They're hard to get."

"The AAUW is for women, young lady," said Frank, ignoring the NEH fact. "As you can see, I'm no lady." He laughed as if no one had ever said that before.

"You are hardly a man, either," added Samantha.

"Anything else?" Roxanne asked. "My attorney just keeps piling up the information. So, come on. I'll just keep this running." She pulled out a small tape recorder from her windbreaker pocket and held it up. "I'll make a copy for Mary so she can transcribe accurate minutes."

"Shit," said Smithers. Then he and everyone else clammed up.

Professor Belinda C. Rinds, dressed in flowing pastels that covered her painfully thin physique, timidly raised her hand for permission to talk. "Why don't we break for lunch? We're all tired and need a little break." She looked around for approval. "Don't you think?"

"Yes, let's," agreed Deb Young as she grabbed her purse.

Harwood approached the sofa where the minority faculty sat and put on his hat with shaking hands. "My God. What a bunch of ignorant dolts. I wish you all luck and I advise you to retain an attorney." The distinguished professor Harwood walked out the door, and no one saw him again that year at any function, but some occasionally caught a glimpse of him scurrying to and from classes. He moved out of his office to write at home, and until he moved back to Harvard, he only engaged with Mary the Secretary.

For the next two years, a secret cell of the department schemed and created stories about their chair. Young had never married and did not attend one of their churches, so they spread the word that she was an atheist lesbian. Because Roxanne was not married, they suggested that the atheist lesbian had had an affair with her. Furious, Young lost her temper one afternoon and composed a memo to her adversaries. She made the mistake of referring to them as "jealous, bratty children," and that, more than anything else, was her undoing. The old guard's strategy had finally gotten to Young's emotions. Young found herself demoted to a faculty position.

"Rox," said Tone a week after the confrontation at the faculty retreat, "let's get something clear. This is a department with people who have to find some way of rationalizing why you have what they don't. Looks, talent, health, and a hell of a lot of potential."

"You think?"

Tone looked at Roxanne's Byzantine face framed by waist-length black hair. She blinked long black lashes and shifted her weight from one slim leg to the other. Inside her head were enviable brains that worked overtime. She had seriously bucked teeth, but the overbite added to her appeal.

"Yeah. I do. Jealousy mixed with insecurity and anger makes a volatile combination. They're not jealous of each other because they're all the same. Some of these guys are like an army of vindictive, squirmy brained toads."

"Didn't Jim Morrison say that? He was talking about a murderer."

Tony turned to get his mail. "Yes, ma'am. These creeps are capable of a lot of things."

TWO YEARS AGO

The stressful years slid past as Tony and Roxanne adjusted to their dysfunctional environment. Attending conferences got them away from CHU, but into other taxing situations, such as the American Anthropological Association conference in Los Angeles.

They arrived at LAX in time to make the AAA reception at the Museum of Natural History. The two Indians stayed close together, too intimidated by the sea of white faces to venture forth by themselves into the crowd. They ate several platefuls of barbecued shrimp, crab-stuffed mushrooms, and Malaysian coconut chicken curry, then called it a night around ten.

One of the first sessions of the next day featured Barney Southcliffe, a cultural anthropologist who had devoted his career to deconstructing modern Indian identities. His goal was to prove to the descendents of "real Indians" that, because they watched television, drove cars, and lived in houses with chimneys, they were pathetic shadows of the authentic tribal entities who had lived in the misty past.

Despite years of criticism by scholars both Indian and non-Indian, Southcliffe persisted in asserting that "there are no Indians left." His session drew a standing-room-only crowd, although few attendees agreed with him. Professors encouraged their students to witness the strange man, while older scholars attended for reasons of nostalgia.

From where they sat in the hallway, unable to get inside, Roxanne and Tony heard Southcliffe answer a query about "authoritative voice." "Keep in mind," he said loudly, "that there are plenty of writers today who say they're Indians, but in fact no real Indian would be formally educated. The session scheduled for tomorrow that says it features 'Indian scholars' is misleading and dangerous, for a real Indian would not have a degree."

"My God," Roxanne said, shaking her head. Several white scholars stood at the door, snickering softly. As tempting as it was to argue with Southcliffe, neither Roxanne nor Tony had the stomach for a nauseating debate. "Let the white anthros argue with him," said Roxanne. "It's good for them."

No scheduled sessions the rest of the day interested them. None of them dealt with the myriad troubles faced by modern tribes—poverty, pollution, water, fishing, treaty rights, and loss of land. Most of the participants focused on pots and old baskets. Numerous opinions were expressed on burial mound structures and skeletal remains. Apparently, it was much easier to deal with dead people than with live ones.

The cultural anthropologists were little better. With the exception of a few who worked closely with tribes to gather information on AIDS, spousal abuse, and the effects of water loss, most delivered commentary on what Natives were doing and thinking at the time the scholars intruded on their communities. Oglalas didn't suffer from anthropologists quite as much as other tribes, such as the Hopi, at whom nosy tourists aimed cameras and tape recorders during tribal dances, sometimes secretly. Scholars revealed the most intimate religious information in their books and essays.

On the afternoon of the first full conference day, Tony and Roxanne sat on a bench outside one of the meeting rooms and scanned the program. Conference-goers rambled up and down the hallways. Some looked like anxious ABDs, high-tailing it to job interviews. Others appeared to be secure in their positions and spent their time in bars where academic business and gossip took place. Indeed, a good many participants attended only to drink and to escape their spouse for a while.

Tone asked Rox if she had a desire to listen to the session on "Indigenes and Anthropologists: Cultural Scientists' Responsibilities as Owners of Intellectual Property."

She looked at him and rolled her eyes. "Sure. I bet there're a lot of Natives in there discussing how anthropologists can better protect the knowledge that actually belongs to tribes."

"Or we could go hear M. M. Trueblood speak on 'Self's Otherness: The Semiotics of Dehumanizing Difference and Sameness of the Islas Campanas Through Discourse and Intertextualization.'"

She looked at him and made a face. "What?" He read it again. She couldn't muster the energy to respond.

"Okay then, what about 'Wheels' Rims: The Postmodern Social Conditions of the Marginalized Low Riders of Southern New Mexico Borderlands?'"

"I *might* hit you." She reached into her bag for a Twix. "I'm here only because I wanted to see some old friends and I need inspiration to finish my book."

"Then let's go look at the books. Lots of new stuff out this year."

"I get the catalogs."

Tony sighed and tried another idea. "There's a session sponsored by the Association for Feminist Anthropology down the hall. We could listen to the female anthropologists' commentaries about the sexist methodologies used by male anthropologists in textualizing their biased work."

"Screw the feminists. I don't identity with white feminists and don't care to go."

Tone sat in silence for a moment and watched the conference-goers scurry past. "I'm curious. I know some of these women, and they aren't obnoxious feminists who blame men for all their problems."

"Indian women aren't feminists," Roxanne shot back. "White women are privileged, even if they say white men are the enemy. Community should be our focus, not putting down Native men who've been hammered by white men. We have nothing in common with women who want individual rights instead of rights for their community."

"But Indian men beat the shit out of women. I know lots of Indian women who say they're feminists, and they're pretty traditional."

Roxanne gave him a hard look before cramming the program into her shoulder bag. "They're the ones who're mainly white and don't know anything about their tribe."

"You sound like some of those women who're so territorial about the topic of activism they think they're right about everything. They play that 'I'm more Indian than you' game. They worship the American Indian Movement even though some of those guys abuse women."

"Don't you dare compare me to those people."

"I'm not saying you're like them. Get back on track here. The women I'm talking about back home who say they're feminists are full-bloods. And I also said they're traditionalists."

Roxanne stood and stomped down the corridor toward the bathrooms. Tone followed her. "Don't get mad, okay? But Rox, you can't put everyone into the same category."

She pushed open the ladies' room door. Tone watched her until the door closed.

Emerging a few minutes later, she had a changed demeanor. "Let's go find lunch somewhere."

"Rox," Tone persisted. "A lot of these women are talking about how men have dominated anthropology with patriarchal voices. You could use what they say to compare how some non-Indians write compared to how Indians write."

"No thanks. I get too upset at these sessions about Clifford and his ideas about feminists and ethnography. I mean, the way he sees it, if women attempt to be experimental, they aren't really feminists. And if they are feminists, they couldn't possibly understand textual theory." She put her hand in her purse and fumbled for her sunglasses. "Besides, lots of women anthros laid out the case against him and keep the ball rolling. They sure don't need me and my subjective indigenous female opinion to muddy the issue."

"There's a need for Native women's voices in anthropology, Rox."

"Maybe so. But they'll just take my comments and form their own anthropological, biased theories about them."

Tony sighed and followed his friend out the lobby door and into the sunshine. They skipped the afternoon sessions and tour of the Huntington Library and instead went shopping.

The next morning, as they waited for their session to begin, they heard Martina Smith on "Shamans and Shells: Witches and Spells of the Selvas of Central Argentina." Smith had studied the Selvas for years and, despite being expelled from the village for asking too many questions, had published numerous papers on ceremonies she had filmed in secret. Sadly for Smith, the medicine people had had enough of her prying, and she now was paying the price of her nosiness: she had lost thirty pounds and her hair was falling out in clumps.

As the audience asked questions and Smith coughed, the other three participants in Roxanne's and Tony's session came in. First came Katherine Dobbs from Montana, a blond-haired, blue-eyed cultural anthropologist who was 1/512 Cherokee. She extended her hand to Roxanne and then Tony.

"How you doing, Katherine?" Tony asked.

"Great," she answered with a bright smile. Katherine was pretty and perky, which made it difficult to dislike her. "Finished my paper last night around midnight. I thought I was done last week but I got nervous yesterday and kept thinking of all the things I forgot to include."

Roxanne smiled back but didn't respond. She got along fine with Katherine, but was annoyed with her claim to Cherokeeness when she looked white and had never lived near her tribe. Katherine wrote about mixed-blood Cherokee identity in metropolitan areas. She started her work as a master's student, then expanded the project for her dissertation, and then a book. She had interviewed over 800 people, none possessing more than 1/32 degree Cherokee blood.

Teague Parkins, a tall Osage with sharp features, walked up behind Katherine. Parkins worked at a prominent midwestern university until the year before when he was turned down for tenure. Despite his two books and numerous essays in prominent journals, the conservative promotion and tenure committee declared him "not quite ready." Several east and west coast schools wanted to snap him up, and he had been hired at Dartmouth.

"Hey Teague." Roxanne gave him a hug. "How's Dartmouth?"

"Heck of lot better than where I was. Hey Tony-man." They shook hands. "Katherine," he said while giving her a high five. "How's the white Cherokee project going?"

Katherine sighed at the insult, but wouldn't play along. "Fine. Book's almost done."

"Hey, what do you call sixty-four Cherokees in a room?"

Katherine's nostrils flared; she'd heard this before.

"A full-blood!"

For Katherine's sake, Tony tried not to laugh. "The gang's all here," he said as he looked over Katherine's shoulder. Terry Renalt, a short Tewa/Kiowa came over, smelling of Brut aftershave. He reflected the sturdy build of both parents, broad shoulders and hips, a substantial gut and bow legs. He directed the American Indian Studies program at Western Oklahoma University and couldn't care less if he was ever promoted. He always seemed unfazed by the racism and academic politics that tore apart his colleagues.

Terry's work on "mixed-blood full-bloods" was nontheoretical and personal and therefore not viewed with much respect by anthropologists. It had been cited many times by prominent non-anthropological scholars in their works on bifurcated identities.

"When did you guys get here?" Roxanne asked.

"Last night," said Terry. "We accidentally missed all these great sessions." The group laughed.

"Yeah, I can't keep up with all the helpful information around here to take back to my people," said Teague.

After Roxanne, Tony, and the others presented their papers, they invited questions from the floor. Few came, mainly because the panel had thoroughly covered its topic. To argue with a panel of Natives about identity would indeed take a brave or foolish scholar.

That didn't stop a few people from offering a challenge to the person they believed to be the weakest link. "I've got a question for Professor Dobbs," said a small brunette woman wearing blue-tinted sunglasses, her hair in a braid that fell to her belt. It was Lucretia Ramirez, an anthropologist who claimed to be Chicana/Muscogee yet could not produce proof of tribal membership. Lucretia believed that one way to prove herself an Indian was to shoot down others and make certain everyone knew she was an authority on Indian women and activism.

"Yes, Lucretia," Katherine said in a low voice. She knew what to expect out of Lucretia.

"You state in your paper that even the Cherokees who look phenotypically white, like you, I mean . . ."

Tony kneed Katherine under the table and snickered.

". . . are Cherokees by virtue of racial connection, not because of any cultural knowledge they may have of the tribe."

"I—and many others—have stated that legally, they are members of the tribe," Katherine responded wearily. "That's the way the tribe set up their membership standards. Provide proof that your ancestor is on the Dawes Roll and you can enroll."

"How can you possibly say that that's an okay thing? There're a million Cherokees in this country and hardly any of them know about the culture. What does that say about the tribe? It doesn't even seem like it's a tribe of Indians. I mean, what does that say about *you?* You sound like you're trying to prove you're more traditional than . . ."

"Lucretia, cool it," said Teague. "This is a very old discussion and an obvious attack on Katherine. She never said it was an 'okay thing.' She said it's the tribe's right to dictate membership criteria. I'm getting tired of listening to you. I'd like to know what knowledge you have about Muscogees. Hell, forget that, I'd like to see proof that you are Muscogee."

Teague leaned over to Tony and whispered, "Look at the rest of the audience. They love it. They came to look at us like monkeys in a zoo. See how they're writing down their observations?" Tony laughed and knocked over his water.

As Lucretia started to answer, Teague looked at his watch and interrupted her. "Well darn it," he said. "Looks like our allotted time is up. Thanks for attending and we look forward to hearing from you." He closed his folder and turned to his panel. "Let's split a taxi and get some seafood."

The group shared a bucket of steamed clams as an appetizer. Katherine imbibed a strawberry margarita.

"Don't you think it's weird that Southcliffe didn't come to our session?" Katherine asked as she wiped off the thick salt around the rim of her glass.

"None of the people on his panel did," said Teague.

"Come on, guys. Why would they come to our session?" asked Tone.

"We didn't go to theirs," said Terry. He had stopped drinking several years ago and turned to positive thinking to stay sober. He refused to dwell on anything negative.

Roxanne sighed. "It's not a matter of them not coming to our session because we didn't go to theirs. Southcliffe has a reputation for not facing off against Natives. He'd get creamed. So he theorizes about us from a safe distance."

Patrons at the other tables gawked at the Indians. Teague stared back at the table of six white businesswomen dining next to them in dresses and heels. "We're Injun anthropologists studying white people in L.A.," he said in a voice just low enough for them to hear. They jerked their heads around and looked away.

"Teague, cut it out," said Katherine. She'd been at his dinner table several years ago when a family with three kids had stared at him all through the meal. Teague finally asked them, "You wanna touch my hair?"

"So how're you two surviving at CHU?" Katherine asked.

"We're still alive," Tony said as he buttered a hushpuppy.

"It's the same old thing, Terry," Roxanne said. "We turned in our annual evaluation forms last week, and I know we'll get destroyed again."

"But you just had a new book out," said Katherine. "Isn't that an automatic superior rating?"

"Not hardly. Anytime we do something big like a book the committee finds fault with the teaching and service categories. I resigned from two committees last year and the committee will pick up on that right away. They don't look for the good points, they just look at the files with an eye for weaknesses. I try every year to make my file foolproof, but . . ."

"The fools get the best of you," interjected Teague. "You should've seen my tenure file. I even showed it to my major professor back at Nebraska and to some friends in other departments. Then I tinkered on it for months before turning it in. I mean, I met every single prerequisite for tenure." He picked up and dropped a clamshell. "I was so proud of that application. There was no way they could have turned me down. But they did."

The group didn't say much. Each had heard Teague's story several times in the past year and there was nothing else to add. It was an outrage and the perpetrators won the battle and the war. Not only did the school deny Teague tenure, he left the university.

"Shoulda sued," said Katherine.

"I tried, Kath. Legal action is just too expensive. Besides, everyone on my side told me that I'd have to leave the university even if I won."

"How could you expect support from the administration you just whammied?" Roxanne asked. "Better to get the hell out of there."

"It's not just Indians who have problems, you know," said Terry, changing the topic. "White people wail on each other. And white women bash each other. You sure you're not just looking for excuses?"

"Right," answered Tony. "Poor whitey. I cry for him every night." He dragged a large shrimp across his plate through the sauce, making a mini-highway. "It's not humanly possible for me to do any more writing. I'm not looking for excuses, but a lot of the people in my department sure are."

"You saw my file, Terry," Teague continued. "Are you saying I'm making up excuses?"

Terry continued to eat while the others watched him. Roxanne spoke first and said what they all thought. "Terry, I like you, but you do say some pretty stupid things."

"Okay, okay," Terry said, smiling. "Just checking." Then the group watched him expertly crack and dismantle his lobster. "You gotta stay happy," he said as he pulled out white lobster meat from the mangled crustacean. Terry shrugged, undeterred by the discussion.

"I'm up for tenure next year," Katherine said. "And I'm really worried about it, too."

Roxanne looked at the blond Cherokee and said, "And how could that be?" Roxanne believed that Katherine had it made at university. She could be part Indian without having to live the harsh reality of tribal life. She lived like a white woman. Nobody in a million years would mistake her for an Indian, not even part Indian. Roxanne and Tony had discussed numerous times the advantages the mixed-bloods who looked phenotypically white had over those who appeared Native.

"Roxanne," Katherine said in a low voice. "You may be more Indian than I am, but as far as my department is concerned, I'm Indian and they treat me like one. They know I'm enrolled. Blood quantum doesn't mean anything to them. I get assigned to all the minority committees. I don't get any special favors. They judge my merit files like they're life or death cases. The committee for next year is shaping up and the people on it aren't my allies. The racism is more subtle where I work, but it's there, all right."

"How's Ross Clipper?" asked Teague suddenly.

"You care?" answered Tony.

"Actually, no. Didn't you see his and Ben Rogers's quotes in the *Chronicle* yesterday? They were talking about the CHU's business connection with the dig over by that new Dick Cheney freeway they're building by you guys. There's a burial but the article says it's small."

"I knew there was a site," said Roxanne, sitting forward, "but I didn't know the details." She looked at Tony, who shook his head. "What do you mean, business connection?"

"Well, if the burials have much in them, it could cost millions since the road will have to wait. Some corporation needs the land, but the freeway can only move so far. They're paying Clipper and Rogers a bundle as consultants."

Roxanne and Tony stared at Teague. "My God," Roxanne finally said. "CHU hasn't publicized any of this."

"Shouldn't you two be the consultants?" asked Katherine.

"What about the tribes?" asked Terry. "Whose burial is it?"

"The article said it appeared very old, hard to identify. It didn't mention if medicine people got brought in."

"Holy shit," said Roxanne. "Typical fricking CHU," Roxanne said, throwing down her napkin. "We're not archaeologists and wouldn't be consultants anyway, but they could have told us. Don't you think, Tone?"

"Gotta go to the can." Tony stood and dropped his napkin in his chair. "I'll be back."

Everyone at the table was silent for a moment.

"How's Pauley Wenetae?" Katherine finally asked. She finished her fried shrimp and scallops and began cracking crab legs. "Still riding your coattails?"

"He's still there, all right. Going up for full next year, I hear."

"Full?" Blurted Teague. "How's that possible? Pauley hasn't written shit."

"You're right about that, but he knows all the right people."

Teague tapped his knife hard against the plate like he was beating a drum triple time.

Roxanne said, "He could run for President with all the people he's brown-nosed."

"What really pisses me off," Teague began in a low tone, "is that I went through a very tough graduate program. Then I tortured myself writing three books. Then I apply for grants like a maniac and struggle through every phase of my academic existence. Here comes Wenetae, who really was in school only because of Affirmative Action, who then wiggles through a crappy degree program, doesn't even work with specialists in the field and now look at him!" He hit the heavy white platter with his knife again. "He makes a killer salary, gets promoted to associate with no problems and he travels the world like he's retired. I want a drink."

Katherine gasped. "No, you don't. Let's get Key Lime pie instead."

"Pisses us all off," said Roxanne. "There are people like him everywhere in this business. You're either a political person or you're not. If you are, then you get what you want. If you refuse to play the game, then you struggle for every little thing you can get. Get over it. At another place you would've gotten tenure."

Tony returned to the table. He sat and smoothed the napkin over his lap. "What did I miss?"

"Like I said," Terry repeated, "you gotta stay happy."

Roxanne looked at Tony and frowned. Terry was right, but also infuriating.

TWO YEARS AGO

"Well, let's see," reasoned Leo Harding over the music at the Pool Masters Bar and Steakhouse the spring prior to the decisions on Tony's and Roxanne's tenure. Harding and his allies met that evening to discuss how they could best maneuver the promotion and tenure committee next year. Who got promoted would determine the direction of the department, and this faction was strategizing as if it were the United States military.

"There's nineteen faculty in the department," Harding continued. "One's the chair. Five are assistants, six are fulls, and the rest are associates. Members can serve only two years, then they have to wait two years before being elected again. That means since Paul Deerbourne and Bob Pierson are off, we can get Ross on as one of the full professors."

"Who's the other full?" asked Johnson Magnum.

Mark Fhardt took a swig of his Bud and looked down at his notes, which stuck to the wet table. "Jerry can't get on for another year and Frank and Ben are on sabbatical. Gee, Johnson, looks like you're the choice by default."

Johnson knew that already and raised his mug in salute to himself.

"Associates?" asked Ross Clipper. "Samantha's off, thank God."

"Looks like it's you, Leo," smiled Mark Fhardt. "Course, if you do it this year, you can't go up for full 'cause you're on the committee."

"That's right," said Rhonda Cartwright. She sat back from the round table, needing to be part of the group, but also finding her colleagues distasteful. In the setting of Anthropology the men were tolerable and safe. Being with them outside the university, however, made her anxious. Her purse sat in her lap since she intended to hightail it after their strategy was understood.

"Why not?" asked Clipper. "There's no rule that says he can't just step off when the decision comes up for him."

"Hmmm." Mark Fhardt shuffled through his pile of papers. "I don't see . . ."

"Doesn't matter," said Frank Smithers as he leaned forward. "There's no other way to construct the committee." He smiled. "There's gotta be two associates and guess what, Leo and Rhonda are the only choices. Next year, Rhonda goes up. Same situation except Belinda goes on because Leo'll be promoted." Rhonda managed a weak smile. "It doesn't matter which one of the assistants gets on because their opinion won't count for anything. Ben Rogers could get on, but he can vote however he wants. Doesn't matter. Since we'll elect you to the college promotion committee for a three-year term, Jerry, this is the only way the committee can shake out. Am I right, Belinda?"

The mastermind of anthropology politics sat opposite Rhonda in the shadow of the large stuffed moose head. Hollow-cheeked and jittery, Belinda C. Rinds wore sunglasses and her hair in a tight bun in an attempt at anonymity. "I guess," she answered quietly as she looked around nervously. Clipper and Harding laughed the loudest, knowing that of everyone, she knew the best.

SIX MONTHS LATER

Although they had met every goal listed in their Documents of Expectations each year they had been at the university, Tony's and Roxanne's quests for promotion and tenure were rejected by the promotion and tenure committee in the Department of Anthropology.

They didn't just reject the candidates without commentary; the committee gave them pages and pages of critique about their work's value (for Tony: "Is anyone much interested in work about Indian populations besides Indians?"), notes on their attitudes (including nasty remarks about their personal lives: "Dr. Badger refuses to socialize with her colleagues at departmental functions, perhaps due to her upbringing"), and strange criticisms of their syllabi ("Undergraduate students cannot be expected to read two books a semester and answer only essay questions").

Roxanne had wasted no time in marching into Renell's office. Tony did the same. Renell knew that the normal chain of events in a promotion decision was to allow the file to make its way to the president's office for a final decision, but the ferocity with which her clients had been attacked in the first round of reviews compelled her to meet with President Brion early. She suggested to him that he take charge of the travesties before the university lost its pants and he faced the possibility of losing his job. Roxanne and Tony never found out for certain, but rumor had it that Brion met with the various committees and explained what the consequences would be if they didn't straighten up.

President Brion ordered Dean Piller to dictate to the College Promotion and Evaluation Committee the importance of supporting Tony and Roxanne, so grudgingly, they did. Seven of the ten committee members gnashed their teeth at having to sign their names on the "pro" line of their assessment letter. Still, they did manage to get off two petty statements: "Professor Smoke Rise shows a small amount of potential" and "Professor Badger appears to like her topic of study." The other three college committee members (two political scientists and one philosopher), on the other hand, were thrilled to see the two Indians promoted. From the dean's office, the file sailed past the vice president to the president's desk.

That ordeal behind them, Tony and Roxanne continued to focus on their work. But not everyone in the department was as diligent. Belinda Rinds had been at CHU for fifteen years and had written a couple of essays and no book-length manuscript, but she hustled tirelessly around campus and ingratiated herself with administrators. People who didn't know any better thought her a spectacular scholar. In the typical pack mentally of mediocre scholars everywhere, her friends who also did little work pooled their votes so Belinda could be awarded one Distinguished Faculty award after the other.

Belinda often could be heard laughing hysterically in her office. Even with the door closed, her cackle echoed on other floors. The odd part was that she usually laughed with students. She invited students to her house, where they'd sit around drinking wine while Belinda revealed confidential information about other members of the department. A graduate student told Roxanne that Belinda had bashed her at a Saint Patrick's Day party. "Roxanne and Tony don't know theory," she had said, "and they sure wouldn't be published if they weren't Indians. I sure wouldn't work with them because they're career poison and you'll never get a job."

Roxanne was mortified at this news. "How many people were there?"

"At least a dozen students. And some from history. Oh yeah, then she said that you tell your classes only Indians should write about Indians."

"What?! I have never said that. Not orally, not in writing."

"Rinds has them thinking that you don't want to work with white students. And she says you really don't like Indian students, either."

Despite the vicious nature of their colleagues, Roxanne and Tony had happy times, too. Roxanne met and married Warren, and Tone married his longtime girlfriend Perri, a Tohono O'Odham from Sells, Arizona. The four ate dinner together regularly and often with the Sweeneys, too, and Roxanne and Warren visited Tony's parents and fished to their heart's content two hours north of Flagstaff at Lee's Ferry. Roxanne loved Tony's parents, Glenn and Arlene. She called them the "Cosmopolitan Hopi and Renaissance Apache." They worked in the school district as counselors and maintained Arlene's family's centuries-old pueblo in addition to their own home.

As long as Roxanne and Tony stayed away from campus, they were happy, normal people. During the academic year, their attitudes changed as surely as the weather. Warren and Perri were alternately sympathetic and fed up with their spouse's complaints. Warren wanted Roxanne to see a psychologist.

"It's an unhealthy environment," Roxanne told Tony about her proposed visit, during a quick lunch at a Thai restaurant that featured only seven tables and huge plates.

"Really? You're going to pay to hear someone tell you that?"

"Maybe. Warren keeps pushing me to talk to a professional. You and I both already know what the problem is." Roxanne forked a piece of chicken. "I've hit a wall. I hate it. I'm gonna quit."

"Have a Gas-X instead."

"I mean it, Tony. Life's too short. Nobody reads my stuff. Nobody cares."

Tony listened to her ramble. For five years now, she'd threatened to quit every month or so. "I have a better idea," Tony said, spooning his coconut ice cream. "Let's stay to spite them. They'd kill to see us leave. Let's just hunker down and deal with it."

They looked out the window in silence for a moment. Crows rummaged in the parking lot, looking for crumbs dropped by patrons of the hamburger place next door.

"Hey," Tony said, perking up. "We should write some grants and start a decolonization institute."

"What?"

"A decolonization institute. A think tank for indigenous intellectuals."

"You're dinged in the head, Tone. No way will our colleagues support a formal decolonization program on a colonialist campus."

"Not anthropology. But listen, we could go to another college. Get psychology, education, and the sciences in on it."

Roxanne played with her food.

"Biology especially. Environmental science and land restoration."

Roxanne perked up. "That's a thought."

"More than a thought. We should look into funding. That'll get us out of anthropology at least part of the time."

"I didn't know you wanted out of the department. I thought you just wanted a fair shake."

Tony glanced at the crows. One found a donut and took off, the glazed treat like a life preserver around the bird's beak.

"I do want a fair shake. Everyone does. This is our way out. Come on. Think about it."

"I have to get out of anthropology."

"Consider my plan. It could work."

Roxanne sat back in her chair and drummed the table with her index fingers. "I'll think about it," she said.

POST TENURE

Roxanne and Tony learned to cope with the gossiping. They worked hard and played hard with their families, taking vacations during summer and winter breaks. Both focused their energies on locating funding for their Indigenous Studies Institute. They discussed collaborations with the School of Education and the departments of psychology, history, physical therapy, biology, and languages. They discovered that a solid, honest proposal brought results.

Their proposed curriculum featured basic courses in policy, history, and economics, including strategies for decolonization in each. Roxanne approached the Department of English, whose faculty agreed that instead of American Indian Literature, a course that focused on identity confusion, place, and humor, the department would offer Literature as Activism, which might encourage critics to focus on stories with messages of empowerment. Faculty from across the disciplines were ready to teach part-time in the new ISI.

The institute's emphasis on environmental protection of tribal lands brought in an U.S. Science Foundation award, enough to build a separate structure, albeit a modest one. The Buick Foundation gave enough for three new faculty members at the full professor rank. The institute's policy and self-determination component garnered a tidy sum from the Indigenous Rights Endowment of the Americas. Local tribes pledged support from their casino revenues for student scholarships and internships; a wealthy benefactor presented an endowed chair in his son's name.

With solid financial support, Roxanne and Tony were poised to establish one of the most successful indigenous studies programs in the United States. But Roxanne had her doubts that it could actually succeed.

"I wonder what the anthro department will do about this, Tone. I mean, we're not only taking their thunder, we're taking Ross Clipper's moneymaking potential. With us gone, who does he have to use besides Pauley?"

"Quit being so pessimistic," Tone told her. "I'm not going to even think about them. I can't spend any more time on their paranoia. I'm on to something bigger and better, and it's their problem if they can't handle it. Here we are, creating something useful that also makes us feel good. It's the right thing to do no mater what our department says. Remember what Ralph Waldo Emerson wrote in *Self-Reliance*: 'Nothing can bring you peace but yourself. Nothing can bring you peace but the triumph of principles.'"

"I'm aware of what he wrote. And I also know that just because we want to do something good doesn't mean it'll get done. It's also been said that if your head's above the crowd, someone will throw a rock at it."

"Who said that?"

"David Lee Roth. And I think that we're about to get pelted."

Monique wanted to visit Tony's wife before interviewing the rest of the individual faculty members. She thought it odd that Perri Smoke Rise was not aware that her husband didn't come to their bed the night before.

"Maybe she really is feeling puny," said Clarke as they made their way through traffic. "The flu wipes me out so bad I can't tell if it's day or night. I lose weight and have to spend a month drinking milkshakes and beer to gain it back."

"You poor baby," Monique said. "One milkshake shows up around my gut."

They headed towards the south side of town to Elk Springs, a small community of fourteen homes between 2,000 and 2,500 square feet built twenty years ago. The houses surrounded a lake that stayed dry most of the year. During the summer monsoons the lake filled and elk came to drink every evening and early morning. Each resident owned an eight-acre parcel that could not be subdivided. On a map, their little piece of the world was one of the white squares bounded by green squares of national forest. This meant that if the Forest Service didn't cut some kind of deal with real estate developers, no one could build within five miles of Elk Springs. The community had electricity, propane delivery and garbage pickup, but residents had to haul water or dig a well.

Tony's house was not a trailer, but it looked like one. Long and rectangular, it sat on blocks to avoid the one-hundred-year flood that hadn't occurred in seventy-five years. There were no pine trees in the lake basin so Tony had planted dozens of fruit and Russian olive trees for shade and windbreaks.

He had also planted a small plot of grass on the side of the house so that he and Perri could lie on soft ground and watch the stars.

Monique stopped in front of the house behind three vans with "All the News at Two!" "World News Three," and "Live at Five," respectively, painted on their sides. The newspeople leaned against their vehicles, smoking or drinking pop. Monique saw that up the rock driveway sat a taupe Expedition, and a mountain bike leaned on the steps. Pigeons cooed from the shelter of the fruit trees.

"News is here," Monique said.

"Careful. Gettin' around those news people is like herdin' chickens," said Clarke.

"Watch me."

"Hey Monique," yelled a tall brunette woman wearing a quarter-inch of television makeup. She looked hopeful as she held out her microphone. "How about some information?"

"Don't have any yet."

"Pleeese?"

"Can't help you, Diane."

"Maybe later?" Her voice rose in pitch, as if she were a little girl and wanted something from her mommy.

"Maybe."

Diane's smile dropped as she stomped back to her van.

The detectives climbed the locked gate and walked to the porch. Monique knocked, and a middle-aged white woman answered, wearing navy Nike pants with a white stripe down the legs, a Hilo T-shirt, and granny glasses. Two golden retrievers came to the door as well, one standing on either side of her. They had been excited to get to the door, but their bodies drooped when they realized their master was not the one who had knocked.

"Detectives Blue Hawk and Clarke," Monique said holding up her badge. "We're looking for Perri Smoke Rise."

"You're not reporters?"

"No, ma'am," Clarke answered in a deep voice.

"Are you sure?"

"Pretty darn sure. My badge." Monique held hers up higher.

The stocky woman looked closely at the badge, then said, "I'm Anne Jacobs. I live next door. Come in." She unlocked the screen door and held it open. "I heard about the murder over the scanner early this morning and came right over to see Perri. I knew she was sick." She motioned with her chin to a back room. "I brought some soup. I make good minestrone. I put in carrots, tomatoes, onions, a little cauliflower, those shell pastas, then I . . ."

"That sounds just great," Monique interjected gently.

"Ah, well, she has a sore throat and congestion. And she's been sick to her stomach. Maybe it's strep or the flu. Anyway, I made a call to the university this morning to find out who died and came back here and woke Perri. She broke down and cried and wouldn't stop. Fortunately, my husband is a doctor and he gave her a sedative. She's back there, sleeping. I left the soup in the crock pot on low because you know how it gets better the longer you simmer it. You want me to get you a bowl?"

"Not now, thanks."

The detectives started for the hallway. Anne followed them. "I called her parents before taking the phone off the hook. They're on their way. She's Tohono O'Odham, you know."

"No, I didn't," answered Monique. She quickly searched her memory banks for what she knew about that tribe. She didn't come up with much except something about a huge Arizona fire that had devastated their lumber economy, but then recalled that was White Mountain Apache.

"They're in Arizona," Clarke offered.

"That's right, young man," Mrs. Jacobs patted his arm.

"I'm from Oklahoma and we got lots of Indians there."

"Well, be careful how you say that."

"What?"

"You said 'we got.' They aren't yours honey, and Tony would be the first to tell you that."

"Oh. That's not what I meant."

"I know, sweetie."

Monique turned away and smiled. After running into unpleasant white folks it always cheered her to meet a good-hearted one who was aware of what Natives went through.

From the doorway they saw that Perri slept hard. She wore a navy T-shirt and baggy gray sweatpants. Monique walked over and removed the washcloth from her eyes and felt her hot forehead. Perri didn't stir. Her long dark hair was tangled, and she looked drawn and dehydrated from vomiting. The two dogs jogged into the room and jumped on the bed. The headboard hit the wall with a clunk. They settled down into the comforter as air from the ceiling fan ruffled their reddish-blond fur. They laid still, their gentle brown eyes watching the detectives.

"Perri told me she thought Tony came in last night because she felt the bed move," Anne said. "Turns out it was the dogs."

"So, she was here all last night?" Clarke asked.

"Well, I saw him and Perri around eight. He was on his way to school and I asked Perri how she was feeling. I had just come from the store as he was leaving, you see. Tony joked about her being a terrible patient and he was going to get away so she could have quiet time. She really did look bad. Anyway, I didn't hear a car come or go after Tony went to school. No lights shone through our bedroom like Tony's headlights do when he comes in or out after dark." She pulled a Kleenex from her pocket and dabbed her eyes. "The last thing he said to me was, 'She won't even know I'm gone.'"

Monique shifted her feet. "Have you seen any strange vehicles driving through lately? Have Tony or Perri mentioned any harassing phone calls or letters?"

"No, nothing like that."

"Did Tony ever talk about the university?"

"No, that wasn't allowed."

"By him?"

"No, her. She teaches first-graders and she always tries to keep conversations light and happy. She didn't want depressing talk during social time. And CHU talk is always depressing, you know. Tony would mention to me in the yard sometimes about how awful his department is. But our conversations as a foursome were always fun and interesting. Tony tells me about his latest book and Perri talks about the kids she teaches and what she's growing in the garden. Tony drops in sometimes to see if we need help with the yard work. He hooked up my new DVD last week. I had wires going everywhere and he knew just what to do. They're good neighbors." She wiped her eyes again and sniffed. "My God. Who would do this?"

Monique sighed. "That's a good question. Mrs. Lucas, if you can think of anything else, please call." She held out her card. Clarke stood by the kitchen counter, looking at what appeared to be a sculpture of an animal.

"What's this?" he asked Mrs. Lucas.

"I don't know. I was over here yesterday and it wasn't there. Tony must have brought it in late in the afternoon."

Monique walked over and looked closer at the foot-high stone-carved figure and saw it was a bull elk with one antler missing. It was dirty, as if it had been in the ground and had only a cursory clean up. Little flakes of red clay lay on the kitchen counter underneath it. Clearly, it was very old.

"Do you have any ideas?" Mrs. Lucas asked.

"Ideas?" asked Monique. "Well, it looks like an elk."

"No, I mean about the murder."

"Not quite yet, but we've just started," answered Monique. "I'd put the phone back on the hook to catch any messages. Turn down the ringer. You don't have to let anyone in. Especially reporters."

"Don't worry about that." She glared out the window at the group of newspeople hovering at the fence like hawks over a chicken yard. "I hate reporters."

MONDAY, 2:00 P.M.

"Hey guys," said Renee Coker, one of the Moose City police officers. She sat at her desk eating a free-range chicken sandwich on whole wheat with sprouts hanging out the edges. She propped her petite feet on the wastebasket. "Got anything?"

"Working on it," Monique answered as she walked past. At her desk she took off her jacket and bobbed her head around to unknot her neck muscles. "Turns out Tony's wife was sick last night. She took some prescription cough syrup and fell asleep. She thought it was Tony falling onto the bed around midnight, but it really was her golden retrievers and she didn't know he was missing until this morning."

"Bummer," Renee remarked as she crunched her blue corn chips. "She shoulda taken some homeopathic tabs."

"Not everyone can stomach your clean food, Renee," Clarke said.

"Should."

The detectives sat on heavy wooden chairs that conformed to their backsides and drank Diet Pepsis as they read files. Monique polished an apple on her pant leg and munched as she thought. Clarke propped his aching foot on a waste basket.

"How's the foot?"

"Oh man. It's sore as a risin'."

"What?"

"A risin'. You know."

"No, I don't."

"A risin' is a boil."

"That's gross, Clarke."

"Yeah, and it hurts, too."

"Well, take something for it." She turned a page in the file. "Seems clear that Tony's a lot like Roxanne when it comes to saving the CHU anthropology department from obscurity."

"Yeah," agreed Clarke. "Tony, Roxanne, and a few others did far more than the others."

"The annual merit presentations I read are impressive. They basically checked off every accomplishment they had listed in their DOEs."

"Their whats?"

"Document of Expectations. It's the way the department awards raises. Every August the faculty member lists what he or she expects to do, then the document is approved by the chair, and then the professor is required to follow through with what they say they will write and teach. But year after year the committees didn't mention all their accomplishments. That kept Badger and Smoke Rise out of the highest category of merit rankings. Listen to this from Roxanne's tenure file; it's written by committee chair Harding: 'You have met all the requirements for associate professor and tenure, but we do not recommend either at this time.' That doesn't even make sense."

"Man, if this happened to me," said Clarke, "I'd whup 'em like egg whites."

"You read *Hannibal?*" Monique asked. "By the guy who wrote *The Silence of the Lambs.*"

"No. Saw the movie, though."

"Well that woman in there, the heroine. You know, Clarice. In this one she's still a hot dog FBI agent, smarter than a lot of the men she works for, but there're a lot of clowns who don't want her to succeed. Harris says it perfectly in one passage: 'they dripped poison into her file at every opportunity.' Clarice just kept on fighting. Roxanne reminds me of her. She's ready and willing to fight these people in her department all the way. She could have just rolled over and brown-nosed a long time ago, but that's not her personality."

"I suspect it wasn't Tony's personality, either."

"Hardly. I figure it like this about Roxanne." Monique held up her hand and extended her fingers. "One, a typical guy thing. They want to screw her in one way, if you know what I mean, and can't so they screw her in another." She put her thumb in.

"I'd buy that."

"Okay, two: they're jealous of her and wish they had her brains and talent. That's a man and woman thing." Monique put down her index finger. Clarke nodded. "Three, they hate her 'cause she's a successful woman in a man's field. That's a man thing, but sometimes a sick woman's issue, too." She put down her next finger, but the other two wouldn't stay up.

"That doesn't make sense."

"Sure it does. A lot of women are comfortable being second-class citizens and they resent any female who claws her way out of the crab bucket. It's the same strategy you see with insecure Indians who are so jealous of any other Indian's success they that go ballistic and attack him more aggressively than they would any racist white person."

"That's sick."

"I just said that. Okay, four. Insecure people who dislike themselves are even more dysfunctional as a group. They feed off each other." She put down the finger next to the pinky and her thumb held it. She popped open another Pepsi and took two deep swallows, then waited until she quietly belched to continue.

"It's easier to justify her and Tony's success because of their ethnicity. If the department were to admit that both spent a lot of time on their projects, then the rest of the anthropologists would have to admit that they would have do the same. It seems to me that researching and writing takes a hell of a lot more energy than teaching the way a guy like Clipper does it, especially when you have graduate students grading your exams. What do the professors do besides show up and talk for an hour or so a couple times a week? The only challenge some of these professors face is boredom." Monique stood and put on her shades. "So. Do you see any similarities here?"

"Between what and what?"

"*Hannibal* and the department."

"Well, yeah. Lots of motives here: jealously, anger, resentment, desire. What's number five?"

"About half the department studies African, Egypt, or Central American topics."

"I saw that. New Guinea and Australia too."

"Right. But the point is that the people who've talked the loudest about these two Indians being losers are the ones who study Indians. So, five, here we got white people getting all bent out of shape because the living representatives of the dead people they study do a better job of it than they do."

Clarke stood, stretched and put on his sports coat. "How do you categorize that? Frustration? Fear? Loss of money if they can't get a research project done? Compellin' combination of motives."

"Yes. And women can be just as violent as men and sometimes more so. And don't forget this new institute Tony helped start. It takes him and Roxanne out of the department and cuts off Clipper's money supply. Clipper has motive because he doesn't have his Indians to use anymore."

The two stood in silence a moment, enjoying the cool breeze from the oscillating fan.

"But is that enough to justify murder?" asked Clarke. "Putting nasty comments in a personnel file is a long way from cuttin' the guy's throat.

"One way of thinking about a crime is to ask who benefits from the crime."

"Well, yeah. I mean, they can be mad and jealous, but is that enough to kill? Even if they get fired or lose some money, is that enough?"

"Crime of passion. And I don't mean love."

"It just seems to me that we're missing something on the money angle."

"Maybe. People will do a lot for money."

"Yes," Clarke said, chewing his lower lip, "they will. Especially if there's a lot of it involved."

"If Smoke Rise and Badger are dead, Clipper can't use them in his grant applications any more. From that angle, killing them makes no sense. We've established the animosities, but there's got to be something else we haven't found yet. Let's go visit Professor Badger."

Heavy traffic caused the trip to Roxanne's house to take thirty minutes. "Damn city," said Monique. There were only two main roads going east and west, and the shortcuts were no longer secret. At any time of the day, cars were backed up at the poorly planned intersections where the train tracks crossed.

"Another earthquake or two in California and we'll really have problems," she said. "All those rich people on the West Coast will come here and drive the prices up so high that cops won't be able to buy affordable housing."

"Looks like Roxanne lives as far away from campus as she can get without leaving the county," Clarke said.

"Smart kid. I wouldn't mind living out here."

Moose City weather was almost perfect, although not as nice as the Oklahoma springs. Monique longed for the intense green of the rolling countryside, and she missed watching the scissortail flycatchers diving for bugs. She missed the dark calm before the raging spring and summer storms. Devastating tornadoes caused most Oklahomans dread, although many citizens secretly enjoyed the excitement of listening to the rain pound their roof and watching the Weather Channel to see the twisters skirt their town. Monique's parents had a storm cellar in the backyard where she and her brother played as children. The small underground room had two twin beds and plenty of toys, like pick-up sticks, pencils, and crayons. The moist cellar was safe and private and the perfect place to think. A twister once swept through their neighborhood and her family holed up in the cellar for half the night, telling stories by light of the lantern. It was one of the best times of her life. The most significant weather she'd seen since moving to Moose City was cold, blowing snow.

They left the congested city behind and entered the road that took them up the side of Mt. Felix, named after one of the men who christened the town. After six miles, Monique turned onto a paved road with a line of mailboxes by the corner. Large pines stood on either side of the road. Underbrush and smaller trees had been recently cleared out by the Forest Service in an attempt to manage fires. Mule deer ran in front of their car; the four does and one buck stopped when they reached the fence and turned to watch the car.

"Neat place," said Clarke. "Lots of animals out in the evenings."

"Yup. The herds come around that big lake up the road. One night I came out here with Steve and stopped counting at eighty elk. This road's a bitch to plow in winter, though."

A log cabin with a green metal roof appeared first. Flowers in the porch pots sat strategically on blocks of wood behind each other so it looked like they were planted on a hill. A white-tailed deer archery target stood next to a fake wishing well. The owners tastefully separated their portion of the world from their neighbor with dowel and range fencing. "Good fences make good neighbors," Monique observed.

"Hey, look at that deer target," Clarke laughed. "They put the horns on backwards."

"This used to be a dirt road," said Monique. "Now they have cable TV."

"Looks expensive."

"It is now. Ten years ago it was easy to get a place here. That's when Roxanne bought her home, I bet. She could probably sell it now for twice what she paid for it."

Three properties away stood Roxanne's house. A carved wooden plaque on top of the wooden fence had the address carved into it. A padlock on the chain around the gate only looked locked, but it wasn't. Monique and Clarke saw a large tan duelly truck parked in front. "Looks like Renell the eccentric lawyer's here," Monique said.

Yeah, I've seen her in action in the courtroom. And she's won the health club's annual racquetball tournament for the last five years. "Crazy redhead."

"I've seen her argue, too. Crazy, but smart."

Clarke got out and opened the gate and felt a poke in his rear, then another in his groin. Two large gray malamutes came out of nowhere to smell him. Another little dog came running from the house. It jumped up to Clarke's waist, and he realized the funny-looking cross between a Spitz and a Chihuahua wanted to be held in his arms.

With all the dogs Clarke figured it was no use going back to the car and getting in, so he waved Monique through the gate. "Got some pals there?" Monique asked.

She got out and the dogs greeted her as well. One of the malamutes shed chunks of gray hair on her trousers. Monique tried wiping the fluff balls off but only spread the hairs around.

"That's some truck," commented Clarke. The four-door, long-bed Chevy was jacked up and wore huge all-terrain 17-inch tires. Fog lights were mounted on top of the cab and under the front bumper, and the roll bar looked formidable enough to prop up a house.

"What? Forty-five, fifty grand?"

"At least."

Clarke was more impressed with the mud splattered over the tan truck. "The owner actually does something with her toy."

The detectives walked up the steps to the covered porch. Pines shaded the entire property, their trunks trimmed of low branches. "About eight cords there," Clarke speculated as he surveyed the neat stacks along the west fence line.

"You gotta burn that pine fast and hot, otherwise it leaves a sooty mess in the flue," said Monique. "I bet she uses that oak over there." Stacks of oak and juniper stood on the east fence and against the barn. "Burns slower. Good for nighttime when you don't want to keep waking up to stoke the fire."

The open garage door revealed a purple Ford pickup with a camper over the bed, a white Land Cruiser, and two mountain bikes hanging from ceiling hooks. Pegboards covered with tools had been hung on the walls, and in the rear of the garage stood cross country and downhill skis and poles in a large wooden base. A plow that could be attached to the Ford during snow season peeked from under a tarp on the outside of the garage wall.

The little dog ran ahead of the two men and turned when it reached the porch. When Clarke put his foot on the first step, the dog leaped into his chest and Clarke caught it.

"Nice catch," said Monique. The little dog wagged its tail crazily and looked up with adoration at Clarke. It licked Clarke's face until his sunglasses fell off.

The covered front porch and low overhang allowed one to sit safe and dry outside during a rain. Potted green plants, flowers, and herbs lined the deck and the wide railings. Wind chimes hung around the roof eaves. They were the tiny tinkly kind and didn't make intrusive noises. Since the wooden door stood open and the screen door was hooked shut, Monique figured Roxanne knew they were outside, and she knocked instead of ringing the bell.

A woman came to the door on light footfalls. She wore a pink spaghetti-strapped top and a flower print shirt that fell to her mid-shin. She wore her dark hair in a loose bun and tendrils hung around her dark face. She wasn't beautiful, but striking.

She stood with her thin arms folded, looking at them with brown eyes rimmed with what looked like bruises. A tiny voice from behind her asked in a two-year-old accent, "Whosit Mommy? Is it Tony?"

"No, honey." Monique and Clarke knew the woman's dark circles were from fatigue. "Yes?" she queried.

"Detective Blue Hawk and Detective Clarke." They held up their badges. "We're here to talk to Professor Roxanne Badger."

She opened the door and motioned with her head for them to come in. "That's me." She extended her hand and gave each detective a firm shake. She kept her eyes on Monique.

"Hi!" said the little one. The girl held on to her mother's dress. Beaded clips adorned her long wavy hair.

"This is Giselle."

"No, I'm Tootie," she corrected. " 'Cause I toot!"

"That's her other name," her mother smiled. "For now."

"Hello, Tootie. Renell here?" Monique asked.

"Yeah. She came over this morning after she saw Perri. I was so upset I couldn't drive. Roscoe drove my car home. Tone and Renell were friends, too. Here, gimme Mr. Happy," she said.

"Excuse me?" said Clarke.

"The pooch. He's Mr. Happy. Those other two need to stay out. They're shedding." The two malamutes sat at the door, their heads cocked to the left.

The bright, cool house smelled like vanilla candles. The front room was inviting, what Clarke thought he'd do with his place if he took the time to think about decorating. He saw nothing extravagant, just interesting things like the light fixture made of deer antlers that hung over the dark-stained dining room table. Huge earth-colored pillows covered the L-shaped sofa. Clarke imagined that Roxanne and her husband watched TV and fell asleep here. Family photos hung everywhere, with two painted portraits on either side of the television. One looked like Roxanne holding Giselle. An elk or big deer hide covered the wall above the sofa with a mountain scene painted on it. Pots, vases, urns, and sculptures of various sizes sat on every available level surface.

The room adjoining the den looked like Roxanne's office. Clarke saw only a portion of a desk covered with papers and a filing cabinet with files piled on top. Ivy, the kind in Roxanne and Tony's CHU offices, hung in baskets in front of windows that allowed Roxanne to see the forest and neighbors around her. The floor in the den was made of flagstone, and the kitchen floor was tiles the color of marinara sauce. That made sense to Clarke. His white floor at home showed every speck of dirt.

"Nice place," he said.

"Took a while to fix it up, but we're happy with it," Roxanne answered.

They moved through the neat and airy kitchen to the back door, which led to another covered porch more elaborate than the front one. A ceiling fan pushed the breeze downwards. Renell looked up first and then stood, her long legs still straddling the lounger. She dressed like a guy, in a white short-sleeved golf shirt, khaki shorts, and sandals.

"Hey, Monique." She and Monique shook hands.

Monique responded, "This is Charles Clarke, my partner on this case."

After shaking hands, the detectives looked to the other person on the porch, a man. He was the same height as Monique, and weighed a little more. He looked like a runner. He had on a sleeveless gray shirt and navy shorts, and his long wet hair was tied back. He smelled like deodorant soap, and Monique quickly placed him in a Plains tribe. His eyes were golden, which made him a mixed-blood. Not too white, though, because he was dark, intense, and definitely wouldn't be mistaken for anything other than a skin. Monique figured he had a white great-grandpa in the family woodpile.

"Warren Brugge, Roxanne's husband," he said in a slow, deep voice as he shook hands. "Sit where you want."

They pulled up wooden fold-up chairs that rocked back when they sat.

Roxanne brought a tray of tall plastic tumblers filled with ice and lemonade. "I'm not feeling too hostessy right now. If you want something else, there're drinks in the fridge." She motioned to the red Coca-Cola refrigerator on the porch. "That old thing works," she answered before they asked. Then she sat in the rocker next to Warren.

"You didn't need to us get anything. Thanks," said Monique. Her glass fit into the armchair holder.

"Need aspwin, Mommy?" asked Giselle the Toot.

"I'm okay, baby. Thanks," Roxanne gave the little girl a hug and kiss.

"So, Professor Badger," Monique began. "Sorry about your friend."

Roxanne's eyebrows went up and back down. What was there to say to that?

"We've interviewed some of your department already. It's quite a crew."

"So that's your term for them?" interjected Renell.

"You know them?"

"Heard about them through Tone and Rox, and actually had a conversation with the university president about their behavior," the lawyer said. "Enough to make my skin crawl for the last decade."

"I think I can understand that." Monique eased back in her chair.

Roxanne's eyes flooded with tears. Warren handed her a tissue. Roxanne stared into her backyard. Monique followed her gaze and saw two squirrels chasing each other around the base of a tree. They chattered and fussed as they ran up and down the trunk, their tiny claws making scraping sounds as they struggled over their turf. Beyond the squirrels stood the corral, where two gray horses also frolicked. One held the end of a piece of hose in her mouth while the other chased her, trying to get hold of it. The two malamutes growled and urged the horses on. Next to the barn stood a chicken coup and fenced yard filled with brush for the birds to hide under. A well-worn path from the house to the corral branched off to a gate in the fence.

"Let me ask the question I have to, Professor Badger. Where were you last night between ten and midnight?"

Roxanne paused to consider Monique. She knew the tall detective was Native but she didn't know what tribe. Roxanne hoped that the officer was sympathetic, but she didn't trust many people, and that included Indians.

"Here with my family. I was at Anthropology working, but I got tired and had a headache so bad I couldn't stand it. I went down the hall to say bye to Tone, but didn't go to his office. I just yelled at him. He said, 'Take a pill and I'll see you in the morning before I leave.' He had a conference in Ohio and was working on his paper. I said good-bye around eight."

No one spoke for a few seconds.

"You got anything on the case yet?" Renell interjected.

Monique considered what to tell them. She glanced at Toot, who was engrossed with putting Hannah Montana stickers onto an empty Coke bottle. "Maybe she should go inside for minute?"

"Toot," Roxanne said, "go get some doggie treats."

After the little girl scampered off, in a low voice Monique told the three sad people on the porch about some of their findings and a little of what members of the anthropology department had said. Then she dropped the bomb. "Roxanne, it appears that you were an intended victim. We traced the steps of the perp and he, or she, also went to your office and found your light on, but you weren't there."

Roxanne inhaled sharply. "Did he die quick?"

"His left carotid artery was severed and he was stabbed numerous times, so yes, he died quickly."

Roxanne excused herself and Warren followed her into the house.

"You know," said Renell as she watched her friends, "this was inevitable. These sickos couldn't stand Rox or Tone."

"Umm, Renell?" Monique said in quiet voice so Roxanne and Warren wouldn't hear. "Did Tony and Roxanne have a thing going?"

"No. Those two," she lifted her glass toward the house, "are rock solid. So were Tony and his wife. Tony's not from this area and neither is Roxanne. They're two Indians in a racist environment and they needed each other. I know they got sick of listening to each other bitch. Tony told me that he couldn't stand to discuss department politics every time he and Rox got together. I'm sure Rox told Warren the same thing about Tony. But they were close, good friends."

Roxanne came back outside holding a white fluffy cat. It had a flat, ugly, and expensive face. Roxanne sat down, and the cat made itself comfortable in her lap. Roxanne scratched its head and everyone heard the Persian's loud, contented purr.

Roxanne sighed deeply. "When I heard that he had been murdered, my breath just blew right out of me. Like getting punched in the gut, you know? The guy who told me smiled. Like he was happy and he enjoyed telling me Tony was dead."

"Who was that?" Clarke asked.

"Some twerp in another department. Louis Ryan, a psychologist."

Monique wrote on her pad.

Roxanne kept her eyes on the yard as if she couldn't bear to face humanity. Nature was a comfort. Monique and Clarke watched her profile.

Warren leaned forward and rubbed Roxanne's shoulders. "You can't keep dwelling on those people," he said.

"I mean, he was *happy*," Roxanne spat it out. "I don't get it. For ten years Tone and I asked ourselves what we were doing to make people hate us so much. We haven't done anything to them. Nothing!" The white cat startled and opened his blue eyes.

"Yeah, you did," said Renell. "And you still are doing something."

Monique and Clarke leaned in to hear.

"You're here." She looked to the two detectives then leaned back and put her arms behind her head.

"Roxanne," began Monique. "I mean, Professor Badger."

"Please. Don't start that," Roxanne said.

"Oh, well. Some of the other professors insisted that we call them Dr. this or Professor that."

"Tell them about the phone call," Renell interrupted.

"Call?"

Roxanne nodded. "Last night, or guess it'd be this morning around three, I answered the phone. I said hello and no one answered. I couldn't hear any background noise. The voice sounded like it went through a machine that makes it distorted. You know, deep and slow. It said, 'You better give it up or you're next.' Then they hung up. I punched 68, but it just rang. At the time I had no idea what the caller meant."

"Was it a man?" asked Monique.

"Couldn't really tell. The voice sounded weird. Could have been a woman, I guess."

"Was it muffled?"

"No. The person seemed to be speaking through a machine that makes you sound like a robot."

"Now do you know what the caller meant?" Monique asked.

"Well, Tone's dead."

"No. I mean the part about 'give it up.'"

"Maybe they meant 'give up.'"

"What are you supposed to give up?"

"I have no idea."

"You don't have anything that belonged to Tony?"

"Yeah. Quite a bit of stuff, actually. Warren borrowed his chain saw since the chain broke on ours. We have his grill and he left a pair of leather gloves over here two weeks ago after the guys worked on the corral."

"And the ice chest," Warren added.

"Yeah. That chest, a salad bowl, and I have about a dozen of his books."

"Doesn't sound like anyone in your department should be angry because you have those items."

"No. So the caller had to mean just 'give up.'"

Monique decided to start on a new tack. "We've learned about this institute that you and Tony have under way. Has anyone been fighting you on this? Any bad feelings?"

"Ha! You're kidding, right? Last fall after we got the go-ahead from the administration to proceed, Clipper, Langstrome, and Smithers were furious when they found out how far we'd gone without them knowing about it. They knew they were in trouble because we'd be leaving the department. Clipper's little empire will go down the potty."

"Did anyone say anything directly to you about it?"

"Of course they did. Clipper told me one day in the mailroom that we don't have the brains to run a program, much less an institute of that size. Langstrome told Tony it was a worthless project. Belinda Rinds called us both essentialists—again—at a department meeting. Lots of things were said. It's all documented."

"I just learned about essentialism," Clarke said.

"Well, this is one way the white anthros have kept grad students from me and Tony. They tell the students that we believe in essentialism, and so the students avoid us. On the other hand, many Natives have information that whites can never get, such as knowledge about religious ceremonies."

"And, I would add," interjected Monique, "it's almost impossible to convey what it really is like being Native. Unless you live with racism, stereotypes, and the reality that we're colonized, you simply can't write about emotional and psychological repercussions of that with any accuracy."

"Very good," Roxanne said. "Really though, I *am* an essentialist at heart. Tony wasn't. He thought the field should be open to anyone who wants to write about us. Personally, I don't know why white people have to be so damned nosy."

The doorbell rang. "I'll get it," Warren said. He returned a minute later trailed by an Indian man with long, unkempt hair. Roxanne was so surprised to see Pauley Wenetae that she couldn't speak. "This is Pauley Wenetae," Warren said to the group.

"I uh. I uh," Pauley began. Then he put both hands to his face and sobbed.

Roxanne and Monique quickly stood. Warren steered the crying man to a chair and had him sit, still crying. "I found out about Tony this morning," he said before snottily blowing his nose. "I flew back. I came from the airport." His eyes looked red and puffy, and his hair was more mussed than usual, as if he already had been through a few rounds of tears and beers on his long flight.

"Mr. Wenetae," said Monique, "I'm Detective Blue Hawk and this is Detective Clarke."

"What happened?" Pauley asked.

"Do you know something about this, Mr. Wenetae?"

"What? No, nothing. All I got was a call from my wife telling me Tony was killed. Who did it?"

"We don't know, which is why I just asked you the question I did."

Pauley sighed deeply. "Oh God. Why did this happen?"

Monique sighed. Either Pauley really did know nothing, or he was now sorry that what he had helped plan worked.

"So you've been out of town?"

"Yes," he sniffed. "I've been in Ontario teaching a three-week class. I only had two more days left so I finished early."

"Do you mind if we ask you questions now?"

"No. Ask."

"How well do you know the anthropology faculty?" she asked.

109

"Not real well. I travel a lot. I don't know anyone very well. I mean, I see them a lot, but I don't socialize with them. I've never been to any of their homes. Until now." He pulled another Kleenex from his pocket and blew.

"So you have no thoughts about who could have done this or why?"

He blew his nose again. "No. No idea."

"Before you left for Canada, did you hear anyone say something unusual, or did anyone behave out of the ordinary?"

"No, nothing."

Monique sighed. "What do you think about the institute that Roxanne and Tony planned?"

"Institute?"

A large woodpecker landed at the suet feeder hanging from the porch gutter and pulled out chunks of lard and seed then dropped a load of poop.

"Mr. Wenetae, I think you should go home. Try and sleep and then call me when you can come to the station where we can chat some more."

"Yeah, okay." He turned to Roxanne. "I'm sorry. I really am sorry."

"I'll walk you out," she replied.

A minute later Roxanne returned and sat. "That's the first time we've seen each other outside of meetings and the mailroom. How did he know where I live?"

"He doesn't seem to know much else," said Renell.

"You got that right in more ways than one," said Roxanne. "I'm shocked as hell that he came over here. He never talks to me, never asks my opinion about anything. Tony didn't know him either."

"Sometimes it takes a serious tragedy even to bring people together," Renell said.

"We're not going to be friends because of this," Roxanne said quickly.

"No need. But at least you can be allies. Maybe."

"Provided he had nothing to do with it," Monique interjected.

They sat in silence, watching the squirrels and the horses.

"I like your place," said Clarke.

"When I first moved to Moose City I rented an apartment that had a view of the mountains," said Roxanne. "It was okay, but loud. I saved some money and got some confidence, then started looking for a home to buy. I drove around for months with a realtor and didn't find what I wanted, so I started going out by myself and found this. It was small with just two bedrooms. But it's got two acres and backs up to the national forest."

The two malamutes concluded their harassment of the horses and ran to the porch. One jumped up on Renell and the other came to Monique. "That's Balto," said Warren. "The female's Scully."

"It really needed work," Roxanne continued. "The owners let their pet goats and cats run through the den and kitchen and the garage door was off the hinges. The home inspector found all kinds of problems. The first thing I did was to replace the drywall in the kitchen, which was saturated with cat piss."

Warren laughed. "That was before I met her."

"Smell was so bad I had to use those smoke bombs they use in morgues to kill the odor. I put on another room for my office, then added the porches and built that barn. The coop was in good shape but needed a better fence so the skunks couldn't get in."

"Lots of work," said Monique.

"Worth it," said Warren. "But now money doesn't seem important."

Blue jays yelled at each other high in the treetops.

"So what's next?" asked Roxanne.

"Well, I need to ask you a few more questions," said Monique.

"We can walk to the chicken coop," said Roxanne. "I need to stretch."

"Want me to go?" asked Renell.

"Nah. I don't have anything incriminating to say about myself."

Roxanne, Monique, and Clarke got up and walked to the horse corral. The two big grays trotted over and stuck their head over the pole fence, nostrils wide in hopes of smelling treats. Monique was delighted and she rubbed one muzzle and then the other. The jealous malamutes jumped on her and the claws in their huge front paws dug into her pants.

"You guys, stop it," said Roxanne. "Go on. Get in your houses." The scolded dogs ran off and sat a respectful distance away. "Malamutes are hard to train. They get wanderlust and have their own agenda."

"I know this is tough," Monique began, "but it's important. You knew Tony well. Did he tell you he was afraid of anyone? Had anyone threatened him?"

"Sort of."

"Like how?" Clarke asked.

"A couple of them, Leo Harding and Ross Clipper especially, were always telling him to improve his attitude and to respect his superiors. They made it sound as if Tony would be fired if he didn't conform. What they really meant was that he should stop writing and become like them. Fat, lazy, and rude."

Roxanne led the detectives to the chicken yard and opened the feed room. She took a small metal bucket and scooped it half full of scratch and then filled it to the top with pellets. She went to the gate and nodded for them to enter. Mop tops with feathers flopped over their heads like water fountains.

"Wow," said Clarke. "Funky chickens."

"That's Jimi Hendrix," said Roxanne, pointing to a rooster with long head feathers. A smaller gold and black stood at her feet pecking at her toenails. "This is Tina Turner."

After Roxanne threw the feed, the shyer chickens that hid under their security brush bolted from their hiding places. Some had feathers covering their legs and feet. The variety of colors and sizes made a scene like a cartoon.

"I like variety. These mops are gentle and the roosters don't chase Giselle. There're probably eggs in the other side of the coop where the birds stay. I'll get you some."

They left the yard and the detectives watched Roxanne put the bucket back in the feed bin. "Is there anyone you think may have done this?"

Roxanne leaned on the coop wall and crossed her arms. A hummingbird zoomed between the three humans trying to get at the bright clematis growing up the coop wall. "Good question. Lots of unhealthy minds around here. There's evil here and Tone knew it. We were always trying to pinpoint where the immorality came from. I think it has numerous sources. Anyway, the administration won't take care of matters. They just let unresolved problems go on and on."

"Why don't you leave?" asked Monique.

"Another good question. The faculty who stay at CHU either do so because they can't go anyplace else, or, like me and Tone, they like Moose City, the mountains and the forests. Like Tone always told me, who wants to work in a city with a billion people and no trees, or to fight pollution and traffic and wait for an earthquake?"

"That's why I'm here," Clarke agreed.

"It's a great environment. Besides, we thought we had a sure thing with this indigenous institute. We have good faculty, we're bringing in visiting professors and have a speaker series lined up. Now that the advertisements have gone out we have dozens of queries from students. It'll be great and it's just what we've always wanted to do—to be academic activists, to teach how Natives can use all this knowledge to better their tribes. You know, to empower themselves and their people."

"Clipper isn't doing that, right?" Monique knew the answer already but figured she'd get a reaction out of Roxanne. And she did.

"Is that a joke?"

"No. What I meant to ask was . . ."

"Things won't change there. Ever. Last week one of Rhonda's graduate students came to my office. I'd never met her, and she hadn't been in my office before. She completed her dissertation this spring on urban Indians or something and was applying for a couple of positions. She asked me, 'Professor Badger, would you write me a letter of recommendation?'"

"What's wrong with that?" asked Clarke.

"To begin with, I knew nothing about her and I told her so. She'd never taken a class with me, much less discussed her research topic, which I should have been supervising. This is the third time this has happened. Students don't want to take my classes, or even be around me, but when it comes time to get a job, they know they need my reputation to help them get it."

"What did you tell her?"

"What I just told you. I won't put up with that anymore. I know she ran downstairs to tell all her little buddies what an unhelpful ass I am.

The interesting part about what's happened to me and Tone these past ten years is that it's hard to prove who's doing it. Tricky little things, like planning the committees ahead of time and making sure neither of us are nominated. Sending complaints about us to the chair—every complaint gets put in our file whether it's true or not. Belinda's behind all of it, I'm sure. The men do most of the talking. She's the gun and they're her bullets."

One of the roosters crowed and the other jumped to the top of the brush pile to out-yell him. The hens ignored them and continued scratching. Roxanne reached down to pet the head of the malamute that disobeyed orders and came over to his mistress. "I've always felt that things in the anthro department would lead to something really bad."

"Like murder?"

Roxanne shook her head. "I can't say that I predicted murder. Punctured tires, maybe. Wrecking our offices, maybe. Putting Ex-Lax in some brownies. Anonymous letters full of libelous statements and gossip. You know, stupid, juvenile stuff."

Monique didn't reply.

Roxanne gritted her teeth, and her jaw muscles flexed. "This may be nothing, but did you know there's an excavation going on by that new freeway?"

"No." Monique looked to Clarke, who shook his head. "We didn't know that."

"It's a burial site and instead of calling me or Tone to look at it, the university—whoever that really is—recommended Ben Rogers and Ross Clipper to oversee the project."

"Do they get paid?"

"For being consultants, yes. As far as I have been told, there are only a few skeletons. If it were a large burial then there could be a lot at stake since it costs millions to build a freeway. If it's stopped, then time is money."

"So, what's Clipper advising?"

"I don't know. He should be consulting with local tribes to determine who the remains belong to. What tribe, I mean."

"Who's paying them?" asked Clarke.

"Corps of Engineers. The city, maybe. I don't know the answer to that question, either."

Monique looked at the dirt as she thought.

"What about Rogers?"

"What about him? He's neutral on everything. It's hard to tell where he stands on any political issue. I do know that he's making a small fortune on this dig. I can tolerate him since he seems to mind his own business and he comes across as decent. He has never mentioned the dig to me."

"Did he talk about it with Tony?"

"No. I mean, Tony never said he did. I don't know why he would. There's no publicity about it all. Very hush-hush." She scratched Balto's head. "Like I said, it doesn't matter anymore."

"No, Professor Badger," disagreed Monique, "I think you're wrong about that."

MONDAY, 6:00 P.M.

Monique and Clarke returned to her vehicle. Monique drove for a while in silence while Clarke held a carton of eggs in brown shells, thinking about the day.

"So how do you like this case, Clarke? You enjoying yourself?"

"Like a tornado in a trailer park. Seriously though. This case is full of strange cookies."

"Most murder cases are," said Monique. "There could be any number of people who committed the murder. Maybe more than one person planned it. There're quite a few motivations for killing Tony and Roxanne. Their colleagues have always worried about them taking a share of the monetary pie. Not everyone can get a merit raise each year, and only one-third of the department can qualify."

"Right," agreed Clarke. "The raises amount to 8 percent of their salaries for each of the last four years, so the result is a nasty competition. Tony and Roxanne made the cut for ten years."

"Some faculty might lose the money Badger and Smoke Rise would get for heading the dig and besides, this institute is taking away whatever prestige that department had."

"Yeah, I think so too." Clarke rubbed his eyes. "I'm gettin' tired. My eyes feel like they got sand under the lids."

"Cases like this are rough and tough. Get used to it because after someone is murdered, raped, or kidnapped, you have to find the perp fast. I feel like we're getting close, so don't poop out on me. I'm wondering about that dig."

"Wonderin' what?"

115

"Roxanne doesn't seem to know much about it and claims that Tony didn't either." Monique took a small bottle of Advil from her pocket, opened it and worked two caplets out with her tongue. "We need to make one more stop."

"University?"

"Nope. Our least favorite place."

"Swell. And I wanted to have a nice night's sleep."

At 9:12 P.M. they arrived at the Moose City Medical Center. They parked in the emergency area and went through the automatic glass entryway. Instead of turning right to ER, they went left down a dimly lit corridor about a hundred feet to the door marked "Morgue" and "Authorized Personnel Only."

On the other side of the door was what Klaus called the "mud room," furnished with an unattended desk, filing cabinets, and lockers. The desk lamp had been turned off, but bright lights illuminated the larger room where Klaus worked. Light from the large overhead bulbs reflected off the cold storage lockers where the cadavers rested. The room seemed lit by the sun.

Klaus looked up from what he was doing, weighing the organs of the body on the table. Klaus had only initially evaluated Tony Smoke Rise and was working on some poor guy unknown to the detectives.

"Enter please. Almost done," he said loudly.

Klaus wore goggles to keep blood and other fluids from spurting into his eyes, and his mask kept things out of his mouth and nose. He wasn't opening the skull on this individual, so he didn't worry about flying bone fragments.

He picked up the heart and put it in the scale that looked a lot like the ones at the grocery store. "Heart weighs 298 grams," he said into his dictaphone. Then he took the organ off the scale and looked at it closely. He cut into it and said, "Ah ha. You guys should see this."

Monique and Clarke walked over very slowly. Clarke lagged behind in case he needed to sprint to the men's room. "See here?" He put his plastic gloved finger next to the revealed cross-section of the aorta and smaller vessels. "Almost completely clogged. Guy had a heart attack and family doesn't

116

understand why. He was overweight and smoked. Lungs looked like they're lined with tar." Klaus nodded to the plastic bag on the table that was half full of Mr. X's soft tissue. "And he drank too much. You should see his liver."

"No thanks," said Monique.

"Good, I don't want to fish it out of there anyway. If his pump hadn't shut down, he'd be dead from a number of other things with a year."

Klaus told his dictaphone about the artery situation before dropping the heart into the bag. He took a suction hose and slurped out the rest of the blood in the chest cavity. Then he twisted the garbage bag and pulled the yellow drawstring tight and stuffed the whole thing into the empty chest. He folded the rib cage back into place and when he pushed down they made a crackling sound. Finally, Klaus stitched the skin with a large needle and thick thread, then covered up the body and pushed him into the cooler. The last image Monique had of Heart Attack Man was of wrinkly feet and a toe tag.

When Klaus turned around he looked up. "Where's Clarke?"

"He needed to go to the can," said Monique. She was feeling light-headed herself. The morgue had an unreal feel to it, like it wasn't a part of life. Death was normal; everyone would pass through a morgue at some point, and Monique knew that. It was the way some people died that wasn't normal. Some people killed themselves with excess food, drink, and drugs, while some perfectly healthy people got murdered. They were alive, then suddenly dead.

They heard the outer door to the mudroom open. Clarke came in and sat at one of the chairs by the desk. His jacket was off and his sleeves rolled up. He wasn't going back to the work area. Klaus recognized the symptoms and smiled. Clarke sat with his elbow on the desk, his chin resting on his fist. He'd wet his hair and his shirt and tie were spotted with water.

"You don't look so great, buddy," said Monique.

"Neither do you."

"Some people never get used to it," said Klaus. "I see all kinds of people look confident about handling a visit to the morgue. They walk in all smiles and within minutes they grow pale and some faint. Ever see a black person start to faint? They look grayish." He opened his Sprite and took a few deep swallows. "Your Captain Saltaine dropped like a swatted fly once when I opened a murder victim's head. Everything vibrated when he fell. I should put up a sign: 'The bigger they are the harder they fall.'"

"He never mentioned that," said Monique. It wasn't surprising. The last thing her 300-pound ex-linebacker boss would want her to know was that he fainted at the sight of brains. "So what can you tell us about Tony Smoke Rise?"

"Well, let us take a look, shall we?"

Monique suffered through the process of slicing and dicing, of watching what was a normal, healthy, and handsome man become even more ruined than he already was. *His soul is gone. It's okay. He can't feel a thing.*

"You okay, Detective?"

"Fine."

"You're swaying."

Monique swallowed and willed herself to watch as Klaus opened Tony's ribcage to investigate the damage to the organs. The he slowly peeled back skin to look at damage done to the neck vessels.

"Obviously, his throat was cut and this carotid artery was severed. That caused the blood to spray on the wall. There are, let's see . . ." He counted the wounds, "About two dozen stab wounds to the chest. About half of those could have killed him if the neck cut had not. Two lacerated his liver. See how much blood is in the abdominal cavity? That's dark blood from the liver. I think this man was surprised at his desk. Like I said this morning, he put up his right arm to defend himself, and couldn't." He held up Tony's arm and scrutinized the deep cuts.

"That's right. Perhaps he tripped over a pile of books behind his chair," said Monique.

"Yes. Yes. Well, the neck cut came after a flurry of strikes to his arm. He may have tripped and then the big slash came, perhaps. Anyway, he put his left hand to his neck. That hand had no marks on it. It was covered in blood, which means he may have tried to put pressure on the cut."

"Oh man, oh man, oh man," Clarke chanted in the background.

"You okay, partner?"

"Barely. Sorta."

"Whoever killed him didn't just want to kill him a little bit," Klaus

118

continued. "I mean the slash to his neck was enough. It was as if the person went crazy and felt compelled to stab him repeatedly. He sat on him and stabbed his chest. When the killer was satisfied, he—or she—pushed the filing cabinet onto him."

"The perp was mad," Clarke suggested weakly.

"Angry or crazy-mad, yes."

Clarke wiped his forehead with a paper towel.

"After the perp killed Tony," Monique said, "he wrecked the office. There was no blood on top of the papers."

"Maybe," continued Klaus. "There's no evidence here of Smoke Rise having any other physical problems. Low body fat, didn't smoke. As we can see, healthy organs. A big tattoo on his chest and no body piercing except his ears."

"Pretty clear what happened." *And how easily he passed from life to death.*

"Let's sit over there, shall we?" Klaus asked. He stripped off his gloves and popped them and his mask into the garbage marked "Hazardous Waste." He dropped his bloody apron into what looked like a normal laundry basket, and the goggles went into the sink. Monique did the same.

"And what about blood tests," she asked. "To see if there's any blood on him, besides his own?"

"Did that already. Nothing. All the same blood type. Tony's. Your killer was lucky not to get cut in the frenzy."

Monique looked at Tony's still, mangled form laying on the cold table. What would he think if he knew he'd be lying there so quickly, long before his life should have ended? Would Tony Smoke Rise have lived his life another way? Taken a different path, perhaps? *Hell, what would I do if I knew the date of my death?*

"Lucky my ass," said Monique.

MONDAY, 11:15 P.M.

Monique arrived home and quietly undressed, then dropped her clothes on the den floor and walked to the kitchen in her underwear, her weapons in her right hand. She laid the Glock, Charter Arms, and Mace on the table, then went to the fridge to see what might be left over from dinner and smiled with surprise to find Steve's homemade pizza on the top shelf. Layers of sauce, cheese, olives, and a variety of other vegetables, mainly mushrooms, were piled on the thin, whole wheat crust. She took a slice, nuked it in the microwave for a minute, then showered it with powdered garlic and jalapeno pepper slices. Eating took less than a minute.

She returned to the fridge and stared at the bottles of Moose Drool beer but knew she'd regret taking a drink this late. Even if it was earlier in the evening, one bottle would lead to another, then to three and probably four. Since she rationalized her drinking habit by telling herself that she ate no junk food and worked out every day, the four bottles of brown ale would disappear within an hour. "Good thing you hate hard liquor," she said out loud. One shot of tequila would give her a migraine.

Next Monique went to the bathroom by the light of the dim night light and washed her face but used a washcloth to quickly wipe her neck and armpits instead of showering, so the water heater wouldn't clank. She planned on getting up early the next morning for a short run and could shower then.

She put on the pair of baggy shorts and a T-shirt that she had left on the bathroom floor the day before and made her way to the bedroom. Steve lay on his side with Foogly the cat happily curled behind his knees and his arms around his stuffed bear. An open copy of *Still Life with Crows* lay on her pillow.

Monique guzzled a bottle of Propel and moved the book, then lay back and stared at the whirling blades of the ceiling fan. The automatic light over the detached garage in the back shined gently through the thin white drapes of the double doors that led to the wooden deck. In summer their tomato plants grew tall amid the crooked-neck yellow squash and zucchini. Although they had buckets of tiny tomatoes, pole beans, and big squashes, Monique longed for the sweet giant tomatoes, cucumbers, and corn she had cultivated easily during the longer growing season in Oklahoma.

"You here?" Steve mumbled.

"No. Go to sleep."

He stayed silent a moment, then sat up, strands of his long hair falling down over his face. "What happened today?"

"Too much and not enough."

"You always say that."

"Yes I do. I learned a lot but not enough to know what happened. How was Robbie's day?"

"Good. He only missed one on his spelling test. And he made an A on his rainforest diorama project."

"He should have. It took me long enough to make it."

"What?"

"I mean, me and Robbie made it."

"I heard it was an Indian anthropologist who got killed."

"Yes," she sighed. "His name was Tony Smoke Rise. He's Hopi and White Mountain Apache. You know any Hopis?"

"Just one guy I played against in a basketball tournament about fifteen years ago."

"What about White Mountain Apaches?"

"None that I know of."

"Sioux?"

"Oh yeah. Lakotas, Dakotas, Assinaboins, Santees."

"Me too."

"I know a cop at Rose Bud. Man, what a job. Murders, rapes, incest, abuse, car wrecks. He should be about out of his mind by now."

"You have to be a little nuts to work there." Monique knew that being a cop on almost any tribal land would be a true test of one's character. "It's interesting how we're both almost fifty and know so many Indians, but don't know a single Hopi or White Mountain Apache."

"Who's Sioux?"

"Oglala. His best friend is from Pine Ridge. Her name's Roxanne Badger."

"I've heard of her."

"When?"

"She was in the paper this year sometime. She wrote a book that won an award and it was in the university news column. I don't remember what it was about."

"She writes about mixed-bloods. Evidently she should be a real superstar in that department but they treat her like shit. Jealousy, mainly."

121

"Is that why Smoke Rise is dead?"

"That's one reason. I'd put money on it. But it's more than that."

"How'd he die?"

Monique flipped over onto her side to face her husband. "Nasty stuff, Steve."

He didn't say anything, so they listened to the hum of the fan a moment. "Okay," she finally said. "His neck was cut and he was stabbed. Many times."

"Did he fight back?"

"Not much. I think he had no forewarning. His right arm has only a few defensive cuts on it, which makes me think the perp got into his office fast and took him by surprise. Smoke Rise was a big guy and surely he would've been able to put up more of a defense if he had seen it coming."

"Who do you think did it?"

"I don't know for sure. But if it's not one of those anthropologists, I'll change jobs."

Steve leaned over and kissed her cheek. "Then I hope you're wrong."

TUESDAY, 5:00 A.M.

Monique Blue Hawk slept soundly through the night, but Roxanne Badger woke for the fourth time and it wasn't worth the effort to try and sleep more. Warren snored lightly and Toot lay between them, her breathing heavy and even. Roxanne got out of bed and padded to the front bathroom so she wouldn't disturb them. Then she went to the front porch, laced her Brooks, and took up her cross-country running poles for a hike. Normally she had the dogs with her, but she had no desire to bother with them when they ran off to explore or chase deer, so she left them in the pen.

She began walking. The first half-mile was uphill. The poles took a bit of pressure off her lower back and knees and forced her arms to work, something most runners neglect. She discovered the benefits of poling after attending a cross-country ski clinic where she was told that competitive skiers run with poles in the off-season to recall their timing and keep their arms in shape for the specific poling motion.

She sped up as she reached the level portion of the trail, the part easily accessed by another short trail that led to the parking lot by the Petson trail-head. She often encountered other runners and hikers there. The easy trail meandered lazily for a mile before another branch where Roxanne usually turned to her right and panted as she made her way up the steep trail used only by mountain runners and hikers who sought challenging climbs.

It still was early and she saw no one at the first intersection. Mule deer saw her, however, and they sprung like a herd of giant rabbits through the scrub oaks and bushes. The rain had stopped an hour before, and the smell of wet bark and grass lingered. The cool air helped clear her head, but that was not necessarily what she wanted. She needed to focus on Tony and her loss.

Roxanne stopped. She thought she heard something, perhaps a small branch snapped by the hoof of a careless deer. Or maybe it was a squirrel or lizard. She knew how loud small animals can be and conversely, how silent the largest, like elk, usually are.

She couldn't catch her breath enough to stay quiet; the more she tried to hold it, the more she needed to gasp. She heard another rustle through the underbrush and she turned quickly. Nothing.

"Far enough," she said out loud before starting back down the trail at a slow jog. She glanced at her watch to see that she'd been gone almost forty-five minutes. She'd make the downhill run home in less than thirty. But she'd need to be careful. Small rocks acted like marbles under her feet. Many people complained about the uphill part, but Roxanne knew that going downhill could be just as arduous and even harder on the quadriceps and knees. She'd fallen on her ass several times and didn't want a dislocated coccyx. So she concentrated on her feet and went slower, placing the poles in front of her with each stride.

She stopped next to a jumble of boulders to admire the view of Moose City. Pines and smaller oaks grew in between the rocks that had settled long ago. From this height she could see the university, which she cared nothing about, but she also saw the mountain range and the lakes and desert beyond. The sky had clouded up for the last twenty minutes, and it would rain soon. The dark clouds reminded Roxanne of the summer monsoons that she loved. She'd often start her run around noon, then watch the sky darken and she'd race home, laughing alongside her dogs before the lightning started.

Then she could shower and afterwards sit on her porch as the rain fell. The lightning knocked out the electricity, so she'd have to turn off her computer and read a novel. She thought about Tony's soul and wondered if he could now see what she saw from a better vantage point.

She put her arm against a boulder. Then she heard small rocks tumble down behind her. She started to turn and before she could move her shoulders to look back up the trail, something thin and hard hit her across the face with enough force to drop her to her knees.

Roxanne's face felt like fire had singed it, and before she could put her hand to the laceration that caused blood to spurt onto the trail, the thing hit her nose, this time hard enough to break it. Roxanne's nose gushed blood where it was struck across the bridge, where bone met cartilage. Her eyes watered and she fell sideways onto the trail with her arms over her face. Both of her legs kicked out and upwards in defense. Her feet collided with a body.

Roxanne blinked against the blood streaming into her eyes. She kicked upwards again and swung the pole that was attached to her left wrist and this time felt a more solid connection along with an exclamation of "oof." She quickly picked up one of the ski poles and poked it in the direction of the sound. The attacker gasped.

Then she heard through the pounding in her ears the quick steps of someone running back down the trail. She recognized the yodeling of her malamutes in the distance. She thought fleetingly that Warren had turned them loose to come get her.

Her face burned and despite the adrenaline and sheer desire for survival, Roxanne could not see enough to stand. The pain forced her to lie on the trail like a wounded deer, an animal that had barely escaped the hunter's bullet.

TUESDAY, 7:00 A.M.

Monique and Clarke met at the office early. Despite her good intentions, Monique felt too tired to run that morning and decided to make up for her laziness by drinking a large glass of carrot juice and eating a banana with peanut butter. When she got to work she picked up a granola bar from the bowl on Renee's desk, a message on a pink paper, then sat down to read more faculty merit files before Belinda Rinds arrived for her interview.

"Hey, listen to what it says in this file," said Clarke. He had taken some files home with him the night before and made enough notes to half fill a legal pad. "It's the merit summary for Belinda Rinds last year: 'Belinda Rinds is an exemplary scholar/teacher. She demonstrates extraordinary talent for delivering informative lectures based on her original research. Further, she exhibits a superior ability to mentor and advise graduate students.' Man, someone's a brown-noser."

"That's not much different than what I'm reading about Ross Clipper."

The phone rang in Earlene's office. "For you," she pointed at Monique. "Line 3."

She picked up. "Blue Hawk here," she said.

"Detective, this is Officer Brandon Lutie."

"Yes, Brandon."

"There's a patient who just arrived here in the ER named Roxanne Badger. She said to call you. She was attacked this morning. Less than an hour ago, actually."

Monique eyes met Clarke's. "Attacked? Where? When?"

"First, she'll be okay, although her nose is broken and the doctor says she'll need plastic surgery on her face from a deep laceration that extends from one eyebrow down her nose to the corner of her mouth. Looks really ugly from where I'm standing. Her eye and lid aren't touched, though. They butterflied the cuts for the moment."

"What the hell happened?"

"From what she can say—she's in some pain—someone hit her."

"Where? Who? Did she say who?"

"She didn't see who it was. She was running up the trail she normally does early this morning, and when she stopped someone surprised her. Apparently that person hid behind a rock. Roxanne had been gone almost an hour when her husband let their dogs go to find her. She hung on to the dogs while she limped a mile to the trailhead where her husband met her. It started raining and she also got chilled."

"What was she hit with?"

125

"Don't know for sure, but it was sharp so possibly a knife. Maybe the intent was to stab her, but she moved and got sliced instead. The second strike may have been with a branch or a fist."

"How's she doing now?"

"Resting. They'll keep her the rest of the day at least. Hey, what about protection? From what her husband tells me about the murder of her friend, well, doesn't she need us watching her home?"

"Yes, yes, she does. Thanks for the news. Clarke and I'll be down there in a few minutes." She pushed the button again and looked at Clarke. "My God."

They grabbed a couple of water bottles and a few more granola bars from the top of Renee's desk, then drove to the hospital, followed by two other policemen who would inspect Roxanne's trail.

They found Roxanne in a private room. Her bloodshot eyes peeked through swollen lids and heavy gauze wrap.

"Roxanne?" queried Clarke. "Man, you look like a leaky pipe that got duct-taped."

"I think I got hit by the pipe," she murmured. The white gauze extended to her swollen upper lip.

"She's out of it," Warren said. His long hair was tangled but Monique wasn't surprised that he had neglected to brush it.

"These men are Officers Gamble and Castle." Everyone shook hands. The two officers stood still with their hands folded in front of them. "They'll take a look at the trail after we find out where it is. Roxanne," Monique asked gently. "Can you tell us what happened?"

Roxanne pointed to Warren so he would speak for her. "She was high on adrenaline when she told me," he said. "I knew where she had been since she goes hiking at least four days a week. Then the doctor gave her pain medication and she talked really fast. Now she can hardly open her mouth. She said she ran the trail she always does. We get to the trail from behind the horse corrals. You maybe saw it last night."

"That wooden gate, right?"

"Yes. You meet the main trail that wraps around the mountain after half a mile, or ten minutes if you're walking. She went up the steep trail that goes up through the boulders. That takes you to the summit of one of the smaller peaks."

Roxanne held up her hand and spoke without moving her lips, "Where the trail meets after the first mile . . ."

"Right. There's a parking lot about a quarter of a mile down the trail. Lots of families hike about that far to picnic. Then they go back. It would be easy for someone to get onto the part of the trail she runs on. There're a million places to hide in the rocks, then they could get out of there quick."

"I run with cross-country ski poles," Roxanne mumbled. "I hit the guy in the legs pretty good with them. I kicked out when I was on the ground and got him in the gut, I think. Couldn't see anything."

"You're saying 'guy,'" said Clarke. "You sure it was a man?"

"Grunted like one."

"Who at CHU knows you run up there?"

"Tony knew, of course," answered Warren. "Mary. A few faculty members in other departments who run. It's been mentioned a lot. Especially after she bought that property. Even the bad guys in the department made comments about the nice area and access to the national forest. They know she hikes early."

Roxanne clenched and opened her fist a few times revealing road rash on her palm. "Everybody knew," she said. "Ross Clipper made a comment once about how he got up just as early to play golf. Like I give a shit."

"We'll have an officer stay outside until you leave," said Monique. "Then one will follow you home and stay outside your home for a few days. These two men will follow your trail and see what they can turn up."

"Hon," Roxanne grabbed at Warren's hand. "Go get Toot, please."

"She's at school," Warren explained to the officers. "I took Toot to school after the ambulance left the house so she wouldn't have to watch all this. But I think it's a better idea for her to stay with me today. She was pretty upset. See you guys later." His keys jingled as he pulled them from his pocket.

"It's raining," Roxanne sighed as she looked out the window. "Tracks'll be gone."

"Yep," answered Clarke. "But you never know what else might turn up."

Monique's cell phone rang. She pulled it from her coat pocket and pressed the talk button. "Blue Hawk here." She listened a few seconds, then her eyebrows went up. She looked at Clarke and didn't blink. "Okay.

We'll be there." She pressed the "end" button. "Tony's house was ransacked this morning while Perri and Mrs. Lucas were at her husband's clinic," she told them.

"Vultures," Roxanne said in a deep, drugged voice. "They knew there was a death and they took advantage of it."

"Pretty early in the morning for a robbery," Monique said.

"Maybe the vultures were waiting for them to leave," Roxanne offered.

"Yes, they certainly were."

"What did they want, I wonder?"

"That's a good question," Monique answered. "But the more important one is, who are 'they?'"

TUESDAY, 9:30 A.M.

Monique and Clarke drove to the Smoke Rise residence and parked in the drive next to the first squad car on the scene. They got out and were greeted once again by Mrs. Lucas.

"Thank you for coming out," she said in a high-pitched, stressed voice. They entered the room to find the den turned upside down. The pretty ivy plant had been pulled from the ceiling and the dirt dumped on the floor. The room's drawers lay on the floor and the cabinets emptied. Amid the chaos stood a short gray man in jeans and a flannel shirt talking to the equally short policeman in the kitchen. The policeman saw Monique and Clarke and nodded.

"Got here about twenty minutes ago," Officer Charles Van Rice said loud enough for the two detectives to hear across the room.

Monique nodded then pushed her sunglasses to the top of her head. "Thanks."

A thin Native woman sat on the sofa, the two dogs on either side of her. She wore a beige V-neck sweater and hip-hugger jeans that would have looked good on her had she been healthy and happy. She was not happy and still felt sick, however. Perri Smoke Rise sat slumped, sad and withdrawn.

Mrs. Lucas leaned down so Perri could see her face. "Perri, dear," Mrs.

Lucas said gently. "These are the detectives who were here yesterday. You were sleeping."

Perri turned her swollen, bleary eyes to the two detectives. "I gave her a Valium," the man in the kitchen said. "She's on her way to pneumonia if she doesn't move slowly and stay calm."

"We're here to help," Clarke said awkwardly.

"Help away," Perri replied. One of the two dogs put his head in her lap and she dropped a hand onto his neck.

Monique and Clarke crossed the room to meet the new people. Mrs. Lucas trailed them like a shadow. "This is my husband, Luther. He's a doctor and we were at his office when this happened."

The short man stuck out his hand and shook authoritatively. "Good to know you," he said.

"Looks like someone wanted something here," Monique said.

"That's what I thought," Mrs. Lucas began. "Thank goodness the dogs were outside in the run."

"Dear, let them deal with it," her husband chided.

"Well, it's true. Whoever came in here would have hurt them just for fun. Most of this is just the house messed up. The bedroom is bad, too. But the televisions, stereo, and Perri's jewelry are all here. That expensive little color TV they had on the kitchen counter is on the floor."

"According to Mrs. Lucas," said Officer Van Rice, "the valuables are here. Drawers and cabinets are all torn apart. Contents are thrown everywhere."

Clarke walked around and tried to recall what the place looked like the day before. He looked at the counter behind Dr. Lucas. "Excuse me," Clarke said as he moved closer. "Where's that carved elk we saw yesterday?"

Mrs. Lucas rushed over to look. All that was left was dirt residue that had fallen off the carving. Mrs. Lucas looked around then went to the other side of the counter and looked on the floor. "Not here," she said.

"That's odd," Monique said. "They left the electronics and took the carving. What else is gone that you know of?" she asked her.

She put her hands on her hips and walked to the den. Perri sat, staring.

"Let's see," said Mrs. Lucas as she scanned the room. "I don't see anything missing in here." The men followed her as she went from room to room and back to the den. She said the same thing. "Nothing missing that I can tell. Just a mess everywhere."

"The boxes are gone," Perri said in a drugged voice.

"What boxes, dear?" Mrs. Lucas asked.

Perri lifted her arm and motioned with a limp finger. "In the office. The boxes under his desk aren't there." From Perri's vantage point on the sofa she could see into Tony's office and had a direct view of his desk. "Two copy paper boxes. Tony brought those boxes home from school."

"Do you know what was in them?" Clarke asked.

"No. Tony brought them here a few days ago. They were dirty and I told him to clean them off before he put them on the carpet. I could tell they were heavy because he had a hard time holding them so the bottoms wouldn't drop out."

"Books maybe?"

"Don't know."

Monique went into Tony's office and looked under the desk. She shined her flashlight and saw the same red dirt on the floor that was on the elk. "Our intruders were after something specific," she said to Clarke.

"Let's go outside a minute," she suggested to him. She told the others they'd be right back.

They walked around the front and back yard. Clarke looked at the woodpiles, the tool shed, and trees, while Monique kept her eyes on the ground. "Clarke, we're looking for that red clay."

"Oh. Okay." They looked for a few minutes. "I don't see anything that's remotely red or pink in this dirt."

"Me neither. Those boxes weren't out here."

Monique and Clarke went back inside to where Perri sat. She appeared to have sunk deeper into the sofa. "Mrs. Smoke Rise, where did your husband get the elk?"

She took a deep breath. "He said it was given to him by a friend and that he was going to have it evaluated."

"Evaluated?"

"Yeah. For his research. He wanted to know its age and that kind of information."

Monique's spine stiffened and she tried not to show her concern.

Archaeologists did need this data in order to learn about the ancient people and cultures they study. But from what she knew about trafficking in artifacts, one also evaluated them to assess their monetary value.

TUESDAY, 11:30 A.M.

After a few more questions for Perri Smoke Rise, Monique and Clarke returned to the station to begin their interviews with the anthropologists.

"You ready for this?" She asked Clarke.

"As ready as I can be."

"Stay cool."

"I'll let you do the talking."

"Thank you."

Monique glanced up and saw a thin, decorative woman talking to the receptionist. "I'll bet real money that's Professor Belinda C. Rinds."

Clarke looked at her watch. "Twenty minutes early. I'll get her." Clarke fetched the nervous woman and she followed him back to Monique's desk.

"Hellooo!" Belinda C. Rinds greeted them in a high-pitched voice.

"Professor Rinds. I'm Detective Blue Hawk . . ."

"And this has to be Detective Clarke. Oh, I know that." She sat without waiting for an invitation then took off her sunglasses and set her purse on the floor. She crossed her legs and folded her hands. Although Belinda had been called to the police station to answer questions, she also had been informed that she was not formally a suspect and that all answers would be voluntary. Instead of balking, she appeared to be eager to talk.

"Professor Rinds," Monique said as she stood. "We need to move to another room. Please come with me."

"Oh, all right." She gathered her stuff and walked behind Monique. Clarke walked behind Rinds.

Monique opened the door to the interrogation room and gestured for Belinda to enter. The professor stopped for a few seconds to look into the stark, gray-painted room. The large table had nothing on top of it. "Sit here, please," Monique said, then pulled out a wooden chair at the head of the

131

table. Clarke closed the door, and Monique and Clarke sat on sides opposite each other.

"So, Professor Belinda Rinds," Monique began. "How well did you know Tony Smoke Rise?"

"Well let's see," Rinds answered as she scooted her bottom around in the wooden chair in an attempt to get comfortable. She wore fruity perfume, and the wide scarf she tied around her neck and over her left shoulder was too big and kept slipping off. "He got here about twelve years ago under the Target of Opportunity. That means he was hired because he's an Indian. You know—one of those minority hires."

"What do you mean 'those'?" asked Monique.

"Oh, he and Roxanne—that other one—got computers, travel money, reduced teaching loads, and even semesters off." She twisted her long beaded necklace with nervous fingers.

Monique opened a file. "Says here that everyone in the department got a computer. And the machines were replaced every three years. You also have a university computer at home and a laptop. Plus a projector. Correct?"

"What are you reading?" Belinda asked demurely as she peeked over her chic reading glasses.

"Your department file. And notes from my meeting with your chair and from a phone conversation I had with Deb Young last night," she lied.

"You called her?" She looked from one detective to the other. "Of course you did. Never mind."

"According to the old and new chair," Monique continued, "everyone in the department had equal access to travel money. After looking at Tony Smoke Rise's file, it looked like he was given less money to travel than anyone else in the department besides Roxanne Badger."

Belinda's pantyhose felt tight. "But why are you telling me this? You should talk to Mark Fhardt."

Clarke couldn't stifle his laugh this time. She pronounced it "fart" loud and clear.

Belinda saw her chance. "Oh God, I know. It's just an awful name isn't it? I mean that poor guy must have to . . ."

"Professor," Monique interjected sharply. "The reason I'm asking you is,

I'm wondering how it is that you managed to get a semester off three separate times in the last ten? With full pay?"

"Oh. I chair the graduate committee and have more graduate students than anyone in the department." She sat up straight and smiled big since this was her claim to fame. Having lots of graduate students showed that she was popular and admired and sought after.

Monique wasn't impressed. "So?"

Belinda's face drooped a bit. "It's hard work. I have to keep files straight, mentor students, make sure they're studying for comprehensive exams, write letters of recommendation."

"Just a few more questions, Professor. Where were you night before last between the hours of ten and midnight?"

"I had guests over."

"Who?"

Belinda squirmed. "Some colleagues."

"Who?"

"Some of my students," she said softly.

"Students were at your home that late?" asked Clarke.

"It was a graduation party."

Monique never attended a graduation party at any of her professors' homes, but what did she know? Maybe this was common practice. "I'll need a list of names."

"What for?"

"They're witnesses for you and you're a witness for them. What size shoes do you wear?"

She looked down, clearly embarrassed. "Eleven. I have big feet."

"Another thing, professor. Roxanne says her area of specialization is cultural change among Oglalas." Monique looked at Belinda and she nodded. "And Tony did population statistics." Belinda nodded again. "You list your specialties as in the archaeological arena."

Belinda answered, "Unh huh."

"Mounds in the Ohio Valley," Monique finished. Belinda nodded again. "Interesting. Ohio."

Belinda interpreted her comment to mean Monique was impressed. "Yes, I have quite a bit of training . . ."

"So why are you mentoring six graduate students who specialize in Tony and Roxanne's areas?" Monique interrupted. "She's working on Indian identity issues and cultural change, and Tony worked on populations. That seems like an odd thing to do. To appropriate another professor's students, I mean."

Belinda's cheeks flushed. "Wait a minute. Tony and Roxanne are difficult to work with. They make students do too much work, and their standards were too high. Students have to work with a professor they can trust and get along with and Roxanne was especially tough on them."

Monique reached into her coat pocket and pulled out a roll of Mentos. She knew Belinda was lying and would keep talking if she let her, but this was growing tiresome.

"According to student records and class enrollments, neither Badger or Smoke Rise have taught a graduate seminar in years because, according to sources in the department you effectively keep students away from them. You pressure the chairs to schedule your classes at the same time they attempted to teach their graduate courses. We've also been told that you say other untruths to your colleagues and graduate students."

Clarke also had Belinda figured. "We spoke with one of your former students. He had a few innerestin' things to say about what goes on at your parties. Looks to me like someone is tellin' graduate students bad things about her colleagues. Not nice to gossip, professor."

Belinda, for once, became tongue-tied.

"I think that's all we need for now." Monique and Clarke stood.

"Thanks for your time," Monique said. "And if you should recall anything important, please give me a call." She held out her card. Belinda took it and stuffed it into her bag. "Officer Scott will show you out."

Belinda walked out without another word, which was unusual for her. She was used to having the last one.

"That woman lies like a fat boy eatin' biscuits," Clarke said.

"What?"

"Think about it."

"That makes no sense, Clarke."

"You got no sense of humor."

Monique smirked. "Whatever. Looks to me like our victim was being murdered for years," she said.

"What a pack of ghouls," agreed Clarke.

"Yeah, and I bet someone in this pack of ghouls knows who the murderer is. Or maybe several of them do. Now we wait until they turn on each other."

"Creeps like this always do. Sooner or later," said the perky voice of Megan the FI. She arrived at the interrogation room with her hand in a bag of Cheetos. She took her hand out to display orange fingers.

"How you doing, Meg?" asked Monique. "I see you're getting your daily dose of vitamins and minerals."

"Cheetos and a peanut butter sandwich, five days a week."

Clarke made a face. "So you got anything to tell us?"

"Not really. Just that I made a plaster cast of the butt print in the flower bed."

"Hey, great. Now we can measure asses."

"Yes," Meg agreed. "You certainly will."

"Where you wanna go eat, Monique?" Clarke asked.

"I don't care as long as it's not hamburgers again." Monique stood and was in the process of putting on her jacket when she heard a booming voice by the front desk.

"I need to see them *now!*" The detectives watched as Ross Clipper stomped his way over to the door of the interrogation. He wore the same T-shirt and shorts he had worn on the day before, but instead of sandals he had on golf shoes that clicked on the hard floor. Blood ran down his cheek and onto his yellow shirt.

"Uh-oh," Clarke said as they watched Clipper march towards them. "Someone pissed in his Wheaties."

"Professor Clipper," Monique greeted him in a cool voice. "What's the matter?"

"The matter? Look at this!" He tucked his chin so the detectives could see the inch-long gash along the hairline.

"How'd that happen?" asked Clarke.

Clipper breathed hard, and now that the detectives had seen his wound, he pressed on it with a folded hankie. "I was gonna play golf this afternoon. I went out to my garage to get my bag. I keep it on my tool bench so the dog won't pee on it. Well, when I almost got to the bench, I tripped over a rope and the bag fell on me."

Clarke looked at Clipper a few seconds, trying to visualize the scenario. "A rope, you say? Was it coiled on the ground?"

"No, no," Clipper answered impatiently. "It was tied to the top of my golf bag, then it wrapped once around a leg of my tool bench, then other end was tied to a tool box on the ground."

"I don't get it. Why do you have a rope winding around your garage?"

Clipper sighed deeply and stared back at Clarke. "Because I like an obstacle course in all my rooms. What the hell do I look like? An idiot? Someone else did this. Last night sometime."

"Professor Clipper," Monique said gently. "Are you certain . . ."

"Yes I'm certain!" He looked from Meg to Monique then to Clarke. "It was strung across where I'd have to walk to get my clubs. The person who did this knew the bag would fall right on my head."

"Was your garage locked? How could someone get in?"

"There's a door on the side that was unlocked. I checked. Someone could have gotten in easy. And the light's unscrewed, so I had to fumble around in the dark."

"Did your wife go anywhere today?"

"No. Hey, if she had, she would have seen the rope."

Monique knew that. "Who knew you'd be golfing today?"

"Just Jerry Langstrome and another guy from history. But it doesn't matter if I was golfing or not. I'd trip over the rope just getting into my car."

The group stood quietly for a few seconds.

"Well," Monique said. "I suggest you get that looked at. It may need stitches. I'll send some policemen over to your place now. Is that okay?"

"Where's that Roxanne Badger?" Clipper asked in a low voice.

"Considering that we were with her last night and that she too was attacked early this morning, I feel fairly certain that she didn't set you up."

"Attacked? How so?"

"I can't discuss that now. I'll have some men check for prints at your house. Try not to touch anything. You should have left your car in place and called police."

"Yeah, okay. But she still could have come over in the middle of the night." Clipper said hesitantly.

"Anything's possible, Professor," added Clarke.

The three watched Clipper make his way to the door.

"You know, guys," said Meg as she eyed Clipper and crunched her mouthful of Cheetos. "That rear end looks awfully familiar."

TUESDAY, 1:15 p.m.

Monique and Clarke had discussions with more faculty members after their Taco Bell lunch. They all said the same thing: Roxanne and Tony were privileged people who wouldn't be published if not for their race and who refused to socialize with their well-meaning colleagues.

Rhonda Cartwright was the most evasive. She arrived looking tired and fidgety. Her baggy clothes were wrinkled, and her hair hung limply around her pale face. Fleshy and frumpy, she looked the physical opposite of the thin and tidy Belinda Rinds.

"And what was the trouble between you and Roxanne?" Monique asked. They'd been at it for twenty minutes, asking how she found out about Tony's death, how long she had been at CHU. The two detectives were growing tired just being in her presence. She sat leaning forward, speaking slowly as if on a sedative, her hands clutching her hemp purse. Clarke sat with his arms folded, watching her closely while Monique did the talking.

"Well, Roxanne is hard to get along with."

"Hard how?"

"She's demanding." Rhonda's eyes roamed around the room. Monique thought her eyes were light brown, but it was hard to tell.

"What did she demand?"

"She always wanted new equipment. I remember once she wanted a phone with caller ID on it. None of us have that."

"People usually request caller ID for a reason," Monique said. "Mainly because they get too many calls, or they get calls that aren't important."

Rhonda sat without speaking.

"Tell us about Tony. How well did you know him?"

"I didn't. Not really. He wouldn't talk to me."

"Why's that?"

Rhonda shrugged. "I don't know."

"Did you talk to him?"

"Well of course I did. But he never initiated any conversation."

Other than the issue at hand, neither detective could think of anything they'd want to talk to her about.

"Where were you Sunday night between ten and midnight?"

"In bed. I go to bed early."

Neither detective doubted that.

"You got a witness?"

"Uh, no. But I did order a pay-per-view movie at nine-thirty. It lasted almost until midnight."

"What was that?"

"The new Harry Potter one."

Monique licked her lips and thought about what to ask next.

"What is your field of study, Dr. Cartwright?"

"I do earth mother."

"Earth mother?"

Clarke stifled a laugh. Rhonda heard him and turned her head sharply to look at him. "And what's funny about that?"

"Uh, nothing. Go on."

"All women are goddesses, detective."

"Yeah, Sharon Stone . . ."

"No. We're the nurturers. We are the propagators, the first ones and the—"

"Sorry," Clarke interrupted. "First ones?"

"Of course. Every tribe began with woman. Every tribe was sustained by women. Each tribe also—"

Monique interrupted. "What tribe are you?"

"I'm not."

Clarke's eyebrows bunched together.

"You don't understand," Rhonda said. "I used to be Indian."

Monique asked, "Used to be?"

"Yes. In my former life. My former self was Iroquois."

"Which one?" Monique asked.

"Which self?"

"No, which Iroquois? That's a group of tribes, not one tribe."

Rhonda licked her lips. "You don't get it." She looked at her feet and held her purse tighter.

Monique thought, *How in hell did you get hired?* She leaned back and propped her arm on the table. "How many graduate students do you have?"

"Um, maybe six. Belinda Rinds has most of them."

"Why's that?"

Rhonda bit her lower lip.

"You can tell us. We won't tell her what you said."

"Well, uh, Belinda likes to pamper her students. She has them over to her house a lot. I won't do that."

"What do they do at her house?"

"I hear they drink and gossip. That's not appropriate for a professor to do that with students."

Monique watched Rhonda as she chewed a ragged nail. "Why didn't Roxanne and Tony have graduate students?"

"They're essentialists."

Monique and Clarke already knew where this was going. "Meaning, they think that only Indians can write about Indians," she said.

"Yes."

"Have you ever heard them say that? I mean, that they believe in essentialism?"

"Well, no, but . . ."

"Then how do you know?"

"Belinda told me."

The detectives weren't learning anything from Rhonda, but Monique tried again. "What do you know about the dig by the freeway? The one that some of your colleagues are working on?"

"Nothing, really. I heard Ross Clipper and Jerry Langstrome talk about it in the mailroom one day."

"And?"

"Ross and Jerry are always talking and laughing. I only heard a few words. Then they saw me and started talking about basketball."

"Do you get along with the rest of the department?"

"Sure. Well, sort of. I mean, I don't socialize with any of them."

"Who do you socialize with?"

"Faculty in women's studies pretty much. I also mentor the Gay, Lesbian and Bisexual Alliance on campus."

Clarke's right foot fell off his left leg and landed on the floor with a whump.

"I see." Monique's eyes narrowed as she considered the woman in front of him. "You got any other questions, Clarke?"

"You say Tony didn't speak with you," Clarke responded.

"Uh, right."

"Did you see any good qualities in him?"

"Well, uh, he worked hard. He did a lot. The undergraduates liked him and he always had an interesting project or grant going. He always seemed cool under pressure, like at department meetings when he could have gotten mad but didn't. He always had logical things to say. His wife is pretty."

"That's quite a list."

Rhonda shrugged.

"Who do you think killed him?"

She looked up suddenly and held her purse like a security blanket.

"How should I know?"

"I asked who you think killed him. Not who did kill him."

"I . . . I . . . have no idea. Someone who robbed him?"

Monique stood. "Tell you what, Dr. Cartwright. Take my card and if you think of anything else, please call me. Anytime. Don't leave town."

Rhonda stood and nodded. She walked quickly out the door, her head down.

"My Gawd," Clarke said as they watched her go. "She's nuttier than squirrel shit. That's one confused lady."

Monique took a sip of cold coffee. "In more ways than one, partner."

The day grew still and warmer. Monique brought in a couple of desk fans so that a continual breeze blew around her and Clarke.

"I think that I've figured out this university thing," Clarke said as he chewed some beef jerky.

"I must be stupid, Clarke. I'm jealous."

"Bingo."

"What?"

"Jealousy and territoriality. Yup. Sums it up."

"You may be on to something. But you know, not everyone in this business is weird."

"Coulda fooled me."

Monique considered that a few seconds. "Not everyone is. But a lot are."

Clarke slapped his palm on the table. "I rest my case."

Monique was in the process of dumping sugar into her new cup of coffee when she looked up to see the tanned and confident Professor Rogers walk smoothly down the aisle between the tables. He moved like an ex-competitive athlete who stayed fit, lightly and without effort. He looked like a professional golfer who hauled his own clubs and did yoga afterwards.

Despite the warm weather Professor Rogers wore a long-sleeved, maroon Izod shirt with khaki trousers. His graying hair was parted on the side and neatly combed.

Ben smiled big, his teeth straight and white. "Hello, detectives," he said, holding out his warm, smooth hand to Monique, then to Clarke.

"Thanks for coming," Monique answered, although Rogers didn't really have a choice in the matter.

"Hey, no problem at all. Happy to help."

"Follow me, please," Monique motioned.

The three sat in the impersonal interrogation room and got as comfortable as they could.

"Terrible thing," Ben said.

"Yes, yes it was," Clarke agreed.

"Nice young man. Promising future."

"Yes," Clarke agreed again.

"So what do you want me to tell you?" Ben asked.

Monique smiled. "Who killed Tony Smoke Rise."

Ben's grin dropped a bit, then he recovered. "Oh, well. I sure wish I knew."

"Can you tell us where you were Sunday night between ten and midnight?"

"At home, in bed. With my wife."

Monique nodded. "How long have you been at CHU?"

"Since 1980. I'd been at University of Illinois before that."

"And your work deals with the people of Peru?"

"Right." He smiled a ultrabright smile. "You've read my file."

"Yes. What did you think about Tony?"

"Like I said. Great potential, great mind. A real shame."

Clarke put his hand to his chin and rubbed his emerging stubble. He watched Ben Rogers as closely as he had watched Rhonda Cartwright.

"So you got along with him?"

"Yes, I guess so. I mean, we didn't socialize and I didn't see him much because we taught on different days."

"You taught on Tuesdays and Thursdays, then."

"Yes."

"What do you do on your days off?"

"Let's see. Sometimes I . . . wait, those aren't days off. I write or do research."

Monique nodded a bit, figuring that Ben golfed. "I see. How much time do you spend at the new dig?"

"A lot. I'm out there every day since they discovered that burial. It's not big but you never know what may turn up."

"They've uncovered items that by law have to be handled in a certain way?"

"Well, just a few bones."

"And what has happened to all the items they uncovered?"

"They have to stay there until we find a medicine person to determine who the remains belong to. What tribe, I mean."

"When will you find someone?"

"We're working on it."

Monique tapped her pen on the desk. "It's been months. Why is it so hard to find a tribal representative? Seems like this is important to tribes. Wouldn't they jump at this chance?"

Ben cleared his throat and sat up straighter. "Well, not always. Navajos, you know, they don't want to deal with remains because of a taboo or something against the dead."

"There aren't any Navajos around here."

"No, but then other tribes cremate the dead and so there aren't any remains."

"That doesn't answer my question."

"Well, these remains are so old that we aren't sure who to contact. Besides, it's not my job. The Corps of Engineers is supposed to call after we give them advice."

"And what advice did you give?"

"I told them there are six tribes in the state and that they should contact the tribal councils of all of them."

"And in the meantime, what happens to the items you find?"

"Like I said, they stay put and we excavate."

"Are they protected in any way? I mean from someone who wanted to remove them?"

"The place is guarded at night so no one can come in and ransack the site."

"What kind of things have you found?"

"Broken bones. Fragmented pots. There really isn't much to it."

"What do you think of Roxanne Badger?"

Ben looked surprised at the change in question. "Uh, well. She's like Tony. Smart, a hard worker. Touchy."

"Touchy?"

"Yes. She gets mad easily."

"She had a hard time with the tenure process."

"True enough. I wasn't on that committee, but I heard it didn't go smoothly. Personally, I think some of my colleagues are a bit too tough. They don't do the same amount of work Roxanne and Tony do, yet they judge them very harshly."

"Why's that, do you think?"

"Jealousy."

Clarke's eyes narrowed as he listened.

"What do you think of the institute they're starting?"

"Great. Good for them. Might boost enrollment."

"Do you socialize with Belinda Rinds?"

"Never. She's not someone I care to be around."

"Rhonda Cartwright?"

Ben laughed. "No. She needs a shrink."

"Pauley Wenetae?"

Ben laughed. "No."

"What's funny?"

"Pauley's never here, for one thing. For another, he epitomizes incompetence. I have nothing to say to the man. He drifts in and out like fog and has as much substance."

"Ross Clipper?"

Ben sighed. "I don't socialize with anyone in the department. They're colleagues. That's all. Besides when we're at the dig, sometimes I see Ross on the golf course or Frank Smithers at the chiropractor and Leo Harding at the credit union, but that's the extent of my contact with them."

Monique asked a few more obvious questions but Ben Rogers answered consistently: he was calm and evenhanded in his assessment of his colleagues and thought both Tony and Roxanne were emerging stars who got bad breaks in the department.

"Well, thanks for your time, Professor Rogers." Monique and Clarke stood and everyone shook hands.

"If there's anything else I can do, please let me know." Then he smiled and was off as smoothly as he arrived.

"Hmmm,' Monique muttered. "What think?"

"I don't like him."

Monique put her hands on her hips. "Why do you say that?"

"You don't like him, either."

"I didn't say that. Tell me your thoughts."

"Other than he's slicker than pig snot, I'm not real sure yet."

"Well, hold those thoughts because here comes another one."

A short, round Black woman of about fifty-five followed Renee's pointing finger to where Monique and Clarke waited outside the interrogation room.

"This will be Mrs. Denicia Donald, custodian," Monique said as the woman approached them.

"Mrs. Donald," Monique greeted the woman. "Thank you for coming. I know you work at night and need to be sleeping."

The three sat. Denicia put her large purse on the ground next to her chair and crossed her stocky legs at the ankles.

"No, no. I need to be here," she answered in a deep, rich voice. "What do you want to ask me?"

"First off, when did you leave Anthropology on Sunday?"

"I wasn't there Sunday. Last time I went to the building was on Friday evening. Me and my sister buffed the floors and cleaned the carpets until about midnight. We were the only ones there."

"Fine. So you haven't been back?"

"No."

"You steamed the carpet in the seminar room on the second floor Friday night?"

"Yes, we did. A student spilled a red drink all over the carpet."

"Are the windows in that room normally locked?"

"No, not in warm weather like this. They're usually open."

"Were they open on Friday night?"

"I'm pretty sure they were." She paused to think. "Yes, they were open. It helps the carpet dry."

"Did you know Tony Smoke Rise?"

"Yes I did. He was in his office at night a lot. He introduced himself one night about six years ago. If he was working at night, he'd put his garbage can outside his door and I'd empty it. But usually he'd ask me how I was doing. I told him about my son who's in college and he'd ask about him. He knew I had surgery on my feet and he and Dr. Badger and some of the other professors sent me flowers."

Monique nodded. "Did you notice anything unusual the week before?"

Denicia shook her head. "No. Same old, same old."

"Did Tony do anything out of the ordinary? Did he come in earlier or later?"

"Let's see. No. But he did have some boxes in his office last week that left an awful mess on the carpet. Normally I don't have to vacuum in there, but he left red dirt everywhere and I couldn't clean it up with the hand held vacuum."

"When was this?"

"Thursday night." She paused to think about it. "That's right, because the vacuum was fixed that afternoon and I had to pick it up. It worked real well and just sucked that dirt right up."

Monique sat up a bit straighter. "Have you emptied that vacuum yet?"

"Why, no. It's in the closet on the first floor."

Monique nodded to Clarke. "Do you know Roxanne Badger?"

"Oh yes," she smiled. "Nice girl. She's like Tony. She asked after me, too. Mary and Dr. Brazzi are the only other ones who talked to me."

"Do you have an idea about who killed him?"

Denicia shook her head. "A lot of the other people in that department aren't nice, if you know what I mean. They leave messes, they don't speak, and they act like they own the place." She looked up quickly. "That don't mean they'd kill someone. I'm not saying that."

"I know you're not. Thanks for your time, Mrs. Donald." She stood. "Please call me if you remember anything else. Here's my card."

"Will do," she answered as she picked up her purse and exited.

"So," Monique said aloud. "Tony left a mess in his office Thursday."

Clarke stretched. "We aren't learning anything particularly helpful."

"Sure we are. We're just gathering the puzzle pieces."

"Yeah, but the puzzle's a snowman in a blizzard."

Frank Smithers arrived shortly afterwards, dirty in a brown T-shirt with faded lettering, blue jean cutoffs, and leather sandals. He looked like he played in the same sandbox as Clipper.

"He looks like he stinks," Clarke said quietly as he approached the interrogation room.

As Smithers drew near the two detectives, Monique sniffed. "Right on."

"Frank Smithers?" Monique asked as she stood and extended her hand. Smithers shook it with a mushy grip.

"Yeah, that's me." His face was filthy, the deep creases filled with dirt. His red Afro was uncombed and uneven.

"You been mowing the yard?" Clarke asked.

"Uh, yeah. Right. Mowing and stacking wood." He spoke slowly as he looked at the Sponge Bob notepad. "This your kid's?"

"Not anymore," Monique answered. "Professor Smithers, where were you Sunday night between ten and twelve?"

He reached over and picked up her empty coffee mug with the Six Flags Over Texas logo on it. "Never been here. I've been to Disney World but not Six Flags."

"Professor Smithers?"

He looked up.

"Where were you . . ."

"I was at home."

"Anyone with you?"

"Nope. Just my cats."

Clarke's butt puckered at hearing that.

"What size shoes do you wear?"

Smithers put his foot in the air so the detectives could see it. "Fourteen."

Monique nodded as she observed the man in front of him. "What did you think of Tony Smoke Rise?"

"Didn't. Don't."

"Pardon?"

"I didn't and don't think about him. He doesn't mean anything to me. Didn't talk to him. Didn't hang out with him."

"Did you socialize with Roxanne Badger?"

"That hard-ass? No way."

"Hard-ass?"

"Yeah. Hard-ass Indian." He stopped talking for a second after he realized who he was talking to. He got no reaction from Monique, so he continued. "She got mad at everything. She's a snob for no reason."

"How is she a snob?"

"Doesn't speak to me."

"Do you see her often?"

147

"Maybe once a week in the hall or the mailroom."

"What do you think about their efforts to start the institute?"

"Ha! Foundations love to give money to minorities. It'll flop. And in the meantime it'll screw up our department."

"What makes you think it'll flop?"

"They don't know anything about running a program. Much less a grant of that size. Who wants to enroll in a program like that anyway?"

Monique tapped her pen on the table. Smithers picked up Monique's black-framed glasses and put them on. "Cool. We got the same vision."

Monique reached over and claimed her glasses. "What's your field of study?"

"Potsherds in New Mexico."

"What is that?"

"Pot parts."

"No, I mean, what's the purpose of studying pot parts?"

Smithers smiled without showing teeth and tried to clean a toenail with an equally dirty fingernail. "I look at the tribes' art. What the markings mean. That kind of thing."

"And what do you do with that information?"

"Document it. It's important work." Smithers gave up his preening and crossed his arms. He looked past the detectives and focused on the back wall.

"What do you think of Pauley Wenetae?"

Smithers smiled. "Not much."

"But at least you think about him."

"Pauley's a strange dude. He's got a great job and doesn't do squat, just like his buddies."

"I was under the impression that Wenetae didn't mingle with Badger and Smoke Rise."

"Who cares? I wouldn't know anyway. Pauley's not around much. I only see him maybe once a month."

"How often are you there?"

"Two days a week. I teach Tuesdays and Thursdays."

"Who killed Tony Smoke Rise?"

"A truly profound question. Maybe a grad student."

"A student?"

"Yeah. Students didn't like him either."

"So, you talk to the students about him?"

"No. But it's pretty obvious they didn't like him. He didn't have any grad students."

"Do students always like their professors?"

"No. But they respect them. You can feel dislike and respect at the same time. Students didn't like or respect Smoke Rise."

"Why would that be if they had never taken a class with him?"

"Some people give off bad vibes."

And smells, she thought. "Are you working on the freeway dig?"

"Yep."

"What's your role?"

"Advisor. In case they find pots."

"And have they?"

"Not yet."

This was not what Ben Rogers had said. "Okay, Professor, that's all for the moment," Monique said in smooth voice. She smiled big. "Stay close in case we want to see you again."

Smithers saluted and sauntered away.

"Don't let the door hit ya where the good Lord split ya," Clarke said quietly as Smithers walked through the exit.

"That's gross, Clarke. "Did you notice the color of the dirt on his feet? He had changed shoes, but he had red dirt or clay on his soles and under his nails."

"Get the fumigator," Clarke said. "That man reeks."

"That and he reeks of something else. He reminds me of Clipper and Rinds."

"How's that?"

"All of them are confident in their political stature. They know their place in the hierarchy of CHU. A bunch of mediocre little fishes in a mediocre little pond. They've got their pecking order all worked out."

"And what was Tony?"

"One of the fishes who wouldn't play along."

Monique and Clarke ordered a pizza and read more files until it arrived. Then they sat in silence as they ate.

"Who else do we have to see today?" Clarke asked.

"Harding said he had to leave town this morning to visit his sick sister. I need to make sure she is sick. Brazzi and Langstrome are up next."

"That's the woman who owns the restaurant too, right?" asked Clarke.

"Yes. And Brazzi's an ally."

"Better be. Any more self-righteous commentary about how awful Tony and Roxanne are and I may hit someone."

Monique sat clenching her teeth as she listened to Jerry Langstrome say familiar things: the uncollegial Roxanne and Tony were given preferences over more qualified scholars.

Langstrome breathed heavily as he sat, his pot belly more impressive than a woman nine months pregnant. He looked sixty years old, but his file said forty-three.

"And you're one of the professors hired to advise the Corps of Engineers?"

Jerry wheezed as he spoke. "Yes. I'm a physical anthropologist."

"Like Ross Clipper," said Clarke.

"We both study diseases."

"Such as?"

Jerry wheezed a few times as he thought how to respond. "Scurvy, rickets."

"Aren't those health issues brought about by vitamin deficiencies?"

"Well, yes. But a lot of the old skeletons we look at tell us that ancient populations suffered these problems and so we know how to take preventative measures today."

Monique gave him a stare. "I'm curious. The causes of these diseases are well known. You don't need to study old Indian bones to tell us this information."

"Sure I do."

Monique cleared her throat and mentally counted to three. "How well did you know Tony Smoke Rise?"

"Not well. Didn't talk with him much. He didn't like my work and so we stayed away from each other."

"What did you think of his work on population studies?"

"He exaggerated his findings."

"What do you mean?"

"His estimates of the populations at contact are too high. He said the populations were higher than they really were."

"And how do you know?"

"Because."

Monique sighed. "Because why?" Clarke picked his teeth with a toothpick as he waited for an answer.

"There's no way that many Indians were killed."

"How many?"

"Smoke Rise claims about 75 million in this hemisphere in 1492. Almost 7 million in the United States alone. Then by 1700 there were less than five million. We know there were only about 250,000 in 1900 or so. No way that many people disappeared."

"And why not?"

"We wouldn't have killed that many. That would have been genocide. My country doesn't condone genocide."

"Is that right?"

"Damn right."

"And what are your estimates?"

"I'd say there were only a few million in the entire New World at contact."

"That's quite a difference in opinion."

Jerry nodded. "Look, detectives, you need to understand that Tony and his sidekick Roxanne use their so-called studies for political purposes. They've always tried to make political statements and there's no room in academia for that."

"Considering what Indians must endure, political activism for Indian scholars is a logical course of action."

"Endure what?"

"Poverty, disease, stereotyping. Things that you wouldn't put up with. Why should they?"

"It's unethical to use your academic position for personal gain. And that's exactly what they're doing with that Institute. They'll preach about racist white people. They're anti-American and should be deported."

"To where?"

"Iraq. Afghanistan. Some place over there where they hate America."

Monique blinked a few times. Clarke tensed as he watched her nostrils flare. Then he relaxed when she crossed her legs.

"Where were you between ten and midnight on Sunday?"

"At home. My brother's visiting. We were playing poker until late."

"What size shoe you wear?"

"Eleven."

Monique and Clarke had had enough and dismissed Langstrome after telling him to stay in town.

"Another old know-it-all," Clarke said.

"He's younger than you, buddy."

"I may not eat for a week. If I start looking like that, kick me in the head."

"I will."

"You know, it's innersting that the people who hate Tony and Roxanne accuse them of doing things they're doing. I mean, the population thing sounds completely political to me."

"It is, clearly. The higher the population of Indians here at contact means that someone has to be accountable for why they disappeared. In these political times, hell, this great country can do no wrong. No genocide, no racism, no discrimination existed in our pristine history."

"You're sarcastic."

"Yes I am. But Langstrome isn't."

Samantha Brazzi sat ramrod straight as she gestured wildly with her hands explaining the idiocy of the department.

"They are all idiots!' she yelled in her thick Italian accent. "Tony Smoke Rise and Roxanne Badger are our lifeblood! Smithers, Harding, Clipper, Langstrome are all peons! I hate them! I hate them all!"

Monique managed to calm Samantha down, but she remained undeterred in her assessment of the faculty. "Markus Fhardt! Maybe he did it! Ross Clipper, him too! They're all concerned only with themselves! I think they all did it together!"

Clarke tentatively asked her another question that inadvertently set her off: "What makes you think they all did it?"

"Because, young man, they are all idiots! They are jealous, sad, pathetic ugly people. They want what Roxanne and Tony have."

After she left, Monique wiped her sweaty forehead with a Kleenex. "Good Lord. What a woman."

"Yeah." Clarke watched Dr. Brazzi maneuver her way through the desks to the exit, her Sophia Loren hips swinging madly. "Like two wildcats fightin' in a burlap bag," was his assessment.

"Like *what?*"

"Uh, nothin.' But you know, of all the things I've heard so far, what she says makes the most sense. That crowd was green with envy over Badger and Smoke Rise."

Monique took another drink of cold soda. "It sorta looks that way, doesn't it? I mean, why else do you try to kill both of them? But I don't know. I still think there's another kind of green on the table. Let's take a drive."

TUESDAY, 4:00 P.M.

"Turn here, turn here," Clarke said to Monique. They drove down the bumpy, red-dirt road that threatened to tear the undercarriage out from the Impala. "Man, we shoulda rode mountain bikes."

"And we would have swallowed dust for three miles," Monique reminded him.

"There's the freeway over there," Clarke said as he observed the line of traffic about a quarter of a mile off. "So they plan to build an off-ramp that connects to this new road they're building."

"It'll be a wider road leading west that'll bypass town and the railroad. Over there is where the new Sam's Club will be built."

"Great. Let's expand onto every bit of forest land so we can pollute more. How can Moose City support all these people?"

"Same as every other town in this great nation, partner," Monique answered. "That must be the dig site."

Monique drove cautiously to the edge of the obvious area of activity. Dozens of mounds of red dirt sat piled along the recently carved dirt road. A large awning propped by four poles covered a hole in the ground. Monique and Clarke saw the bent backs of several people who were working in it, which meant the hole was about four feet deep. Ross Clipper was standing at the edge of the hole. He wore the same clothes they had seen him in earlier. Blood was clearly visible down the front of his yellow T-shirt.

A hundred feet beyond Clipper were three bulldozers, busily ripping small trees and bushes from the ground, creating the path the road would take.

Monique parked and the two climbed out. Dust swirled around in the dry heat. Monique would have to wash her hair as soon as she got home.

"Wish I had a scarf," Clarke said as he coughed.

Clipper was unable to hide his surprise at seeing the two detectives. Monique didn't fail to notice his expression.

"Dr. Clipper," she said. "I thought you were golfing today."

"Uh, changed my mind, detective. Thought I'd come out here to make sure all's well."

"And is it?"

"Looks like it."

They looked into the hole and saw Smithers and Langstrome with their little whisk brooms brushing away dirt from some bones. They had already uncovered five skeletons in the 20 by 20 excavation.

"Wow," exclaimed Clarke. "Who are they?"

"Uh, local tribe's ancestors," Clipper said.

"What are you gonna do with them?"

Smithers blurted, "Nothing right now. We have to keep watch over them. Someone could come and take them at night."

Monique said nothing. Clarke, however, said, "Who's gonna watch them?"

"Uh, the Corps of Engineers security guards," Clipper said.

"Come on, Clarke," Monique said.

"Well, how do you know they'll be here to guard them tonight?" Clarke persisted.

"Just will," Clipper said.

"Clarke. Now." Monique ordered.

"One more question. Where are the items buried with these people?" Clarke asked.

"No items," Clipper said. "Just the people."

"And how old . . ."

Monique grabbed Clarke's arm and squeezed hard. "Now."

Clarke got the hint. "Okay. Happy digging."

The two walked back to the car. Red dust blew in when they opened the doors.

"You dummy," Monique chided.

"What?" Clarke dusted himself off, which only made his lap dirty.

Monique started the car and drove off fast enough to make certain to raise dust that would blow back on the archaeologists. "It's obvious what's happening here, and you just kept on."

"What's obvious?"

"They were surprised to see us out here."

"Yes, and . . . ?"

"They lied about what they found. They're up to something."

"Right. And?"

"Now they'll be more careful and will hide what they don't want us to see. If you hadn't alerted them to what we're interested in, they'd just keep doing what they were doing."

"Maybe."

"No maybe about it."

"You can look at this another way, Monique."

"And that is . . . ?"

"Now they'll screw up."

Monique shook her head. "They already have screwed up."

WEDNESDAY, 4:00 P.M.

Tony's parents and two brothers arrived in Moose City from Phoenix. It was too expensive to fly from the Flagstaff airport to the connecting flight at Phoenix Sky Harbor, so they drove the 150 miles to the Valley of the Sun.

Besides, the Flagstaff-to-Phoenix commuter planes were like flying logs. Even if passengers didn't have to use the barf bag stowed in the seat back in front of them, they still felt nauseated the rest of the day.

Tony's two brothers appeared angry and intense as they entered the America West terminal. Both men were tall like their parents and wore their hair long and loose. They had on black aviator glasses, jeans, boots, button-down shirts, and enough silver jewelry to sink a boat. Other passengers in the waiting area gaped at the Smoke Rise family as if they were the Beatles. The family boarded the larger plane and after a two-hour, uneventful flight, was met by Warren, who led them to the parked car where Roxanne and a police escort waited.

The Smoke Rise family stared at Roxanne's bandaged face as Warren introduced the short, gray-haired Officer Gamble and explained what happened to his wife.

Tony's youngest brother, Ross, rode with Gamble while Warren drove the rest of the family. Roxanne leaned back in the co-pilot's seat. "Perri's not doing so well," Roxanne mumbled. "If it's tough over at Tony's, come stay with us."

"Thanks," said Glenn Badger. "But we need to stay with her right now. You don't look so great yourself."

"I got pills. My first surgery's next week."

They drove in silence for a few moments.

"There're more people coming out," Glenn said. "Can you handle four of them? I don't want them staying in a hotel."

"Sure," said Roxanne. "Who is it?"

"Some elders," was all Glenn would say.

For three days Tony's family trickled in to Moose City. Some flew, but most drove non-stop from Arizona and California. About a dozen stayed in hotels, a few others stayed with Renell and Roscoe. Two elder medicine men and their wives arrived late the second night as Glenn had said they would, and they slept in Roxanne and Warren's spare bedroom and in Giselle's room.

Then the unexpected arrived two days before the funeral. Warren opened the door to find Roxanne's mother Lucy, her brother whom she had not seen in eight years, and three older Oglalas. Warren stood in the doorway, stunned.

"I'm not Betty White, deary," said the dried-up old woman.

"Right. Come in. Let me get Rox."

"Mom," Rox said as she got to the front door. She stepped forward and hugged her frail mother. Lucy stooped from osteoporosis and her hands were stained yellow from tobacco. Roxanne then embraced her younger brother, who looked like a man in withdrawal. Shawn Badger was taller than Roxanne but weighed less. He had the physique of a drinker who didn't eat much. Still, Shawn looked better than he had the last time Roxanne saw him.

"A councilman called and let us know. Someone from here had called him," her mother said. "I'm sorry, baby."

Roxanne wondered who would have called.

"Your face," her mother said.

Roxanne reached up and touched the bandage that circled her head. "It'll be better in time. Come on in."

The other Indians on the porch were two cousins and Arnold Old Bull, the spiritual leader Roxanne had known for over thirty years. "I thought I should come," he said. "Bad things happen here."

"True enough," said Roxanne, tears crowding her eyes.

Clearly there were too many people at Roxanne's place, so she paid for rooms at the nearby Shady Oaks motel, a small, clean place next to a shopping strip. The accommodations didn't matter much since everyone preferred to stay together during the times they were awake.

Everyone shuffled to the back porch. Warren got out the folding chairs and card table. The Hopis came out from their rooms where they rested. One of their wives held Mr. Happy, who looked as content as a full tick. They had spent a good portion of the day wandering around Roxanne's yard and walking up the trail with the malamutes and Giselle in tow. When the two old men walked out to the porch in their traditional clothing, their hair tied back in Hopi fashion and heads bound with red cloth, the Oglalas jumped to their feet.

Everyone shook hands and said hello.

After hellos and how-are-yous, one of the old Hopis said to Old Bull, "We need to talk. Come out by the horses."

Roxanne handed Arnold a Pepsi as he followed the Hopis into the yard. The horses pricked their ears and watched, aware that power approached.

Friends and family nibbled the burgers that Warren cooked on the grill. Everyone seemed content to eat finger foods. Pickles, olives, and chips disappeared quickly.

"Roxie," said her mother behind her.

"Mom. I'm glad you came. I really am." They sat at the kitchen table.

"How's your face, sweetie?" She coughed a phlegmy cough.

"Hurts. I'm not looking forward to surgery but I'll be sorry if I don't do it. The cut's pretty deep. Luckily it didn't get a muscle. Or an eye." She touched the bandage that still covered most of her face.

"I never thought this kind of thing could happen at a university."

The coffee pot steamed and burped. "Why not? Academics are just like any one else. Maybe more knowledgeable about certain things, that's all. How's Shawn?" Her brother had found kindred spirits in the two horses and had stood in the corral petting them all afternoon.

"Same. He comes and goes with his drinkin'. Just like his dad. And me before I quit. It's hard to tell when he's gonna binge again."

"Hasn't he been in detox?" Roxanne reached for her vial of Percocet and took a tablet with a swallow of Mountain Dew.

"He's been in there more than not. Some people are addicts and there's nothing to do about it except live one day at a time. I quit smokin' too and crave a cigarette every wakin' moment."

Roxanne rubbed the back of her neck.

Her mother asked, "You think that if you get away from here you'll be happy?"

"I don't know, Mom. Things have been so unhappy at this place that I can't imagine a normal environment." She told her mother about the institute. "I believe that I'm on the right track now. It's a complete focus on what tribes want and need. I can finally say I'm being useful."

Mother and daughter sat with their hands on the tabletop, their fingers touching.

"You know, I always thought that getting tenure would be the best thing that could happen to me. I worked my ass off, started having headaches, and became a real bitch. Now that I have tenure, it doesn't seem to mean much."

"Honey, you deserved it."

"Yes, I did. But I never thought the rest of my career would turn out like this. It'll be another fight for full professor, and who cares if I get it? Look at who has it at CHU. Big fricking deal."

"I hope it works out. But you shoulda left here long ago, baby. And Tony."

"And Tony."

Roxanne reached for her vile of Percocet, then pulled her hand back after she remembered that she had just taken a tablet. She exhaled and the tears began. Her bandages quickly became wet. She leaned forward, her arms out to embrace her mother, who was eager to comfort her baby girl.

SUNDAY

The families spent the next day discussing funeral arrangements and talking about their loss and who might be at fault. Tony's family thought that he would be buried in Arizona, and when her time came, Perri could be buried next to him. Everyone else nodded in agreement. Perri sat with her hands in her lap, nodding and smiling if someone spoke to her, but she continued to take Valium and mainly stared at the floor.

Several friends from her past called Roxanne, including former chair Deb Young, her community college professor Bill Reath, and her doctoral advisor Lenay McGraw. Other scholars came to town, including a journal editor, the senior editor of the press that published two of Tony's books, chairs of other anthropology departments, and scholars who had known Tony since graduate school and always wrote him letters of recommendation. These were his allies, who periodically called to check in, to find out the latest incredible events in the CHU anthropology department. All of these friends were white.

Thirty dinners from a local Mexican restaurant arrived at Roxanne's house. When Tony's mother asked who sent them, the delivery man said, "From the anthropology department, in honor of Tony Smoke Rise."

Roxanne and Warren, who sat on the big den sofa, said in unison, "Send them back." The young man balked, but Warren tipped him and his attitude lightened. "Send them back," he said again, softer. They didn't want food from those people. They didn't need it anyway. Food came from Tony's friends and admirers all over town, as did flowers and notification of monetary contributions to charities in Tony's name.

Roxanne leaned against her kitchen doorframe, scanning the immense buffet of meats, fruit, rolls, pies, and casseroles. One of the Hopi women stood quietly next to her.

"Not everyone is bad," she said. "You and Tony have many friends."

"I know," she answered. "But the bad people keep trying to take up their slack."

MONDAY, 1:00 P.M.

Tony's funeral day began clear and bright. Mourners developed aches from a sleepless night followed by dozing in the early morning that wasn't enough for tired bodies and minds. They drank coffee and juice, knowing that if they didn't, their headaches would worsen. Family and friends managed to dress. Two limos picked up Tony's family.

"Come with us," Arlene Smoke Rise told Roxanne.

Roxanne shook her head. "Better go with Warren." She gave Arlene a kiss on the cheek.

The church was large enough to accommodate those who wanted to say goodbye to Tony. Roxanne recognized the mayor, the county superintendent, the supervisor of the school district, and CHU's president. Her blood boiled when she saw that the anthropology department was represented by all of the faculty.

She felt comforted at the sight of Detectives Blue Hawk and Clarke and especially of her friends who had flown in to pay their respects. Part of what kept her going was the normal people outside of CHU. Still, her breath quickened at the sight of her anthropology colleagues.

The first two rows filled with family and other Indians. Renell and Roscoe sat in the third row behind Roxanne and Warren and next to the out-of-town friends. Giselle the Toot had stayed with a neighbor so that Warren could tend to his wife; he felt unsure how Roxanne would react to the funeral, especially since on the way to the church she had taken two Percocets on the heels of Vicodin. Samantha Brazzi and Paul Deerbourne sat close to the front, and Pauley Wenetae found a place in the middle, with Ben Rogers and his wife just ahead of the rest of the CHU contingency, which clustered together towards the back.

The detectives sat behind everyone in hopes of gathering information. "Guilty parties rarely laugh at funerals," Monique said to Clarke, "but hope springs eternal that the perp'll do something to give himself away. Keep your eyes open." She was eyeing Rogers's wife, whose funeral jewelry looked gaudy even from fifty feet away.

"You're fidgeting, Monique," commented Clarke.

"No I'm not."

"Yeah you are. Don't you go to church?"

"Nope."

"Why not?"

"Churches make me nervous."

"How come?"

"I don't like how people who go to church behave."

"You mean while they're in church?"

"No."

"You mean when they're out of the church."

"Not all Christians act Christ-like. And Christians did more to wipe out our people and cultures than any other group. Yeah. I have problems with that."

"Not everyone is a hypocrite, Monique. A lot of people mean well."

"I know that, Clarke. I may not be a Christian, but I am religious and I have morals. I know a hypocrite when I meet one. These days, we're surrounded by them." She studied the huge wooden cross on the wall behind the flowers and the casket and the minister, who began his remarks about Tony Smoke Rise, a man he didn't know.

After the minister gave his commentary, one of the Hopi men stepped to the podium and spoke at length in Hopi. The Indians in the front rows who represented various tribes sat at attention, while others who sat in the back shuffled their feet in annoyance.

Ross Clipper, sitting on the aisle with his wife and Belinda Rinds, sighed, swallowed, and drummed his fingers on his knee. He felt hot and thought he might have the beginnings of a sore throat. He listened as the elder Hopi began a song with a strong rhythm that caused heads in the front rows to bob.

Clipper leaned in to whisper to his wife, "Catchy beat." She nudged him away with her elbow. Clipper coughed.

He coughed again, this time choking, sucked another deep breath, and began to sweat. He opened his mouth, gasping for air, and his hands tore at the tie around his neck. Then Clipper reached for the pew in front of him, twisted to his left, and fell forward, collapsing headfirst into the aisle. The song continued.

"Oh my God!" shrieked Clipper's wife. "He's bleeding."

Indeed, blood ran freely from a cut above his eyebrow.

The singer stopped and squinted to see who was screaming. Clipper's cronies rushed to him. The first two rows of mourners turned to look; none stood but Roxanne, who leaned heavily on her friend Renell. A crowd formed around Clipper.

"I'll call 911," yelled Mark Fhardt, but instead of doing so, he bolted for exit at a full run while looking over his shoulder at Clipper. He turned just in time to hit the doorframe with enough force to crack the wood. He fell backward and landed sitting up, then fell over sideways, unconscious.

Now a panic struck the rest of the anthropologists. Jerry Langstrome and Frank Smithers also headed for the exit, stepping over Fhardt on their way out of the church.

They disappeared through the door just as Belinda Rinds yelled, "I know CPR!" But as she kneeled down to feel for Clipper's pulse and a breath, she realized she didn't want to give him mouth-to-mouth. Too late—all eyes were on her. She forced herself to put her mouth on Clipper's and give a few shallow, inadequate breaths. She couldn't do it.

"Belinda!" screamed Clipper's wife. "Do something!"

"Well, I . . ." She felt nauseated and stood up. After a few seconds of indecision, Belinda turned to follow in the same direction as Langstrome and Smithers.

Trying to make her way around Rhonda Cartwright, she stomped on Rhonda's sandaled left foot, shattering all five metatarsals. Rhonda howled in pain. Tripping, Belinda fell forwards, her hands outstretched to catch her fall. As often happens with mountain bikers, skateboarders, and roller-skating kids who fall, the delicate bones in her wrists snapped. Rinds and Cartwright screamed a duet of agony. The crowd toward the back of the church became agitated, looked around at each other, and stood to leave. Only Ben Rogers remained undisturbed, sitting calmly in the pew while his wife clung to him like a life raft.

Meanwhile Clarke called dispatch for two ambulances, and Monique tried to get to Clipper. She was a certified Emergency Medical Technician and could perform CPR. But she couldn't force her way through the crowd that surrounded Clipper in a tight mass, wailing and bemoaning the tragedy of it all. By the time she reached him, Clipper's soul had floated up and out of the building.

Roxanne watched the chaos through a drug-induced haze. She spoke loudly to Tony's parents. "Maybe I should . . ."

"Stay where you are," ordered Warren.

Renell leaned in to whisper, "Do what Warren says. And don't talk so loud. You're acting drunk."

The mourners in the back of the church begun to calm down, sinking into the pews in shocked silence. An ambulance ferried Clipper's body away. Another attendant dealt with Rinds and Cartwright. Fhardt lay unmoving on a gurney, an oxygen mask covering his nose and mouth. His pulse was faint and one pupil appeared dilated.

"May be a concussion," the EMT said to Monique. "Might be worse."

"No more golf for Fhardt," Clarke said quietly.

Jerry Langstrome and Frank Smithers had run from the church toward Jerry's car. Wheezing and sweating, Jerry jumped in to drive while Frank struggled to undo his tie. Jerry headed towards campus, where Frank had parked his car.

"What the hell happened back there?" asked Frank.

"Those Indians," Jerry gasped.

"What do you mean?"

"They did it." He sat close to the wheel, both hands gripping it tightly.

"How could they do it? It's impossible."

"No, it isn't. You know what happens to people who handle skeletons and burial things. We were around all those bones."

"Yeah, I know. But they're just bones. Hey . . . are you okay?"

Jerry wiped his brow with his palm. He sweated as if in a sauna. He couldn't quite get a lung full. "My arm hurts," he said as he grabbed his left shoulder with his right hand.

"Pull over, Jerry."

"Chest . . . hurts." Jerry sagged toward Frank, pulling the steering wheel with him.

"Get your foot off the accelerator!!"

The car went faster.

"Jerry!!!"

The 4Runner sailed across the shoulder, narrowly missing a parked car and its driver, who was struggling to change a flat, then careened towards Anthropology. The car sped across the greenway, skidding tires leaving dark furrows in the perfectly green grass.

Frank tried to pull Jerry out of the way so he could get to the brake, but too many cheeseburgers and Heinekens made Jerry a big boy. Frank looked up just in time to see the 200-year-old oak that stood by the sidewalk in front of Anthropology rush forward to meet them.

Jerry's heart was destroyed by the steering column that drove through his chest. Frank, who had had no time to think about a seatbelt, flew through the windshield and over the hood, his neck broken. He was dead before he landed in the middle of a snapdragon flowerbed.

Back at the church, Monique's beeper went off. "Now what?" she asked out loud. She dialed in and Clarke watched her eyes widen. "Let's go." They ran to the parking lot and jumped into Monique's car. She turned on the siren and lights. "Langstrome and Smithers wrecked their car in front of Anthropology."

"How'd you know it was them?"

"Jeff Ogden called it in."

"Man. Did you see Rinds run for it? She sure showed everyone what she's made of."

"We already knew what she's made of," said Monique. She glanced at her partner and pressed the accelerator.

After discussion, Tony's family decided to continue with the service. If Tony was watching from someplace, Roxanne thought, it was with a smirk on his face.

Afterwards the mourners dispersed, then gathered again at Roxanne's home for lunch and conversation. With the exception of a few sobs, everyone preferred to celebrate Tony's life, not mourn it. They spoke in quiet voices about the events at the funeral.

Meanwhile, at the wreck scene, Langstrome's devastated body took an hour to extricate from the crushed vehicle.

"Pretty cut and dried," Clarke observed.

That night Leo Harding decided to soak in his Jacuzzi. He preferred showers, but he needed some help relaxing. While the tub filled, he swallowed two sleeping tablets. He ordered his wife to make him a pitcher of Long Island iced tea, a potent mixture of hard liquors. Harding eased into the hot water and turned on the jets.

"Trudie!' he yelled. "Where's my drink? *Trudie!*"

She brought the pitcher in and filled his tall glass. Then she set it on a ledge where he could reach it. He guzzled it like lemonade while his wife screwed up her face. Before she left the room, the Ambien and booze had already kicked in, and Leo slurred his words.

"I wanna watts TV," he managed. "Get tha portable one."

Trudie fetched the TV with the eight-inch screen. She set it on the edge of the tub.

"Bassball," he muttered.

She plugged it into the outlet next to the sink, set the channel to the Padres-Diamondbacks game and gave him a disapproving look. "You need to sleep, Leo," she said. "This was a terrible day."

"Skoo you."

She went to the kitchen to make herself a sandwich. While spreading mustard on her white bread she heard her husband yelp, half a second before the lights flickered. Trudie ran to the bathroom and found Leo floating face down in his Jacuzzi, as if he had decided to watch the submerged television underwater.

Monique and Clarke went back to the station house after an uninspired fried shrimp dinner at Sizzler's. It was Boy Scout night and every dinner benefited local troops. Both detectives took off their jackets and sipped cold Cokes. Monique's phone rang. Clarke crossed his arms and waited to hear who it was this time.

"You sure? Okay." Monique hung up. "Leo Harding," she said. "Electrocuted in his tub."

"Holy shittoli," said Clarke. "What's going on?"

"You see no pattern developing?"

"Yes, I do. That's what I mean. Let's go see Klaus."

"Well, that's a first. The morgue holds some interest for you now? Let's give them time to get Harding's body over there. I don't want to visit that place any longer than I have to."

"Everything appears to be straightforward," Klaus said to Monique and Clarke two hours later. "Clipper had a massive stroke. He was overweight and smoked. Harding was knee-walking drunk and his wife said he also took Ambien. He no doubt tried to change channels and pulled the television in with him."

"He had a television on the edge of the tub?" Clarke was incredulous.

"Yep. Right on the edge."

"Post hole Digger," said Monique. "What did I tell you?"

"Normally, I'd say a person dumb enough to put a TV on the edge of their tub was so stupid they couldn't find their butt with both hands." Clarke paused, then added excitedly, "Hey, what's Clipper's butt size?"

"Pardon?"

"Whoever fell in the flowerbed left their ass print."

"Easy enough to find out." Klause went to the first table and pulled back the cloth over Clipper's body.

"Hand here. He's heavy." Clarke didn't move. Monique sighed and walked over. She put on an apron and gloves, and together she and Klaus struggled to flop him over like a marlin in a boat.

Klaus took several measurements of Clipper's back and buttocks. "About 24 inches across where he sits. Wider if he actually was sitting."

"I'll call Meg and see what she's got," Clarke said as he walked to the phone in Klaus's office.

Klaus meandered to the body on the next table. "Langstrome here had a heart attack, I think. Hard to tell for sure with just a cursory exam. His chest is mush. But with his health it wouldn't be an odd thing to happen to him. His passenger Smithers," Klaus pointed to the covered body next to him, "didn't have on a seat belt. I don't need to elaborate on the dangers of that."

"Please don't," said Monique.

"I checked with the neurologists about Mr., uh, Fhardt. He had severe swelling on his brain and as we speak they're operating to relieve the pressure."

"How's it looking?" asked Monique.

"According to the neurosurgeon, he might recover."

"Better than being a salad ingredient, huh Doc?" Clarke interjected while waiting for Meg's response.

"Maybe the down time will give him opportunity to write his master-piece," Monique said.

"His what?" asked Klause.

"Never mind."

"Very well. Let's see, who else? Rhonda Cartwright will have surgery on her foot. All the metatarsals in her foot were fractured. Very hard to mend.

She'll need pins. Rinds broke both wrists and she'll wear casts up to her elbows. Quite a day," Klaus said.

Clarke had reached Meg, and they spoke briefly. He said goodnight and snapped shut his cell phone. "Clipper's butt is the right measurement, but it has to match the cast from the flower bed."

"Think there was more than one person in on all this?" Klause asked.

Monique sighed. "Of course. I think several people were behind it. Who would've thought Clipper's ass would give him away?"

"For all we know," Clarke added, "the ones who planned the murder are on these tables."

"Well, then," asked Klaus, "are you finished?"

"Not quite," answered Monique.

"What do you mean?"

"Three of the men I believe were part of the murder were also involved with the excavation," said Monique. "I think they also instigated robbing Tony's house."

"Clipper almost got his head bashed in by a set of golf clubs," added Clarke. "Could Roxanne have done that?"

"Doubtful. I'm more concerned about who was working with these guys."

MONDAY, 10:00 P.M.

Clarke was asleep, dreaming of Sharon Stone in *The Quick and the Dead*, when the phone rang. He mistook it for a gunshot and jumped up, fumbling for the .45 he kept under his pillow. He found it, realized what century he was in, and took a deep breath. He was breathing heavily when he picked up the cell phone and said, "Hello."

"What's the matter with you?" Monique asked from the other end.

"Uh, nothing. I was dreaming about Ross Clipper."

"Clipper? What the hell for? Never mind. I just got a call from Roxanne. Seems her husband went to the post office to pick up his art studio mail. He had a couple of boxes.

"Boxes of what?"

"Don't know, but she says they look odd."

168

Clarke tried to put his pants on while he talked. "So did he leave them at his studio?"

"Nope. They're sitting in Roxanne's home office. I'll be there to pick you up in ten minutes."

They arrived at Roxanne's house forty-five minutes later. Warren stood at the door in his white T-shirt and long navy shorts waiting for the detectives to climb the three steps to the porch.

"Hey," Warren said. "I wasn't thinking," he commented as the detectives came in through the screen door. "I didn't realize until I got home an hour ago that they might be dangerous. I saw Rox's name on them and just loaded them into the trunk with everything else."

"When did you get them?" Monique asked. The night was warm and she took off her jacket as she spoke. The Arizona and South Dakota men sat at the kitchen table eating hamburgers. She saw through the screen door Roxanne's brother standing on the back porch tending to a smoking grill. One Hopi man lifted his Pepsi can in greeting. Monique smiled back.

"About two hours ago. Everyone around here is just moping around, so I decided to go check mail. Rox is in there." He pointed to her office.

Roxanne sat in her office chair while everyone else mingled in the kitchen. She wore gray sweats and a navy tank top. Her bandages had been changed after the funeral, and white gauze still covered her face, but appeared less lumpy than before. She repeatedly crinkled an empty can of Mountain Dew. Three crumpled, empty cans of the same were on the table next to her. The detectives sat in the chairs opposite her.

"Roxanne," Monique said. "Warren said the boxes had been mailed to him."

"Yeah. He just brought them home."

The detectives looked at the two copy-paper boxes sitting in the middle of her office floor. Monique squatted and examined the labels. "Sure enough. Addressed to Warren Brugge care of his art studio P.O. Box. The return address is a post office box with no name."

"At first I thought they were bombs or something. There's no name on the return address and the boxes are beat up. Then I realized that's Tony's crappy handwriting," she said. "They're heavy."

"You know what's in them?" Monique asked.

169

"He e-mailed me last week to say that he was ordering some expensive books and would have them sent to us."

"Why would he send them to you?"

"Well, the books cost a lot, and he's never home during the day and neither is his wife. He didn't want them sitting on anyone's front porch. He also doesn't like having parcels delivered to the CHU office."

"Why not?"

"He mentioned to me about a year ago that he thought someone had rifled through his mail a few times and had opened some envelopes. Tony preferred having mail delivered to his house."

"It's postmarked the Friday before he died," Clarke observed. "It's from Reynolds."

"But Roxanne, you said he ordered books and had them sent to you. There's no indication on the packages that they came from a publishing house or Amazon."

"I don't know what to tell you then."

"Reynolds is two hours from here," Monique said. She asked Roxanne, "What's in Reynolds?"

"Nothing, really. It's a dinky artist colony town with one grocery store. And it has a good Mexican food restaurant and an ice cream parlor with old-fashioned malts. My friend from graduate school lives there. That's about it."

"Who's your friend?"

"Jasper Deere. He's an anthropologist. Or was. He got tired of academia and opened a gift shop instead. Well, maybe it's more of a junk shop that has everything. Jasper has the largest collection of used hub caps in the state. It's in an old warehouse. It's like a huge garage sale and Jasper's always taking apart an engine or cleaning something for resale."

"Did Tony know him?"

"Yes. We went over there a few times. Jasper has lots of tools and car parts. Tony and Warren liked to rummage through all that junk. They always came home with stuff they had to have, but don't need. Perri and I'd go get ice cream while they waded through it. Sometimes Warren found some interesting old calendars or easels."

Clarke scratched his head. "Ok. So Tony mailed these to Warren, not Roxanne."

"Obviously he wanted them to come to Roxanne, but not directly, in case their CHU colleagues were watching what might be delivered to her house."

"Hmm. Right."

"Only one way to find out," Monique said. "May we?" she asked Roxanne.

"Go ahead."

Monique nodded to Clarke. "Have at it, Clarke."

"I don't have any gloves," Clarke said.

Monique took two wadded-up plastic pairs from her pocket.

Clarke took a small folded knife from his pocket, kneeled down, and carefully cut the package tape. He pulled opened the top of the box to expose wads of newspaper. He looked at Monique, who nodded again. Clarke removed the newspaper, revealing objects covered in bubble wrap. He cut through the Scotch tape of the first bundle, then unwrapped it to reveal a small brown pot decorated with elaborate etchings.

"No books," Roxanne observed.

"It's a pot," Clarke exclaimed.

"I knew I brought you here for a reason, Partner," Monique said.

Clarke unwrapped the next item. "Wow," he said. It was a beautifully beaded leather bag.

Monique kneeled down and helped unwrap the rest of the bundles. They set each item on Roxanne's desk, lining them up like objects of study in a museum archive.

"Okay," said Monique. "We got six oddly shaped pots, some little leather bags that might be medicine bundles wrapped in straw, a small elk carving, a dozen carved human figures with remnants of feathers stuck into them, five other carved animal fetishes, four pipes, or part of a pipe, what might be a headdress or bustle, some knives with elaborate handles, and some mystery items that are falling apart. And there is an interesting smell in the room now. Any ideas, Roxanne?"

Roxanne sat still, her eyes looking out from between the bandages. She did not speak.

Clarke looked back in the box. He held it up at an angle to reveal a beige envelope. "What's this?"

Monique leaned over to look. "Looks like a letter with an 'R' written on it. And it also has a printed return address from the Department of Anthropology."

"It's our department envelope," Roxanne said.

"You ever see these items before?" Monique asked.

"No." Roxanne began crying.

"Tony took these from the dig, didn't he?"

"I don't know. I can't believe that he would."

"Roxanne," Monique said as she leaned forward, hands on her knees, "his house was ransacked and the thieves only took a carved elk and two boxes that Perri said Tony brought home a few days ago. The elk and the boxes had red dirt on them."

"Well, big damn deal," Roxanne said defensively. "They were dirty. So what?"

"We went to the dig. There's an area partitioned off. They've found skeletons and grave goods. The dirt is the same color as what was on the elk and the boxes."

"Maybe he had the boxes in his yard and brought them inside."

Monique shook her head. "No clay like that in his yard, or in his neighbors' yards. The dirt on Tony's office floor matches the dirt we saw at the dig."

Monique propped her arm on one knee and casually pointed to the boxes. "I'd bet real money that these are like the stolen boxes Perri saw under Tony's desk."

Roxanne hiccupped.

Monique opened her little Swiss Army knife that she bought a gas station and used the short knife to slice through the envelope. She took out the beige stationery, unfolded it and read, "Rox, you weren't supposed to open these boxes. Since you have, keep these things safe where they can't get them. I'll come over in the next few weeks to take them back to where they belong. Don't say a word about it. T."

"Who's they?" Clarke asked.

"That's the million-dollar question, partner."

Roxanne cleared her throat. "So you're saying that these may have been in Tony's house and that's the reason for that robbery. To get these boxes?"

Clarke answered, "I don't know that they were after these two boxes in particular, but they did get two other boxes. Could be even more of them."

"Tony didn't mean for you to open the boxes," Warren said. "Did he think my studio was a safe house where he could pick them up without you knowing what was in them?"

"He didn't want anyone to know what was inside them," Monique added. "Clearly that's why he sent them to your studio, not this house."

Monique turned to look at the little treasures on Roxanne's desk. "What are these things?"

"It's fairly obvious what they are," Roxanne said. "But I don't know what they mean, exactly."

"Are they valuable from a collector's standpoint?"

"To the tribe they came from, they would be valuable for sure. That's why they were buried with the dead. Looters would sell all this, for sure. For how much, I don't know. I do know that Indian skeletal remains are hot items in Japan and Germany. Collectors don't ask questions about how they were obtained. They just want to know from where and from what tribe."

Clarke said, "That's really weird."

"Yes, it is," Roxanne agreed. "But collecting Indian artifacts and skeletal parts, especially skulls, is a huge, multi-million-dollar business. On the black market, I mean. I know for sure that some collectors in Texas, Oklahoma, and Missouri have them displayed throughout their homes. Even judges who're supposed to enforce the law have skulls and burial objects that tribes say are sacred to them. Collectors don't care what Indians think."

Clarke looked indignant. "I find that hard to believe."

"Believe it. People buy land in Arizona, New Mexico, Texas, wherever, because they know they're Indian burials underneath. They tear up the land and sell what they find."

"Man, that's creepy."

"Where are you from, detective?"

"Arkansas."

"Think about it. Your area and Oklahoma is basically one huge burial ground. Just like Missouri and east Texas. Lush with lots of water, which meant a lot of fish, water fowl, and other game. Tribes settled there one way or the other."

"One way or the other?"

"Over sixty tribes were forcibly removed to Indian Territory. Courtesy of Andrew Jackson's Indian Removal Policy. The old ones aren't still living. They're dead. Where are they? Underground. Who's trying to find them? Looters. It's not hard to figure out."

Monique listened to Roxanne. Although removal of the southeastern tribes took place almost two hundred years ago, the stories she had heard about the displacement still remained fresh in her mind. Other tribes had been displaced and experienced the same anguish.

"I didn't know that," Clarke said. "It's never in the papers. I only read about Boy Scouts and arrowhead hunting."

"Never is in the papers," Roxanne said between sniffs. "Arrowhead hunting is just a smokescreen. Serious arrowhead hunters always get in deeper to the next level."

"Which is?"

"Grave robbing," Monique answered.

"Right," said Roxanne. "They deny it every time, though. Unless Indians get involved and pull a protest, you'll never hear about desecration. A lot of non-Indians see nothing wrong with looting Indian graves, but they'd kill you if you started digging up their grandma."

The three sat in silence. An old Hopi man had been standing at the door.

"It's not good to have those things here," he said in a severe Hopi accent.

"You're right about that," Monique answered.

"You need to be taken care of. Take those things to where they belong and in the morning we have to tend to you. And to everyone in the house."

Roxanne looked at Monique then at Clarke. "He means that we have to be cleansed."

Clarke's eyes widened. "What for?"

"These are burial items."

"You mean they have a spell on them?"

"Sort of, Clarke," said Monique. "Just go with it."

"Well, okay I guess. I probably need it anyway."

It was fine with Monique, too. She'd also have her uncle Leroy Bear Red Ears cleanse her when she returned to Oklahoma.

"We all do," Roxanne said. Then she burst into tears.

Warren sat next to her and gave her a hug. "It's okay, Honey."

"Why did Tony have these things?" She asked between sobs. "He wasn't going to sell them, was he?"

"Let's not jump to conclusions," Monique interjected as she handed Roxanne a Kleenex. "Tony may have had a good reason for doing what he did."

"Man, I hope so," Warren said quietly. Roxanne blew her nose.

"I guess we'll take these things to the station," Monique said. "And we need to ask the elders in there about how to store them so we'll all be safe."

"Man, we never have to go through all this with dead white people," Clarke said.

Roxanne leaned back in the sofa so she could look at the ceiling. "That's the problem with you white guys. You don't know how to relate to the dead."

Did Tony? thought Monique.

TUESDAY, NOON

The sun beat down on the Impala. There was no wind and little traffic on the highway to Reynolds.

The two officers had completed their cleansing ceremony. The old Hopi man started it, then Arnold Old Bull finished it. Afterwards they ate a large brunch of corn bread, fruit salad, and elk stew, courtesy of the successful hunter Tony Smoke Rise, who had given Roxanne and Warren several packages of frozen meat the previous fall.

"Well, I feel good. You feel good?" Monique asked Clarke as she drank a large swig of canned tea.

"I guess. How am I supposed to feel?"

"Good. How's the foot? Still feel like a raisin?"

"Not a raisin. A risin.' You know, like a big pimple."

"Gross. Whatever. Nice of Old Bull to look at it. You need to give him something for doing that. He won't take money, but a new Toolman would be nice. I noticed that his knife blade had broken off of the one he has now."

"Yeah, okay. No wonder there aren't many Indian archaeologists," Clarke commented. "They'd be doing ceremonies all the time."

"I think that's part of why they avoid this business. The death aspect, I mean. Why they'd want to be archaeologists in the first place is the real question."

It was sometimes bad enough working in law enforcement. Monique couldn't imagine purposely wanting to be around dead people. And physical anthropologists made that decision. So did coroners. Maybe it's a personality disorder, she thought.

The detectives talked calmly on the road to see Jasper Deere. They didn't know how Jasper was connected to the murder, but since Tony had come to Reynolds to mail the packages, perhaps he had stopped by to see Jasper.

They reached the turn-off ramp and the large truck stop at the crest of the hill. They passed small houses built like ski chalets and others that looked like nothing more than mobile homes held together by duct tape and tires on the roofs.

Monique drove another half mile down a potholed road until they reached a cluster of neat, but small, older homes. They were meticulously landscaped with decorative rocks and plants that fell over the terraces or climbed up the house walls. Some yards featured bronze sculptures, while others had brightly colored, gaudy carved figures of animals and flowers.

"Artist community," Monique commented.

"That would account for it."

Monique drove a few more blocks and stopped in front of a huge cinder block building with a metal roof. A giant painting of a cattle drive was pealing away on the west wall. A chain link fence surrounded the property, including a dirt parking area that Jasper rented out for boats and RVs. On the west side were shining piles of hub caps of every make and size.

"How'd he get all those hub caps?" Clarke asked.

"Found some, then traded for others."

Monique parked and the two got out, sans jackets. The sun beat down, making the day pleasant in the shade, but not in the direct sun. The front porch was long and covered by a thick wood overhang shingled with metal sheets. The detectives took the steps two at a time and entered the cool warehouse.

"Holy shit," Clarke exclaimed. "This looks like twenty antique places rolled into one."

The detectives stood with open mouths, staring at the numbers of items in the store. Posters, calendars, car tags, paintings, rugs, and Indians painted on sheet metal adorned the walls. Shelves laden with pots, tools, ceramics, kitchenware, televisions, and radios filled one side of the building while the other side featured furniture, ovens and refrigerators, and other appliances, plus a vast array of car parts, wagons, roller skates, skis, and other sports equipment. The front counter was crammed with candy, earrings, books, and seed packets.

"I've never seen so much stuff in one place," Monique said. "This is bigger than that junk store in Cache."

"Where's Cache?"

"Oklahoma. Where Quanah Parker's Star House was moved. You know, he was a Comanche war leader. There's a junk store in front of it and it's filled with things you wouldn't believe. Everything from moldy bread to old photographs to dog shit on the floor."

"Sounds like great shopping. So where's Jasper?"

"No telling. He may be smothered under something."

They walked around the immense store, looking at knickknacks, picking up tools and antique kitchen gadgets. Finally a large, bearded man wearing dirty white T-shirt, jeans held up by suspenders, and high-tops emerged from a side room. "Help you?" he yelled from across the expanse.

"Yeah," Monique yelled back. They wandered through the aisles, around motorcycles and old tables until the met roughly in the middle of the building.

"Detectives Blue Hawk and Clarke," Monique said as she showed Jasper her badge. Clarke held his up and Jasper checked both. He looked younger up close, although he had definitely let himself go.

"We're investigating the murder of Tony Smoke Rise," Monique said. "You know him?"

"Yeah. I sure did. I thought I'd see you tomorrow."

"Why's that?"

"Because I was planning on coming to see you, that's why."

"No kidding?"

"Tony. I've been sick about it." Jasper talked like a backwoods boy, but the detectives already knew that he had two Ph.D.s, one in anthropology and the other in French literature.

"Didn't see you at the funeral."

"I don't go to funerals."

Monique asked, "Can we sit someplace and talk?"

"Yeah, hang on a sec." Jasper took out a small walkie-talkie and pressed the button. "Hon, you mind watching the front for a while?"

"No I don't, darlin'," the feminine voice answered.

"My wife," he explained. "Come this way."

They followed Jasper as he led them through the maze of coats and dresses, their hangers held up by green rope. He came to a heavy door that he unlocked. "Come on in," he told them.

Jasper entered first and turned on the bright overhead lights. Monique and Clarke followed and both gasped. The room was a treasure trove of pottery, fetishes, paintings, and wood carvings. Turquoise, coral, and silver necklaces and belts filled the glass cases. One section featured old and tarnished squash blossoms. There were no windows, and the door was heavy with several locks.

"These are the valuables?"

"Yep. And before you ask, there're no burial goods here. It's all artwork."

"Where'd you get all this?"

"Bought some of it in pawnshops. Traded for some of the other things. I go to other shops and buy pots and rugs. A lot of times I find things underpriced."

Monique asked, "So you buy them and mark up the prices?"

"I know what these things are worth. I don't gyp anyone."

"So . . ." Monique paused to make a point. "You know what things are worth, yes?"

"That's why you're here, right?"

"It is. You talked to Tony last Friday?"

"Yeah."

"What about?"

"Tony brought me items to look at."

"Such as?"

"Pots, skulls, fetishes."

"And what was your assessment?"

"Clearly they were burial items. The skulls could go for anywhere from $100 to $500 on the black market. The fetishes at the top of that range, same with the carved animals. There was a pipe that would be a couple of thousand at least. All told, it was a nice package for disreputable sellers and buyers. But Tony was mainly concerned about the sacred aspects of it all. You know, would the tribes need the items back."

"Tony wanted to return them?"

"Yes. But he didn't know who to return it to. That stuff belonged to the Noituac tribe."

"I'm not familiar with that tribe. Why didn't he contact them?"

"No one to contact."

"Why's that?"

"They're extinct."

They all stood in silence a few moments while Monique and Clarke absorbed this fact.

"No one around at all?"

"Nope. Not even mixed-blood descendants that we know of. That tribe pretty much got wiped out by smallpox 300 years ago. They probably got buried or cremated by the survivors who went off and died or intermarried into another tribe. We'll never know."

Clarke asked, "What was Tony thinking by sending the items to Warren?"

Jasper sighed, then blew his nose in a hankie. "I didn't want them here. I won't handle burial items. And I don't want bones around me. Bad juju."

"Is that why you're no longer an archaeologist?"

"That's most of it. The other part is I hate academics. Small minds, big egos, and no backbone."

"I can understand that," Monique commented. "Where were you Sunday night between ten and midnight?"

"My wife and I were next door at the neighbors. Sam and Janeen Odem had their fiftieth wedding anniversary. We were there until three. I'm still hung over."

Monique wrote their names on her pad. "So the burial items Tony brought you came from the freeway excavation in Moose City?"

Jasper said, "The CHU people knew the chances were good that they'd get away with selling the items because they didn't have to answer to any tribe. So Tony decided to bring the items here until he could convince another tribe to rebury the stuff on their land. He wanted to keep them safe."

"Safe from the guys from his department."

"Correct. Tony was convinced that the ones working on the dig wanted to sell what they could. In fact, he noticed that some items went missing from the dig a little at a time. There were at least 150 full skeletons there when Tony first arrived at the site. Twenty disappeared the first weekend. Then twenty more."

"We just saw about fifteen the other day," Monique said. "Ross Clipper and Jerry Langstrome were digging at the site."

"They took more, then."

"How'd the Corps of Engineers not know about all this?" Clarke asked.

"Easy," answered Jasper. "They left the excavation up to the CHU people, who in turn made it appear as if there were only a few skeletons. They hid the remains or covered them with dirt, then stole them when no one was around to watch."

"Wait a sec," Monique said. "How did Tony know all this? He wasn't a part of the dig."

"Oh hell yes, he was. They were paying him a bundle."

"Who's 'they?'" Monique asked.

"Clipper, Langstrome, Rogers."

"Rogers?" Monique looked at Clarke. "I didn't know he was a part of the dig."

"Hold on," interjected Clarke. "What were they paying him to do?"

"To tell them about what they were finding in the ground. And even though Tony didn't tell me this, I say it was hush money."

Monique was speechless.

Clarke shifted his feet and leaned on a glass case. "Why didn't Tony tell Roxanne that he was involved in the dig?"

"Possibly because she'd want in on it," Monique surmised.

"You mean, the money part?"

"Hell, no," Jasper interjected. "Not her. She'd go ballistic over how it was being handled. She can't control that temper of hers and Tony wanted to deal with it by himself. If she were involved, then she'd be out at the dig every day making an issue of everything."

"But wouldn't that be a good thing? I mean, people need to know about the dig, right?"

"Yes, of course. But Roxanne would try and dictate where everything should go, and that's not how to handle repatriation issues. Tony planned to tell Roxanne about it this week. Really, Tony thought he could handle this quickly and quietly."

"He still sent them to Roxanne via Warren."

"He wanted to get the more precious items tribes might need for ceremonies away from the CHU guys. All of those things are worth a lot. He couldn't keep them here because I don't want burial goods around me." Jasper blew his nose with his hankie. "He thought he could be sneaky enough to save what the CHU anthros uncovered. Too bad he underestimated their greed."

"How greedy were they?"

Well, an authentic medicine bag from an extinct tribe could conceivably get a couple thousand dollars. It depends on who is buying. Those fetishes may also have great religious significance and that hikes the price. A full skeleton could go for three or four thousand. Add on the burial goods with them and multiply that by 150 skeletons or more."

"What's that all add up to, maybe two million dollars? That's a lot of money," Monique said, "but not that much after you divide among all the people selling the items."

Jasper smirked and crossed his arms. "You're right about that." Jasper put his finger in his ear and tried to dig something out. "I got about a dozen more boxes out back."

"What boxes?"

"Each has a skeleton in it. Tony brought them out here a few at a time. I let him put the boxes in the shed out there since that's as far from me as he can get. He said he was going to come back for them."

"Is that a fact?" Clarke asked.

"Yes sir."

"And you were just going to keep them out back?"

"Yep."

Monique chewed her lip as she pondered what he'd said.

Jasper looked at Monique and took a step closer. "Now you think I'm in on something."

"Not necessarily."

Jasper ran his tongue over his top teeth. "Haven't you found any other motives for killing Tony?"

Monique cleared her throat. "How long have you known Tony and Roxanne?"

"Ten years. I hear all about CHU. Nothing they said ever surprised me."

Monique said, "We need to see the boxes, Jasper."

"Yeah, I know."

The detectives followed Jasper to the front of the store where he introduced the two to his wife. Clarke stopped short at the sight of the buxom blonde with a flawless complexion. "You're Jasper's wife?" he exclaimed as he looked her up and down. She wore a nylon stretchy top and tight jeans with a belt clinched tighter than Scarlett O'Hara's girdle.

"Dang right, Detective."

Monique took Clarke's arm and pulled on her gaping partner. "Let's go." They followed Jasper around the shop to the large metal outbuilding in back.

"You know," Clarke said to Monique in a low voice, as Jasper walked ahead. "This may be the end of it. If the guilty parties are dead, that is. What else are we supposed to do besides find a home for the remains of these poor Indians?"

"I want to look at Ben Rogers again. And there's still one big piece missing. Why did they try to kill Roxanne? Who attacked her? She wasn't messing with their bones."

"True," Clarke agreed. "Maybe people thought Tony had confided in her. Maybe they thought she had some of the items."

They were twenty feet from the shed when Jasper stopped. "Bones are in there."

"In there?" asked Monique.

"Yup."

"You coming?"

"Nope." Jasper stood with his hands in his pockets. "I don't go near them. Tony put them in there and he was supposed to take them out."

"How did he get all this out of the excavation without the others seeing him?"

"He said they were already boxed up and Leo Harding had them in his garage. Tony stole them."

"Oh, man," said Monique.

"You didn't know about it, because Harding certainly couldn't report the theft to the police."

"My Gawd," Clarke added.

"Leo Harding?" Monique asked. "He was electrocuted in his tub yesterday."

"No shit?" responded Jasper.

"Television fell in."

"What a dumb ass."

"Not up until that," Monique answered. "He stayed in the background and out of the way of the murder."

"He wasn't part of the dig," added Clarke.

Jasper smiled. "He didn't need to be, did he? Since he wasn't formally connected with the team, attention wouldn't be on him, now would it?"

"How did Tony know?"

"Tony's pretty sharp. Knowing him, he surely followed those guys."

The detectives left Jasper standing in the dirt drive as they approached the shed. Clarke opened the door and found a dozen boxes, stacked in three piles, that looked like the ones delivered to Roxanne's house. Monique lifted the top of one with a forefinger and saw a brown skull, the empty eye orbits staring up at her. She dropped the lid and jumped back.

"Jasper," she called to him. "Are there only bones in the shed?"

"As far as I know. Only bones."

Monique felt her heart race. "Look in those boxes please, Clark," she asked.

Clarke looked in that box, then moved to the next pile. "Skulls with the other bones underneath. Jasper's right."

Then he asked her more quietly, "What do you want to do with Jasper?"

Monique answered, "I think he's straight."

"So we call for someone to transport these things to . . . where?"

"We should talk to Renell. She knows the NAGPRA laws.

Clarke looked around at the boxes and wiped his hands on his pants. His face paled a bit. "We're going to need another ceremony."

"I'll call Roxanne so she can set it up. I think those Hopis and Arnold need to come out here, too."

"Jasper will probably welcome them."

"Yes, indeed," Monique agreed.

In October the judge announced the decision in a lawsuit filed by Tony's family. They would be awarded three million dollars from CHU in damages for not properly dealing with a hostile work environment.

The anthropology department's surviving members involved in the scheme against Tony and Roxanne—Belinda Rines and the still comatose Mark Fhardt—were put on forced leave from their jobs, and would also face criminal charges for conspiracy to commit murder. The other conspirators were deceased.

After the verdict, Monique and Clarke approached Roxanne in the hall. "Congratulations," Monique said.

"Yeah," Roxanne smiled. "His family deserves it." Her scars had faded to pink lines and she looked happy and healthy despite an underlying shadow of sadness.

"Are you doing okay?"

"Great. The second surgery should remove the deep scarring on my cheek. And I'm three months pregnant."

"Hey, good for you!"

"We can finally sleep all night. And I've been thinking a lot. I plan on spending time with the people that matter—my family. I know that I'm always going to run into critics. That's the nature of academia. But they aren't the ones who matter."

"I never knew there was so much to learn about higher education outside the classroom."

"Be glad you're a cop and not an academic." She swallowed. "I wish Tony was here."

"So do I," Monique and Clarke said simultaneously.

184

The night of the verdict, the newly appointed department chair, Ben Rogers, and his wife Marge dined in the Tanglewood Country Club's "Cork Room." The dining room was so named because the ceiling and walls were covered in brown cork. Marge was dressed elegantly and smoothed her outfit continually to make sure it made the right impression on the other golfing diners.

"To us," Ben said as he raised his glass. They were on their second bottle of wine.

Marge appeared puzzled. It wasn't their anniversary.

"I'm happy for you, dear. You've always wanted to be chair."

"For fifteen years," he agreed.

"You deserve what you finally got," she said. "How's your back today?"

"Still sore sometimes."

"It's been months. You fell pretty hard. You should watch the trail more carefully when you hike."

"Yes, I should. But I was trying to get a picture of the deer and I forgot how easy it is to slip on those little rocks. Too excited, I guess."

"Well, now you're the chairman of the department. And a big raise. Maybe cheesecake tonight?"

"Honestly, I didn't think they'd ignore me like they have."

"Those people you work with? They overlooked a lot of qualified faculty. You're not the only one they ignored."

"No, I mean I was ignored in the investigation. The murder. Roxanne's attack."

"Well, of course. You didn't have anything to do with those things." She sipped her white Zinfandel, set down the glass, and smoothed the napkin over her lap.

Ben swallowed the last of his wine, then laughed. He leaned forward slightly and said in a low tone, "Margie, I planned them."

"What?"

"Well, me and a certain lady made most of the plans, and the others did what we told them to do," said Ben, looking coy. He grinned big, his capped teeth dazzling against his golf tan.

"You murdered Tony Smoke Rise?"

"I didn't say that."

"You attacked Roxanne?"

He shrugged. "Thought it would work. She was too quick."

Marge sat up straight. Her long silver earrings swayed back and forth with the motion. She gave her husband a look he hadn't seen before.

"What's with you?" he asked, then cut a chunk of the sirloin and dipped it in steak sauce. "I had to protect myself." His smile dropped. "That stupid Clipper. Unreliable. I thought he was going tell someone about what we were up to at the dig. So I rigged a little surprise for him in his garage. Or I should say, Leo rigged it."

"Leo put that rope in his garage?"

"Yeah. He also wanted to climb the wall that night, but Ross made him flip for it."

"Flip a coin to see who'd kill Tony?" Marge looked stunned.

"And Roxanne. If she had found out about the extent of what we located, she'd have swarms of Indians down here. She can be a bulldog bitch, Marge."

Rogers leaned over the table and spoke softly. "Tony stole the best artifacts. Look, he found out about the dig and it was only a matter of time before he told Roxanne. So we paid him to advise us, but it also was enough to keep him quiet. Then that twerp took what would've been worth hundreds of thousands of dollars."

"Tony did? He took the artifacts?"

"You think he was a saint? Hell yes he took them. He took, I don't know, a dozen skeletons. Hundreds of artifacts. He snuck in at night and stole them from us."

"How do you know he was going to sell those things? What if he was keeping them from you so he could return them?"

"Return them to who? An extinct tribe?"

"That's not what happened, Ben. The papers said that Montana tribe offered to rebury the remains. And, according to the papers, there were quite a few other tribes willing to take them. That was the decent thing to do."

Rogers tapped his knife on his plate and ran his tongue over his teeth. A piece of steak was lodged between his veneers.

Marge stared at her husband. "I'm going to tell the police what you did."

"I don't think so. I won't be able to buy you nice shoes from prison, Margie. I got two boxes back that Tony took and there's good stuff in them. And with Smithers and the rest gone, there's a lot more for me. For *us*."

Ben smiled his smooth smile. He put another big chunk of meat dabbed in sauce in his mouth, coughed, and inhaled sharply.

"You shithead. You son of a bitch."

Ben didn't answer. The meat was firmly wedged in his windpipe. He stood and put his hands to his throat in a futile attempt to breathe. He fell onto the table, knocking over the plates and glasses, then dropping in a dramatic free-fall to the floor.

A physician at a nearby table rushed over and tried the Heimlich maneuver. Then she attempted a tracheotomy with a steak knife and a ball point pen, but Rogers kept flailing so hard that the bystanders couldn't hold him.

Coroner Klaus removed the sirloin at the autopsy and determined that the cause of Ben Rogers's demise was a common one: asphyxiation by choking on an unmasticated piece of meat.

Although she was not fired, due to lack of evidence, Belinda C. Rinds continued to invite graduate students to her house. Many naive, wide-eyed students believed her fabricated tales about Roxanne and Tony, but because she would not stop blabbering about them, and herself, she became boring, and after a while they stopped visiting her. So she began calling acquaintances on the phone and talking until they hung up. She cornered people at the grocery store and jabbered until they walked away. From all reports, she lost weight because she talked instead of eating, and it appeared that she was talking herself to death.

"Good catch," Monique yelled to Robbie after he had run to grab a wide toss of the orange Frisbee. The family had walked to the local park before meeting Roscoe and Renell for an early dinner. "Throw it back to Dad. Keep your elbow up. Okay, nice."

The day was cold but still. Runners made their way up and down the street while dogs and their owners played in the park.

"Hey, Mom," Robbie said as he jogged over to her. "We haven't come to the park in a long time."

"I've been pretty tied up with that case, baby." *Baby*. She wondered how much longer she would be able to call the gangly person in front of her that name. In the past year her son had grown three inches and was beginning to look and sound like a young man. She almost cried. "We need to come over here more often."

"So the case is over?"

"Yep. All clear." Marge Rogers had told the police everything after her husband choked away her motivation to remain silent. The boxes of burial goods collected by Tony and the boxes confiscated from Rogers' home were now being stored at the Museum of the Plains Indian while NAGPRA officials addressed the complicated issue of ownership and reburial.

"You had to deal with more bad people." He did not look at his mother as he traced the lettering on the Frisbee with his finger.

"Yes, honey."

"There're bad people out here." He looked around the park at the other Moose City residents who also had some to enjoy the day. Monique gave him a hug. The last thing she wanted was for Robbie to become paranoid.

She looked at Steve, who shrugged. Her husband had a hard time explaining human behavior to their son. So he left it up to Monique to talk about the tough things. "There always has been and there always will be. That's the way the world works."

"And you're gonna take care of the bad ones?"

Monique stroked her son's hair. "That's my job, Honey. All I can do is try. But you know what? The world is also full of good people." Monique did not want her son to become suspicious of everyone he met. On the other hand, she knew what could happen to those who were too trusting.

"What you do is dangerous, Mom. Something could happen to you. I hear you and Dad arguing about that."

"I know, Robbie. I deal with tough situations and I see a lot of bad things and bad people. But I'm careful. You don't have to worry."

"Dad does."

Monique sighed.

"What if something happens to you?"

Good question, she thought. And one she always hoped he wouldn't ask her.

"I'm very careful. And my job is to find out how people were killed or hurt. I'm not usually in the line of fire."

"How do you know the difference between someone who is good and someone who pretends to be?"

Monique sighed. "Sometimes you can't until they do something that surprises you."

"Why do people kill? I don't get it."

"Don't think about that, Robbie. All you can do is be kind to others, try and be helpful and give people some benefit of the doubt. But not completely. That's the tricky part."

Robbie twirled the Frisbee on his index finger.

"But you know what? It isn't up to me to take care of the bad guys all of the time. Sometimes I don't have to do much at all. Good usually wins out."

Robbie continued to twirl. "Does it?"

Be honest, she thought. "Well, not always. But I think that most of the time it does."

"Most of the time?"

"Yes. Yes, I do."

THURSDAY, 3:00 A.M.

"What's the matter?" Steve asked Monique. His wife was awake and thrashing. She kicked him in the thigh and made him jump.

"Just thinking," she answered. "The funeral. It was on purpose."

189

"Not again. Moni, no one killed those men. They died because it was their time. They got hurt because they were careless. That's all."

She ignored him. "The way those people were hurt and died . . ." Monique watched the blades of her ceiling fan slowly swirl. The night light allowed her to see the outline of everything in their room. "That couldn't be a coincidence."

"Sure it could." Steve stroked Foogly, who also awoke and demanded attention. "There're plenty of elders with power, but I don't believe any of the Indians killed the anthropologists."

"Hmmm."

"I don't think they'd stoop to that level."

"I would."

"Moni, if you had that kind of power, then you'd think differently."

"I always want to punish those who act badly. Am I wrong to be glad those creeps are dead? And hurt?"

"Are you really glad?"

"Pretty much."

Steve did not respond.

"Am I bad?"

"Moni, revenge can be ugly. If everyone wanted an eye for an eye, then the entire world would be blind."

"Don't preach, Steve."

"I'm not."

"Geez. Where did you get that bit of wisdom about eyes? Your book of wise sayings?"

"No. A bumper sticker."

She didn't respond. Steve stayed quiet to avoid an argument.

"I wonder about Arlene Smoke Rise," she said finally.

"She's not a religious leader."

"No. But she has connections. And she's different."

"We have witches in my tribe, and she's not a witch, Monique. She didn't do anything and neither did those Hopi men."

Monique bent her left knee and pulled it to her chin, stretching her back. She did the same with her right leg.

Steve drank some water from his bedside bottle. "There's one way to find out. It's the middle of the week so tickets might be cheap."

"You think I should?"

"Please. You need some peace of mind."

Foogly loudly purred, as if in agreement.

Monique left for the airport late that next morning. She landed at Phoenix Sky Harbor, rented a car, and began the three-hour drive to Flagstaff. The puddle jumper flight would have been faster, but the potential for getting airsick was high, and a single Dramamine would knock Monique out for the rest of the day. So she made one stop in Camp Verde to pee and to buy a bottle of water, another of Propel, and a bag of pretzels. As she zoomed upwards to the mountains, she ate and drank and watched the San Francisco Peaks loom closer. She wondered what she'd do if the Smokerise family wasn't home. Part of her hoped they weren't. Maybe she'd go for a hike. An hour and a half later she parked her car in front of the Smoke Rise home. A cool mountain breeze whipped her hair into her face and she took a deep breath, filling her lungs with clean high-altitude air.

Monique rang the doorbell and heard heavy footsteps before a young man who looked like Tony Smoke Rise opened the door. He had on the same jewelry that Tony wore the night he was murdered. Monique's stared at him.

"Detective," the man said in a low voice. "I'm Brett. Tony's brother. We met at the funeral." He did not appear surprised to see her.

"Yes, yes we did. Sorry. You surprised me."

"I look like him with my hair pulled back."

"You certainly do."

Glenn Smoke Rise came to the door with a smile. "Come on in. Arlene, look who's here." He reached out, took her hand, and shook it heartily.

Arlene Smoke Rise wore a purple turtleneck that set off her dark coloring and made her look peaceful. "Detective Blue Hawk. It's good to see you." She, too, shook Monique's hand and gave her a hug.

"Sorry I didn't call first," Monique apologized. "I woke up in the middle of the night and, well, my husband suggested I fly down here."

"That's fine. We got back from Hopi yesterday."

They sat on the big sofa and looked through the large front windows at the San Francisco Peaks. "How are you?" Monique asked.

Arlene nodded and took Glenn's hand. "Fairly well. The circle keeps turning around. What about you, Detective?"

"Well, um. Odd things have happened in Moose City and I was wondering . . ."

Arlene stood and gracefully walked into the kitchen. "I'll get tea," she said as Monique watched her disappear into the next room.

Glenn crossed one leg over the other and pulled out a pack of Wrigley's from his pocket. The sticks were tiny in his big hand. "Gum?" he offered.

"No thanks."

He took his time unwrapping the stick. He looked at Monique and smiled.

"Mr. Smoke Rise . . ." she started.

"Detective," he replied. "Call me Glenn."

"Okay, Glenn. Call me Monique. Look, I'm wondering about a few things."

He held up his hand. "There are bad people in this world," he answered before she asked. "Some are born bad. Some were born good and learned to be bad. Doesn't matter. They're still bad." He rolled up the gum and put it in his mouth. "The people who killed Tone and who wanted to kill Roxanne were bad. Only one person stabbed Tone, but a whole group of people had the spirit to kill him. They had been killing Tone and Roxanne for years in the only way they could. With words. Then when it became clear that words weren't doing the job, they found an excuse to do the thing that bad people do best. They ended a life."

Monique couldn't argue with that reasoning. "Why so many deaths all of a sudden?"

"Bad people are linked together."

"Their spirits know each other," Arlene added as she brought in tea for the four of them. She sat on the sofa next to her husband.

"They do?"

"Probably."

"One dies and the rest think they're next," Brett added. "They don't have any concern for anyone else, you know. Their guilt and their fears cause

192

them to make mistakes. And sometimes their bad feelings for themselves and for their mistakes cause them to hurt themselves."

"We have nothing to do with car wrecks and electrocutions," Arlene said.

"What did you have a part of?"

"Nothing," she answered with a smile.

"Nothing?"

"No. How could we?"

"Seems like too much of a coincidence."

"Coincidences happen," Brett said.

"Another man from the anthropology department died day before yesterday. Choked on a steak."

Arlene shrugged. "Maybe the fat man had bad dreams the night before he had a stroke in the church. He was tired and confused. Just being in the room with my dead son made him panic. The man who hit the wall got scared for reasons of his own and he wasn't looking where he was going. The one who had a heart attack and crashed the car was fat too, you know. All them were used to taking the elevator. Tone told me so."

"I see. So then everyone else got scared and . . ."

"The mind is a wonderful and terrible thing, Detective. Some may have thought there was some kind of 'Indian curse' and they were next. And they were. Except they did it to themselves. The man who choked may have been feeling guilty too. Or maybe he simply inhaled his meat for no good reason."

Monique looked at Arlene, mulling her words over. "And so those medicine men had nothing to do with any of this?"

"No," said Arlene with her intense look. "Hopis can't do things like that. And wouldn't if they could."

"And neither do Apaches," added her husband. "We don't have to."

"They sang at the church, then everyone seemed to go crazy. What did their songs say? What were the words?"

"Detective, the songs were only a plea for balance."

"Balance," Monique repeated.

"That is a logical request," Arlene said. "It's not up to us mortals what justice should be."

"What comes around goes around," Brett added.

The four sat in silence for a moment. All appreciated that the others didn't mind spaces between words. Monique looked out the front window. She could see the aspen leaves on the San Francisco Peaks changing to yellow. "Arnold Old Bull isn't Hopi," she said.

"Can't speak for him," Arlene said.

"He wouldn't intentionally behave badly," Glenn added.

"Do you know him?"

"No," Arlene interjected. "But he's honest. I can tell."

Monique didn't doubt that.

"Detective. Good people have a way of rising to the top," Arlene said. "Even in death. These bad people thought they could hurt Rox and Tone, and then they'd be on top. Doesn't work that way." She looked out the large window. "Look up there on the mountain. Leaves are turning."

"So this is it?"

"We've accepted it, Detective. Indians always have to deal with death and racism. From coast to coast, from north to south, Indians are persecuted and killed. Look at the murders in South Dakota after the Wounded Knee takeover in the 70s. Look at the Northwest and the elders who are jailed for violating salmon fishing law even though the fish are theirs by treaty. Land, fishing, and water treaties are being broken as we speak. White people still come in and steal our cultural knowledge and secretly tape our ceremonies for their own benefit."

"The difference between us and those Indians," Glenn added, "is that we won a lot of money from CHU for what was done to our son. That doesn't happen every often. Now we can establish what Tony would have done: we have a gym, a scholarship fund, and a new shelter for abused women on the way. And all in Tony's name."

Monique hoped she wouldn't cry. "He would have approved. I didn't know him, but I think he would have liked what you have done."

"Yes, he would approve."

"We also got a nice gift from Pauley Wenetae."

"Flowers?"

"No. He gave three endowed scholarships for Indian students in Tony's name. The students get a full ride through school. The first student begins next fall. Then there are two more right behind that one."

194

"Pretty generous considering how much tuition costs at CHU." *And just how much does Pauley make, anyway?* She thought.

Brett could tell what she was thinking. "Casino tribe. And his uncle is on the tribal council. He doesn't even need to work."

"But what Indian student would come to the anthropology department now?"

"Pauley's gift is not set up for the anthropology department," Glenn grinned. "It's specifically for the law school."

Monique laughed. "I guess Professor Wenetae is smarter than I figured."

"No, he's not." Arlene said. "But he carries a lot of guilt and confusion."

"Well, he certainly deals with it nicely."

They sat in comfortable silence for a half a minute. Monique wondered if Tony was hovering above them, listening.

Arlene spoke. "Stay and have lunch and then go see how the leaves have changed and drive through Oak Creek Canyon on your way back to Phoenix."

"I'll show you my brother's photo albums," Brett said, proudly.

"I'd like to see them. I need to see what he was like."

"Life must go on. And we must live it," Glenn added

Monique looked at Arlene, then back to Glenn. "I will."

And she meant it, too.